The
OUROBOROS

The
OUROBOROS

Howard Coale

Ticknor & Fields

New York 1991

For information about permission to reproduce
selections from this book, write to Permissions,
Ticknor & Fields, Houghton Mifflin Company,
2 Park Street, Boston, Massachusetts 02108

Library of Congress Cataloging-in-Publication Data

Coale, Howard.
      The ouroboros / Howard Coale.
          p.   cm.
      ISBN 0-89919-977-1
      I. Title.
      PS3553.014097   1991   90-15475
      813'.54 — dc20   CIP

Printed in the United States of America

BVG 10 9 8 7 6 5 4 3 2 1

The author gratefully acknowledges the Oxford
University Press for permission to reprint from the
Oxford English Dictionary definition of *ouroboros*.

ou·ro·bor·os (ôr′ə-bôr′əs) **n.**
The tail-biting snake, the eternal
circle of disintegration and reintegration;
it devours, fertilizes, begets, and slays
itself, and brings itself to life again.

The

OUROBOROS

1

Every time I try to talk about Kate I find myself falling into oblique and deceptive descriptions. In my mind, every fragment of her is wrapped tightly inside a gauzy protective layer, like the seed of a lichee nut, or some ancient insect caught behind a wall of amber. This is because, in many ways, I am a victim of my own past attitudes, having stored impressions exactly as they were received, complete with the emotional fingerprints of that time. So that when I pass my eyes over old landscapes I peer through a blurry window pawed by a former self.

You see, I'm not trying to tell you about Kate now, that is, Kate as she exists today; a woman I don't know, a lawyer, who lives somewhere in the Southwest stalking endlessly back and forth in front of an inanimate jury, her words delivered in a voice of soft, steely certainty. Rather, I am talking about Kate *then:* a person who's been blurred in my head like a coin that's been in a pocket too long. So that remembering her precisely is a battle with my own gray and compact brain. She is there, though. Somewhere, scattered in the corpuscles behind my eyes, drifting in fragments through the arteries, is the whole story. And it can be gathered, like seeds picked off a lawn.

In some ways, it was as if I were already trying to remember her the night I first saw her. Sitting on a piano bench, leaning back on a battered upright piano, facing out at the party, not dancing but thinking, I was already preparing myself for such a woman that night. It was midwinter in a big barn not far from college. Beneath the rafters, hooting and spinning, were my fellow students.

It was a time when the world beyond the campus called forth with a rhythmic threat not unlike the sound of drums heard deep in a forest. Outside, in the great outside, there were signs of civilization, but no sign as to what my position would be once I arrived. For all I knew (and I was beginning to suspect), the world of adults was filled with bitter men and women, plagued with disappointment and ready, like savages, to devour you before any thought of welcoming had crossed their minds.

At that time, many of my friends were seeking mentors. There was a premium placed on great teachers who would shield their favorites from the others and ease them into the realm of adults. This was the plan for many. A protected apprenticeship. And it seemed for a long time as if every person old enough to have developed wrinkles, from somber professors all the way down to sarcastic, two-bit pool hustlers in town, had been turned into somebody's mentor. There were none left. No more guides, no matter how far down the scale of wisdom you went.

So I had begun to form an idea of a woman in my mind. A

different sort of human being. A twin, ignorant like me, but wise about her own sex. Because sex was for me the darkest region in the outside world, and women always seemed to see into it farther, as if it were the domain of their private god. So, all gloomy, without a mentor, I watched the dancing of my peers and wished I could conjure up an image of this being: my new friend with a female body. But it was unnecessary. She was already in the act of arriving.

She came through the doorway, dressed completely in red, with red-and-white sneakers, and danced immediately, with a furious expression on her face, as if she had been dancing out in the snow and someone had just directed her toward the door. I watched her and thought, That is the kind of woman I should learn to fall in love with.

We didn't meet that night. I talked to a young woman I barely knew. Then I walked home with my hands jammed in my pockets and my head full of tiny plans and notions of success.

In many ways, my courtship of Kate is not a romantic story. I spent a great deal of time wandering into her house and up to her room, knocking on her door, being let in, sitting on the one chair, and talking to her mildly about whatever came to mind. This went on for a month, with me gradually memorizing the objects in the room, piece by piece, and reciting them to myself in the shower or walking down the street, as if they had some meaning in and of themselves. The box of cotton. The bottle of skin lotion. The bowl full of bracelets. I wasn't in love with her, but I suspected it would happen soon. In the meantime, the things she held in her hand, or brushed against on her desk, or glanced at, or thought about with little improvised pictures in her head, held my attention the way the props in a three-ring circus fixate the audience long before the lions have moved into the spotlight.

Around this time, around the time I was sitting in her chair and facing her, thinking she was a striking woman, but still not in love, or not recognizing my emotion as love, or not, in the mood of college, wanting to burden it with the portent of that word: around this time I began to lose interest in studying. This worried me, because I had always found it easy to do the necessary work. I had a peculiar talent for doing well in school; it was almost automatic. But it had begun to worry me. There was the feeling that whatever I applied myself to I might succeed at, and although that made me feel good, there was the sneaking suspicion that things were going to be difficult anyway.

But since I had seen Kate that night in the cold barn, with its darkened rafters and her dancing on those old timbers like a jagged flame, she had replaced the apprehensions in my mind with an unfamiliar sensation of other, open-ended possibilities.

Then, a week after my last visit to her room, she arrived, out of the blue, at my place for the first time, and did not wait for me to knock on her door and sit gazing at her bowl of bracelets.

I lived in a dilapidated boarding house near campus. She walked up the stairs and through the second-floor hallway, which smelled of cedar, except when you passed the bathroom, and then there was a smell of soap, but just for a moment. She came to see me.

My room was shadowy and the walls were painted in a dark, opulent green. It was the kind of green that is mildly nauseating when you first see it, but when you look closer, much closer, on a bright day, it resonates with a deeply satisfying aqua blue, and suddenly you find yourself forgiving the nauseating green color altogether. The blue in the walls was particularly hard to see in the autumn and winter, and on that day when Kate arrived it lingered beneath the shadows, and the room felt as green and dingy as the unlighted edges of a pool table. But I knew the blue was there, and my embarrassment at being barged in on by this woman was slightly alleviated by what I knew was possible in other seasons. So I turned on my desk lamp and pointed it quickly toward the ceiling.

My bed was squat and overstuffed, like a large arthritic pet wearing a poncho. A bureau stood against the wall, stained the same color as the shadows, almost invisible except for its shiny knobs. Piles of clothes lay helplessly about the floor like ash heaps. Indeed, I was most embarrassed by the odd darkness of the place, its underground feeling. And on top of that was the peculiar issue of my room's hollow anonymity. It could have belonged to any random, murky personality.

— Hello, Harry, she said, moving to my desk and turning over the books there.

She had a barely discernible smile on her face, almost trembling. Yet I knew her well enough by that point to know it was a welcoming smile. Regardless, I felt invaded, like the whale that just had Jonah shoved down his throat. On the other hand, she was radiant, not only with her own beauty, but with some sort of conspiracy of purpose.

— I thought I'd come and see you here. See what your place was like.

As she moved about the desk I noticed a hesitation in her stride, a numbness, as if she were bored with the act of walking. But her hands were honestly reaching out and feeling the edges of things, retrieving things for her eyes, and her face was relaxed as she glanced across the room and through the window to look beyond the scraggly trees outside. She moved toward me.

— Will you come with me? I'm going to buy a sweater downtown.

Standing still, arms at my side, I looked, I imagined, like a statue commemorating someone who saw something incredible. Not because she looked incredible, but because she came very close to me, breathing softly, while I, stark still, let her take my hand.

— Harry?

— Yes?

— Will you . . . ?

— Go buy a sweater?

I kissed her, just after saying "sweater." And I didn't stop kissing her. I put my arms around her and picked her up, and with her mouth pressed to mine I carried her toward my bed. And as I carried her, with my arms around her sides, just below the ribs, my hands pressing up against her back, I felt her firm sloping back beneath my hands and a thrill went through me. Against the green walls her hair appeared white and soaked with light. Inside her mouth there was a small world in and of itself, with an overarching canopy and a lower curved valley of white mountains divided by a red river of a tongue, a place I had never been before and in which I was already getting lost.

But the carrying ended, and we fell onto the upward curve of the bed. As I drew my face back from hers I found myself looking at her hair, which I was holding in my hands like some magical substance I had just discovered on a beach. She watched my eyes looking quietly at her hair in my hands.

One day we walked together, she to her class, I to mine. And suddenly, after being very quiet walking down the long hall, she spoke to me.

— Harry, I'm thinking of going to China.

— China? I said.

— Yes, to study Chinese.

— When?

— Well, they say if some of us wanted, we could go before the end of the year, and finish our degrees studying in China.

— Where in China? I asked, knowing nothing about China.

She changed the subject, pointing to a marble bust of some long-haired, high-foreheaded man that glided by as we walked down the hallway, his daring nose jutting out defiantly.

— That's Voltaire, said Kate.

I looked at the bust and thought, I know nothing about him. As his white face floated by, a head-shaped stone, I thought of Kate in China, and mocked the idea momentarily. I knew as much about Voltaire as I did about China, solely because I hadn't taken a class in either. But I realized, only after we had passed his head, that Kate looked like this man Voltaire sometimes, turning around quickly with a quick smile on her face, or looking up briefly from studying, interrupted, but ready with a sharp thought hovering on her lips. She seemed always ready. Expressions looked preformed on her face, as if she had considered for every circumstance how she would react, and had prepared her responses long ago, maybe in childhood. Yet in her eyes there was a spark of impertinence toward whatever forced her to do this. And it struck me, although I knew nothing about him, that this guy Voltaire, given just his face, his arched and sharp expression, had probably been the same way. A politician, a balanced arbiter, but a secret rogue. A two-sided kind of talent, like Kate; somebody with an almost seamless instinct for the order of things, yet for whom inside there swirled a mischievous lust for risk.

— China? Where in China? I asked again.

We saw each other almost every day for a month. But I wasn't in love, and it angered me. I rushed from my classes to meet her, but with a vengeance. She never saturated my life, so I was left with the aching need to be with her. When dogs hear strange sounds, they tilt their heads. That's how I listened to her. She was plucking a minor key in me, but I couldn't name it. It annoyed me. And one day, out of the blue, she looked me in the eyes and, with a pat on my cheek, said she was leaving. She was going away to the other side of the world. An island off the coast of China.

— Taiwan.

— Oh, I said.

— I'll live in Taipei. I'll find an apartment. It's a great chance to learn the language. The Oriental languages department offered it to me.

— That's wonderful.

We were in her room. I was looking out the window. A squirrel was dashing about on a tree outside. Through the windowpane I could hear it chattering. Its tail was flipping back and forth. An obese man wearing a red parka came out of the house next door and delicately walked across the frozen ground. The squirrel stopped and held its tail in an S curve. The man walked under the tree and bent down, very slowly, to pick something up, and he froze there for a few long seconds, bending. There was a moment of no movement. The bending man and the squirrel and all the trees, and the houses and the street, were all motionless for one terribly long second. And I almost was caught up in it too, the overwhelming stillness, and the arched, hairy curve of the tail, until Kate rustled something behind me. Then I saw, refocusing my eyes, the icy tendrils of frost my breath had fogged onto the window.

— They say it's a polluted city, said Kate. It's an island, like England. A small island with a long history. And Mandarin is spoken there . . . I mean, they care about their language and they want people to come study. And also, I have a feeling it's time for me to go do something daring.

2

The lake at the far end of campus was murky and still and was often visited by people in distress, or lovers, or those whose dogs could not be suppressed and were brought there, unleashed, to bound around the perimeter like demons. It was supposed to be bottomless, a joke that was kept alive only because the lake was an unavoidable "natural spot," and there was a general sense that there should be some sort of myth or stupid story floating about in order for it to be a respectable place. It was known to be about twelve feet deep at the center, but "bottomless" was supposed to signify something altogether different from depth. It meant, Wouldn't it make our lives better if it *was* bottomless. And that desire, aligned with a variety of other hopes, seemed to make the old puddle precious, even amidst the wilting trees, the trampled path, and the dark mud that hemmed in its brown water.

This is where I found myself walking the day after Kate said she was leaving. I was sorry for myself, but, I felt, for a good reason, and smiled as gently as possible at the tongue-waving dogs that barreled by me on the path. I was being abandoned. She was soon going to the other side of the world. And I thought of her assiduous studying of Chinese and how I was aimless and had nothing, except half-memorized quotations from various books, to sustain me after graduation. Furthermore, the lake itself was annoying, for as I looked at its placid surface it ushered up thoughts only of itself, its limitations, as opposed to more active bodies of water, like rivers and oceans, which seem to gossip about places of importance.

Two runners glided by, their shirts stained with sweat. They jogged along the path and onward over a slight hill and down. The sound of their feet faded. But afterward, over the hill, I heard voices.

— What does it matter, as far as you're concerned?

— What the hell do you mean . . . "As far as you're concerned"?

— Give me a break, George.

As I came to the top of the path I saw a man and a woman, off the path a bit, close to the lake. The man held on tightly to the woman's hand. The woman's face was red. She started to pull her hand away, but the man held firmly.

— Let go.

— No.

— Let go, George.

— Listen, I told you we had to talk . . .

She gave one big yank and he almost tripped on a rock as she pulled him forward. They had obviously been there awhile, arguing together.

— George, you don't understand.

She pulled again. This time, though, his other hand came around, palm open, and slapped her loudly on the face. There was a shocked silence, and they both shuffled toward the lake. Her heels sank into the mud.

— You fucking jerk! she yelled.

He looked stunned and suddenly much younger. His mouth dropped open in a childish manner. His hands jiggled tensely, as if he expected her to hit him back. And she did hit him, but not until she had pulled one of her feet out of the mud, shoeless.

— You fucking jerk! she yelled, and her hand came crashing down on his head. Then she said it again, but syncopated with each blow.

— You! . . . Fucking! . . . Jerk!

She hit him in the side of the face with long, sideways arcs of her right arm. And he, facing her, and thereby also facing the lake, staggered backward, awkwardly defending himself with his left hand, which fluttered about the left side of his face.

She then gave him a big heave in the chest, which sent him ambling backward. Her stockinged foot minced along, touching the ground ever so delicately as she turned and limped back to get her shoe, heavily favoring the shoed foot when she reached the edge of the mud. And even as she was bending down, almost as if she were yelling at the lake, she shouted out again.

— What a jerk! You're such an ass! she bellowed, yanking her shoe out of the mud.

— Never hit me . . . never, *ever* hit me!

I began to walk past them as quickly as possible. I figured they'd turn around and, although cursing each other, would probably notice me. So I thought it was a good time to leave and resume my own thoughts about Kate. I started down the path.

— Hey you! the man yelled.

— Yes? I said, turning around.

— You standing there the whole time?

His face was screwed up into a parody of disgust, annoyed on behalf of himself.

— Well, um . . . I said, smiling but still walking away.

It seemed like a minor incident. I was trying to appear as if nothing surprising had happened to me recently, but something in my face made him rush to my side and point his finger menacingly at my nose.

— Peeping fucking Tom!

— What?

— You get a kick watching people talking privately . . . huh?

He grabbed hold of my shirt. A button popped off and zipped past his ear. He blinked. The woman watched, her hands on her hips.

— Let go, I said confidently.

I was sure there was some sort of arranged justice here. He had hit her, she had retaliated quite effectively, and he, in his humiliation, had turned on me. It was obvious. It also seemed obvious that such a man would be the weaker in a fight. So while he held on to me with one arm, shifting back and forth on his feet nervously, I stood as solidly as possible and stared him in the face. He had a pointed chin, and I focused on it, since I was uncomfortable looking him directly in the eyes.

— Let's go home, George, said the woman.

I wondered whether or not these two had anything to do with the university. The guy seemed meek and unsure of himself in an inarticulate way, yet he was hard to place. He reeked of a kind of ambitious ignorance.

— What makes you think you can stand around and stare at people? he said.

He was getting more upset rather than less the longer we stood there. I readied myself for a fight, checking where his feet were to see whether I could catch him off balance, and noticed he had skinny legs and socks that drooped down over his sneakers.

— Give it up, George. Let's go home, this is stupid, said the woman.

At the moment she spoke her eyes met mine, over George's shoulder, and suddenly I felt that I was very attracted to her. She had black hair and green eyes and a full face, like a voluptuous, bawdy angel from a tapestry. Her eyes opened up, and she gave me a flat stare. She bit her bottom lip slightly, and smiled. And at precisely the same moment, as I was enjoying her smile, George's knotted hand, like an angry little hammer, came crashing down against my cheekbone. I fell with a great muffled thump into the leaves beside the path. It was over in a second.

— Christ Almighty, George! she shouted.

— Get up and I'll hit you again! he yelled down at me, much as the woman had yelled at the lake.

I was surprised to find that I had no desire to get up and fight. In fact, I felt an odd wave of joy. All was very peaceful in the low world of leaves and grass. My head throbbed, but all seemed right and in order. I felt safe and content, as if, having lost the fight, I'd reached a version of the good life, staring out sideways at the stagnant, bottomless lake. A small amount of blood surged from my cheek and down the side of my face. It was a strange, uneasy epiphany.

— You really hurt him, said the woman, and I heard her feet move through the leaves toward me.

— No, I'm okay, I said, waving my arm above my head, although I still looked out at the water.

The man laughed lightly. I couldn't see him either. Glassy and smooth, the lake held my attention while I thought over the events of the last couple of seconds. He had me by the shirt. And then the button popped off. And in the middle of my review of these pictures the woman bent her head down and looked at me, her black hair falling softly, her eyes even more entrancing at such close proximity, dark inside, very dark, surrounded by swirling eddies of green, like two small, verdant planets.

— Are you all right? she whispered.

— Yes, I said.

— Why are you smiling? she asked with soft, pudgy curiosity.

It was as if we were talking to each other in bed late at night. Tasting the blood on my lips, I looked up at her and a surge of gratitude for her tenderness came over me. I was a stranger to her. Yet it was as if we were lovers meeting secretly.

— Let's go, said the man, chuckling.

— Well, she said whispering again, you seem all right . . . Sorry about what happened . . . I mean . . . sorry about what George did.

She waved goodbye down at me, and I heard them move off through the leaves and disappear together.

Wonder of wonders was Kate's strange room. The walls were yellow and the floor slanted down ever so slightly toward the windows. The ceiling sloped upward on both sides to a high peak interrupted only by three smooth arches in which the windows were set. Light poured in, even when the sun was on the other side of the house, and lit everything, down to the tiny oval photographs of Kate's parents on her desk, as if from behind. A single bulb produced a luminous orange glow at night, and the three windows stood solid and black like an inky triptych overlooking everything. Her bed was covered with a red shawl initialed all over with intricate black designs, like tadpoles. And by the bed there was a lamp with a minuscule shade that provided a rosy dusting of illumination on the bedside table. There was a hatrack with no hats. Behind the hatrack there was a large white Chinese scroll on the wall. Placed around the scroll were black-and-white photographs of friends from home. A girl, smiling, sitting on a stone wall with trees behind her; a young man, skinny, his left hand in his back pocket, his eyes askew with mischief, very long hair, and a mole a little off center on his forehead.

That night we went to a movie together. I told Kate a little of what happened at the lake. But not all of it. I didn't know how to explain the contentment of lying in the leaves, bleeding. She felt my cut and was curious, but not overly fascinated by the story. It was probably my fault, she remarked. We left it at that.

It rained very hard that night. We came in soaking wet. But when I looked into Kate's room, things had changed. Everything was in boxes.

— Harry, I'm leaving in three days, she said, almost angrily. I'm sorry I didn't warn you, but . . .

— I thought you were leaving in a week.

— No. Three days.

She immediately began to take off her clothes, pulling at her sweater, her shoes, and then her pants.

— What the hell are you going to do with your life anyway, Harry? What's to become of you after I'm gone? she said, as if these were standard questions she had to mark off her checklist.

— I don't know. I'll get my degree soon. Then maybe . . . I
don't know . . . I'll go to New York.

— And what will you do there?

She covered herself with a towel, then slipped out of the
room to turn on the shower. I heard the water begin. It seemed
such a luxury to come out of the rain and get into a shower. All
that water pouring down on the skin. She came back from the
bathroom for a moment to pull a bottle of soap off the bureau.
Then the door to the bathroom shut and the stir of the shower
softened, lifting the rain outside back into prominence.

The three black windows now were stark and magnificent. I
felt the scab on my cheek and wondered about the man who hit
me. And I wondered about the woman, bending down to look
in my face, and her beautiful eyes, and for a moment I felt
guilty because I thought, After Kate's gone, who knows, she
might truly like me, because that guy's a real bastard. Possibly
they had started the argument again, not far from here, behind
a window that glows down on some wet yard. And either they
were arguing or they were screwing madly. Whatever they were
doing, they had to be aware of the rain. Intently I listened to
both the shower and the rain, intently enough so that maybe,
even while they were making love in some dim room, the green-
eyed woman might look up and think of me briefly. Intently
enough that I might force her, by dint of my thoughts, as a result of her peculiar tenderness, to think of me even while she
rolled with him on some rumpled bed and, despite him, remember the moment she whispered to me while I, albeit the
loser, bled on the ground. Then I wondered for a moment
about the feel of her body.

I watched the water leak down the other side of the windows,
and aimlessly timed its descent, betting myself that this drop
would get to the bottom in ten seconds, and that one would remain hanging until it gathered more water. But Kate came into

the room again, her legs gliding smooth and pink beneath the white towel. She came toward me, opening her towel like a shell. I embraced her, and I felt her hair combed in straight wet rows.

— It won't matter, she said. You won't remember me.

— That's ridiculous.

— Come on, really. You don't know me that well, Harry. You'll know me less when I'm gone.

— We'll see, I said, and noted the fatherly tone in my voice.

— When you graduate, if you feel like it, for the hell of it, come see me in Asia.

— Nope, I said. I'm going to New York. I've got things to do when I leave. I'm graduating soon.

We fell into bed and her clean body unraveled out of the towel. We attacked my wet clothes, attempting to free me from them. My shirt, missing one button, opened freely. My socks shot off, one, two. And finally, after wrestling with my pants as if they were ropes around me, several long moments later I was as naked as she.

I was lying in bed with Kate and noticed that the scab on my cheek was throbbing. It was dark, and in the middle of the night, all soft and curled next to me, Kate began to talk out loud in a hazy dream voice. First she champed her teeth up and down. A *chop-chop* sound. Then she spoke in Chinese. At least I thought it was Chinese. Her words curved in blurry bursts, some with little spikes of intonation, some guttural. And I stared up at the light bulb in her room. It was reflecting a tiny spark from a streetlight outside. That was the only light. Rebounding softly through the room were her words, whispered mostly. It sounded as if she were giving a speech in front of some honored assembly, because she chose her words with great care.

Then she stopped. I could make out her blond head glowing delicately next to me, and I felt a shudder. It was as if we had been invaded while we slept; not by an army, but by this lilting, cryptic language. What dropped into my mind were pictures, with bold English below them, "See Spot run," like an admonition. Language is so personal, particularly when it comes from the mouth of a sleeping lover. How peculiar that she should speak that language here, in bed with me, I thought. It's not our language. It certainly isn't mine.

3

She left. And come on, let's admit it, I hadn't known her that well. And what I did know of her I had romanticized way out of proportion. So when she was gone I found myself wondering whether I had been in love at all. I looked forward to my graduation with a certain amount of distaste. I would be released upon the world, and all I could see of myself in the mirror, or in my own fantasies, was a vain and directionless young man without any sense of what could be done with the tremendous wealth of an education that had been poured into his head like liquid tin. Thousands upon thousands of dollars had been spent by my hapless family in the pursuit of making me a decent entity, separate from them, but armed and ready for the struggle for success.

I looked around and was not impressed by my fellow students. Those who didn't seek a secure life were in fact seeking to secure other people's admiration, which in turn offered them a kind of security. Art became one of the last sacred grounds for them, and many wanted to be artists with a suspicious enthusiasm. Art was pursued, if at all, solely for its ability to mimic the possession of mysterious prowess. A finessed prowess. The title ARTIST was worn like a talisman against being boring. Like garlic around the neck. But ultimately it was just another way to camouflage oneself, to take on the appearance of the not-ordinary, while secretly preparing for an ordinary life. Inside myself, unhappily, I found only a small spark of honesty, surrounded by dense, colored clouds of superficial desires. So when Kate left I felt foolish. For a while I believed love, or the aura of love, had redeemed me, like confession. Devoid of any deep direction, I pursued Kate's heart with a degree of honesty. It was real, this making love to the same woman all the time, this effort at creating a union. But she had gone. No tears. She had just gone away.

When I departed from college I felt dropped into vacant territory. It was a cold and apprehensive time, mid-February, and I felt ejected from the university like an errant cinder from a huge chimney. It was the middle of winter because I hadn't completed certain papers, and when I finally did complete them, I found myself arriving at the end of my education in a dark and snowy time, without comrades, and without the benefit of an embroidered celebration.

It was a quiet and gloomy transition, and involved my taking one long walk across the icy campus carrying thirty pages of a paper on Aristotle. I gave it to my professor, who sat alone in his office, the tweed on the shoulders of his jacket spiky and raised, the radiator hissing in the corner, the faces of grave, bearded men on the wall peering through flat glass reflecting drifts beyond the window.

Outside, as I walked home across the snow, a calm descended upon me. I had done it. I was now free. Along with the crunching below my feet came ideas of other places. I thought of Kate. Asia glimmered above the snow, a sandy place, I imagined, where the land was engorged, and almost dripping with sunlight. Strange buildings stood there, their pointed tops needling the air, and in the distance someone somewhere sang something unearthly and indecipherable. A mirage. And in this dark late evening light, the bluish light of snow and evening together, Asia appeared as a hot and rippling world, full of reds and browns and oranges. Through its peculiar buildings, in this mirage, I saw a dart of bright yellow, a tiny spot of fire. It was Kate's blond head, and it moved quickly, from place to place on a distant street.

I heard her speaking. She was speaking very fast. But I couldn't understand what she was saying. I thought, as my feet crunched in the snow . . .

— Now I must find a place to live in New York City. I've got to get away from thoughts of her. I'll do some sort of work in New York. I'll work hard. There'll be bars and clubs and Central Park, where women will be roller skating. And I'll take the subway and nonchalantly get off at the right stop, lifting myself from the seat and gliding out the silver door, a newspaper under my arm, no trace of perplexity left behind.

But I stopped and stood in the snow. I looked ahead and saw Kate again in my mirage. She was standing next to an ancient chipped fountain, the kind you might see in an old photograph, in a ruin, but still bubbling. The sun poured down and lit every shadow, and the sand was blazing. The light made her squint. And finally, just barely, I could make out what she was saying, as if she were giggling through the snow, and it had come straight through the earth and found its way to me.

— It's winter over there, she was saying . . . But he's coming. I know he's definitely coming.

And I wondered about the strange feeling that I wasn't in love with her, but that somewhere deep I was feeling a need to concentrate and fasten my hopes on her. My heart was ready to be launched on a holy crusade. And at last as I listened to her speak in that warm world that hovered above the frigid landscape, love, even unsure and as of yet unfelt, seemed to be the only unadulterated path of integrity in my life.

4

The Pacific Ocean, from above, has no borders and no limits whatsoever. Blue stretches out to meet blue, a flat expanse of water inhabited by creatures hidden below dim waves. But on top there's nothing. It's just flat, flat, and onward flat, heaving and swaying way below.

From above, from the rounded window, from the air tightly held in suspension inside and not rushing past, as it is outside, the blue Pacific Ocean is a place you can go as a visitor, but only to gaze, slack-jawed and jealous. It's like the swimming pool of an infinitely wealthy neighbor, off limits and gorgeous, glittering with that opulence of better lives lived thoroughly by other people.

The entire airplane, I remember, was filled with bright red and bright blue seats. The uniformity of the seats was broken by a fabulous array of different heads: pink bald heads, black-haired shaggy heads, gray-haired heads, some with hats, and small children's heads poking sideways into the aisle. And then there were the languorous and disciplined movements of the stewardesses, like antelopes recruited for a military task.

Departing is generally a self-contained event. Even if you are sad about leaving, even if you have no idea when or if you will return, the sadness in departing has a bitter, self-supporting logic to it. The finality of lifting up and off familiar ground, the ground you've muddied your feet with, of then flying through the open air, combined with that middle world of sky, where you can't see anything above or below, presents a complete equation to one's head. There's something succinct yet essentially unhappy about the beginning of a trip. There's that tension. But soon you become lulled into an itching, joyful hope, because the unhappiness (which comes from being separated from home) is smoothed over by the rare event of a straight path. You know that you are going *somewhere*. And because it's so hard to find a straight path in anything, the unhappiness melts slightly, and you're left with a dull sense of opportunity. You begin to suspect, gradually, that something important lies ahead. And you believe you've earned it because, at heart, you're still melancholy. You become convinced that you're on the way to being healed.

I had not seen Kate in almost seven months. It was so long that I barely remembered her face, and when I did it was usually from an odd vantage point, like looking up at her from somewhere very close, just below her chin. Over the Pacific, I spent a great deal of time wondering about her. Having written a hasty letter describing my plans, I'd left the United States quickly, wanting to leave myself no time to reconsider. Then Taipei appeared below the plane like a smoggy little jewel of cement, a filigree of sooty trees.

She was waiting under the fluorescent lights, her blond hair cut short and her eyes like blue headlights in the dark-eyed crowd. She was vigilant and waiting. I watched her for several moments before she saw me. I was jumbled around in the disembarking crowd, and poked my head over the others to catch her attention, and saw, each time I looked, an older woman than I remembered, with her yellow sweater bunched up around her shoulders.

She was standing, relaxed, a foreigner, but comfortable. And as I emerged from the long tunnel from the plane, I exhaled the last speck of North American air that had been trapped in the fuselage.

— Harry!

I rushed forward and kissed her. Her cheek was cool.

She kissed me and swung around and pulled me toward the large glass doors.

— Come here, she said, laughing.

She pulled me into a corner behind a pillar and we kissed, my hand turning white because it was wrapped in my duffel bag's strap. I had forgotten that her lips felt polished.

I felt slightly shocked that she was so happy to see me. And I was also shocked at how it made me feel. It wasn't something, I suppose, that either of us had expected.

We hailed a cab and swept several times around a complicated series of pristine, circular roads until we were on a highway headed toward the center of Taipei. The signs were in Chinese, white slashing characters on backgrounds of green.

Kate was quiet sitting next to me, the window open, her hair blowing about her forehead. Her dress, white and smooth, was pushed up on her thigh. There was a relaxed sexiness about her. She had a soft smile, and she looked straight ahead, over the seat and through the windshield.

— Harry, I can't believe you're here.

— I can't believe I'm here either.

I was feeling suddenly stronger near her. Hovering above the highway were vapors of foreign heat, and the smells of Taipei, of mangoes and smog, and of trees I'd never smelled before. And yet it was Kate with her sharp blue eyes and her uplifted, forward-watching face who had significance. She was finally coming into sharp focus for me. How was it that I had ever believed I wasn't in love with her?

Out the window, across a level expanse of low concrete buildings, I saw a modern red pagoda rising above a dull gray neighborhood.

— So it's all right? Me coming here and staying with you and all?

She leaned over and kissed me.

— Of course. Don't be ridiculous. I was hoping.

The cab driver asked something, and Kate replied in Chinese, in a very distinct voice. He then swerved the car down an exit ramp and we plunged into the city.

— There's just one thing, Harry. We're sharing an apartment with somebody. I hope you don't mind. There's a lot of room. We couldn't afford it by ourselves. He's very nice.

— Who is he?

— A German guy. He's studying sword dancing. It's one of the martial arts. I've heard he's very good.

— Oh.

We shot along a tiny street, narrowly missing several people. The buildings were low and had dark, oily eaves that hung over the sidewalks. Dogs and chickens roamed about, and shops stood open with vegetables and vats of snowy bean curd sitting open to the sun.

The Ouroboros

My eyes drifted back to her, and I found myself surveying her beauty, the way everything about her, the way she crossed her legs, the curve of her waist underneath her dress, her shoulders, her thighs, spoke of a terrific confidence.

She caught me looking at her legs and smiled and raised her eyebrow, but we hit a bump, and her attention jogged back to the street.

— Wei Chi Bei Lu, she said to the driver.

He grunted and turned down a small street. There were ginkgo trees lining the sidewalks, and the pungent odor of the fruit squashed on the street came through the windows. The leaves filtered dusty sunlight down on the asphalt. All along the street identical five-story buildings stood tight together. They were of a prefabricated modern style and looked hastily constructed, with dulled yellow and blue panels along the balconies. Plants were everywhere, bulging from windows, hanging from balconies, and even poking up over the edges of the roofs. Encircling and covering all this was a heavy, moist gray air, filled with invisible bits of soot, so that the street and its wealth of plants and the blue and yellow panels on the balconies were seen as if through a veil.

Kate told the driver to stop. Her building had a red door, with a big white Chinese character painted on it. We went up the narrow staircase to the third floor and Kate fumbled with the keys. But before she could find the right one, the door swung open.

In the doorway was a very tall man with a large handlebar mustache. He wore nothing but a tiny pair of shorts.

— Vell-come! he almost shouted, and it echoed in the stairwell.

— Harry, this is Frederick. Frederick, this is Harry, said Kate.

Frederick came forth to embrace me, somewhat stiffly, and

his face lunged first right, then left past my face, as Kate edged around us, smiling. Frederick's body emanated a musky, earthy smell, like bark.

— Teas? he said, grinning. I've just made some teas.

He turned immediately and padded barefoot around the corner into the kitchen.

Kate tugged me into the apartment. We were in a large white room with one table, some bamboo mats, windows that opened out onto a square concrete balcony, and a few doors leading off into other, gloomy rooms.

She and I stood together silently in the big room. I brought her to me and kissed her, for real this time, and my duffel bag dropped to the floor.

— Teas! said Frederick, coming around the corner with a wicker tray and a few rattling china cups.

We all sat down at the unsteady bamboo table. It stood near the balcony window, and we could look down Wei Chi Street, at the people walking and the hawkers selling steaming food from metal carts, and the palm trees hovering in the sky.

— And so . . . you've come to Taipei to be with Kate, said Frederick cheerfully, pouring me some tea. You knew each other in co-ledge. Now you are together ah-gain. This is roman-tick. Definitely roman-tick.

Kate glanced at me.

— I'm divorced, Harree, said Frederick with a serious nod in my direction. In case you are thee-inking that I am alone. I *am* alone.

— Oh, I said, not quite sure how he wanted me to respond.

His accent reminded me of old war movies. But he spoke well, with a fluid inflection.

— Frederick is studying Chinese sword dancing, said Kate to me pointedly.

— Yes, I heard. How is that?

— How is it? A lot of work. Just work. No screwing around. You go, you work, maybe . . . maybe, you get better. But it's hard. I'm there every morning.

— Where?

— At the Chiang Kai-shek Memorial. Outside. Six every morning. I was a librarian, you know. Before I came here. Not anymore. In Berlin I attended library school. But — and he made a caricatured face of nausea — it makes me ill. It makes me ill and I have to leave. Too many books. Too much this, he pointed at his head.

Kate looked at me over her cup as she sipped.

— So you decided to come here and study sword dancing?

— Well, yes or no. Other things. There were other things. Other ray-zons.

He waved his hand as if to shoo away unpleasant and unhealthful vapors. Then he looked at me and took a long, deep breath. When his lungs were full, and his thin chest was expanded, he rapped his bare, lightly hairy chest and exhaled.

— Just this, he said.

— Your breath?

— No. My body. Do you know the word see-metry? he said.

— Symmetry?

— Yes. See-metry. I go away from books, and — he smiled and cocked his head — I find see-metry. Right here, in China.

— In Taiwan, said Kate. You mean in Taiwan.

— No. China. Ask anyone, Kate, said Frederick, a little peeved. This is Chi-naa. China and Taiwan are always one.

He took a big gulp of his tea. And then, after a moment or two of staring forlornly at his cup, he became suddenly jovial.

— Look. Some more Americans, he said with a chuckle.

Down below on the street three bicycle riders rode through

the quiet neighborhood, all clad in black, all gravely looking ahead, riding in single file. A few old women stared at them as they passed. They looked uncomfortable and out of place.

— It's the Mormons, said Frederick with a harumph, his mustache blown upward.

And, shaking his head, he took a delicate sip of his tea.

5

On that first evening I didn't go out to see the city. Lying on the mat in Kate's room, with no shirt on, I watched my chest rise and fall. I thought of Frederick's rapping of his chest, and his allusion to symmetry, and I listened to the voices in the street below.

No sooner had we finished our tea than Kate had to leave to go to her class for a couple of hours. We'd kissed each other and I'd walked her to the bottom of the stairs, but I came back up. I'd been thinking about her all the time since she'd left. I thought, This woman is beginning to make me feel whole. I'm in China, and I'm beginning to feel whole because I've spent three hours with Kate.

Then Frederick walked into the room and sat down on the

chair that faced the mat bed. He raised his hand, as if to keep me from speaking.

— I must talk with you, he said, almost in a whisper. I've been thee-inking. I feel I should say a word. I thee-ink I can see why you are here, and I must speak. You're here for a ray-zon. You are like me. You are a seeker. Yes? You've come to seek some sort of enlightenment. Yes? You've come to be with your woman, sure, but also . . . I can sense it . . . you've come, like all of them from the West, to seek an answer. Ha! he burst out, almost as an aside to himself, that's funny. There isn't any!

He said this with such sudden, heretofore hidden, contempt that he seemed to surprise even himself. Then he stopped, narrowed his eyes, and focused his attention on me again. I had a suspicion that he was trying to provoke a reaction. But I didn't say anything, and I suppose he took this as a cue to continue.

— You've come to find some diss-a-pleen, some spiritual practice, to focus your spirit because, like all Americans, and yes — he conceded with a shrug — many Europeans too, you're a lost soul.

He sighed and rubbed his chin. Then he crossed his thin legs. Jet lag had made me weak-headed, and in the silence I heard the voices outside again. Two women in the courtyard below were arguing in high-pitched jabbering. I looked back at Frederick.

— Maybe I'm wrong, he added circumspectly. Maybe you've come just for love. That's okay. But let me tell you a little about myself. I lived in Berlin. But I speak English well because from nineteen seventy-two to the summer of nineteen seventy-five I lived in Caldy-fornia. I worked in a library in Mill Valley. Have you ever been to Caldy-fornia?

— No.

— Well, it's great. But if I had found see-metry there, I would not have had to come here. Although what I said a moment ago, you know, when I said, "There isn't any answer"?

— Yes.

— Well, don't listen to that.

— You didn't mean it?

— No, I was mostly kidding. A part of me gets cynical when I'm talking about this subject.

— What subject?

— Enlightenment. I mean, it's long past the sixties and the seventies. But still, people are always thee-inking . . . *The Mysterious East,* he said in a low, quavering swami voice. They cannot get it out of their blood. It comes from Marco Polo. From Carl Jung. The whole bit. You know what I mean?

— Sort of.

— In me, there is still a seena-cism. But I was not being fair. I am, in fact, now in the process of finding, I think, I hope, true see-metry through sword dancing . . .

— Frederick, I appreciate what you say. But I came to be with Kate. That's all.

— Yes, yes, I know. I was just talking, he said, nodding his head slowly. But he watched me out of the corner of his eye.

— Let me take you someplace, he said all of a sudden, slapping his knees.

— Where?

— A nice place. Near here.

— All right.

So I got up, threw on a shirt, and we went out. We didn't say a word to each other all the way down the stairs. Outside, Frederick nodded and smiled at people along Wei Chi Street, and they all waved and smiled back. When he grinned you couldn't see his upper lip; it disappeared completely beneath his mustache.

A dog followed us. It was a grubby, earnest animal that trotted by our side. We went through the throngs in the market, and down a cobblestone street. Then we turned a corner and entered a long expanse of manicured gardens and paved paths. In the middle stood a massive, bulky structure of molded white concrete about fifty feet high. It bore a resemblance to a tremendous pagoda, but much of the detail was approximated in plaster, as if a coating of thick white glue had been poured over the building, and there remained only rounded evidence of what was embalmed.

— This is the most bee-ootiful place in all of Taipei, said Frederick with a sigh, looking up at the building with reverence.

The dog raised its leg gently against a small tree at the edge of the yard and, while peeing, glanced at us sheepishly.

— A monument to a great man, Harry. It is the Chiang Kai-shek Memorial. I come here every day to practice. You see? Over there.

He pointed to a group of darkly clad people at the foot of the steps, off to the side near an immaculate row of hedges. They were gyrating about in a high-stepping formation.

— Come. I'll show you.

We walked into the inner courtyard, but Frederick saw something up ahead in the group of dancers and became disturbed. The closer we got, the more he frowned. He watched the dancers intently.

Each person in the group had a long sword, and they all spun about in long steps. A male voice emanated from a tape recorder on the ground, counting time.

— Eee . . . Ur . . . Sahn . . . Su . . .   Eee . . . Ur . . . Sahn . . . Su . . .

— Our master's voice. Sometimes he can't be here in person, whispered Frederick.

At each beat, the swordsmen swung into a new position and

their swords whooshed through the air. They wore billowy black pants and bands around their heads. All of them were Chinese, except one lone figure in the back. Frederick's eyes fastened on this man. He was pale and pudgy with red hair tied in a braid behind his head. He minced about self-consciously, and attempted to keep up with the others.

— Ach! Frederick spat loudly. I thought so. It's him!

The man, out of earshot, spied us and waved, but immediately he was drawn back into the motions.

— Scheisse, said Frederick, looking down. He's waving at me. What an idiot. Bad form. Very bad form.

Frederick turned and strode off, gesturing to me to follow. The red-haired man saw us go.

— Free-derick! Oh, Free-derick!

The voice was desperate and thin, and was full of humiliated nuances.

We kept walking.

That night the sounds of the city became hushed. Kate had finally returned from her class, and I sat in her room at her little desk and played with the Chinese dictionary. As she tinkered around in the bathroom, preparing for bed, I began to feel a little uneasy about sleeping with her. Since I arrived that morning we had hardly had any time together. She had come back from her class late, and we'd spoken only briefly before she began to get ready for bed. And now there were a lot of soft preparatory sounds coming from the bathroom: running water . . . silence . . . silence . . . running water . . . silence.

I gave a shot at some of the Anglicized versions of the Chinese words in the dictionary, sort of to myself.

— Ow, ow, meow. Ow, ow, meow . . .

— What? said Kate over the water, through the bathroom door.

— Nothing, I said.

It hit me that I still had my clothes on, and no doubt she would come wafting out of the bathroom smelling of oils, partly naked, expecting to see me in bed already, with my arm tossed over the sheets. But here I was, sitting at the desk, fully clothed, playing with a dictionary. And then there would be the undressing in front of her. I didn't know if I was up to it.

China, China, China, I kept saying to myself, and started to take off my clothes. How far should I go? Down to my underwear?

The noises in the bathroom sounded final. She was winding up things in there. I heard the cabinet shut, and there was the brushing of teeth. Then, with a quick opening of the door, she emerged, and she was absolutely beautiful. She was wrapped in a black silk robe. I had taken off only my shoes and unbuttoned my shirt. I felt as if I'd been caught trying to escape, even though I was actually still trying to arrive. We stood facing each other for a moment, and then I moved to her and took her in my arms, at the same time cursing myself. Why did elegance of movement and things like that seem so important at times like this? But I pushed back her robe and it dropped to the ground. And there she was, gleaming.

The first thought that came to my mind was an unusual one. I thought of gods in various religions and how they are pictured: sometimes in elaborate shapes, with stern yet merciful faces. And sometimes the sky is dark, or they're coming out of the sea, or they're coming up over the ridge of a mountain with their arms spread, sending off sunbeams.

6

In the morning, against the white sheet, I saw Kate's pale breast. The sheet surrounded it and it rose, almost as if it had been singled out, above everything, its nipple like the surface of a smooth rosy planet, like Mars seen from a great distance, floating on a hill of milk. Her chin also jutted up from the covers, but lower than her breast, and her mouth was slightly open. Still, the breast rose and fell as if it were the only living thing in the room.

She woke up and turned her head. Her eyes blinked, and her breast withdrew into the covers.

— Hello, my sweet, she said.

— Hello, I said and reached under the covers, looking for and eventually finding one of her knees. It was knobby and warmer than my hand. Then I found her thigh and I held on to it under the sheets. Everything is going to work, I thought. It was wise to seek her out, even in another country.

From then on we were always together in the mornings, drinking hot soy milk under the tents in the Kung-yuan market, or jogging together around the cinder track near Tai Da. We were the American couple who lived on Wei Chi Street, and gradually we merged into the patterns of the city.

But I was nervous around her. All added up, we really hadn't known each other long, that is, in actual face-to-face time. There were those months at college when we were together, but in such a cool and detached manner, it seemed now, that I didn't really know this new Kate.

She now made me feel as if I were truly in love, as if we were bound together. But still, underneath it all, I was tense. In some deep recess of my mind I found myself searching for that last bit of her that I knew was somehow denied me. There was something about her that was always on the edge of not being given. She was very affectionate, and she said she loved me, and I had run my hands down every inch of her body, but something inside her eluded me.

She was nervous around me as well, even when we merely were walking together down the crowded streets, when no talking was possible because we were trying to hurry somewhere, or we were separately watching things; even then, there was an electric mood, a kind of febrile, sexy knowingness. We were agonizingly aware of each other's presence. If my hand happened to bump hers as we walked side by side, we would both freeze for a just a second, and I'd wonder whether it was right to casually grab her hand.

And moving about the apartment, or lying in bed, collapsed and naked in the afternoon, we'd be all alone in the apartment, and suddenly I'd be stricken with a fear of making a false move, of saying something horrible out of the blue, or of doing something, something selfish or stupid, and ruining my chances of getting whatever I was hoping to get from her. But that fear would pass.

For the first month I didn't have anything specific to do, and thoughts of Kate would flood me and I'd go about gasping for breath as I walked about Taipei.

I wanted to stop lusting after her; not just her body, but all of her. If I was alone, sitting at the bamboo table, doing something like reading the paper, she'd come in and I'd secretly get angry, because I was trying to get some peace, but when she was around everything in me would gravitate toward her and concentrate on her.

So I took to stealing out of the apartment and wandering by myself around Taipei, sometimes taking buses to the outer districts, sometimes just looking in shops, thinking about my future and secretly snuffing out any thoughts of Kate, because that time alone was mine, and if I started to think about her then I'd lose even that silence, and she'd be with me, maddeningly, all the time.

That's how I got my first job in Taipei.

In my wanderings one day I met an Australian guy at a newspaper stand named Roger Theef. After that, we'd often bump into each other there and would stroll around Taipei aimlessly together, talking about things like politics and, sometimes, in a humdrum way, more lofty subjects, like philosophy. Even though I'd studied it in college, I made a pretense of having read things that I hadn't, and Roger pretended he'd read it all. Sometimes it was agonizing. But Roger was always in a hippity-hop mood, swaggering and grinning, and liked to talk about the "philosophies of the world." He saw every philosophical, political, psychological, and scientific idea as being of equal

weight, all the way from biblical proverbs down to foggy
snatches from Dianetics and stress management. He would bob
about from one to the other with hyperactive enthusiasm.

— What do you think Jesus would have thought about creative visualization? Roger would say as we browsed through the
Chinese bookstore on Ho-Ping Lu. I mean, do you think that
his miracles could be due to an extraordinary power of creative
visualization?

I have no idea what he was doing in Taipei. He had a job that
involved lots of money. He knew government officials. He wore
tennis shoes. They were always very clean, as were his teeth.
Optimism, for Roger, was a way of life. It was like a birthright,
but one you had to use, like a talent, for fear of losing it. And
because he had so much of it, because it came out of every pore
on his body like some malodorous cologne, he threw around his
optimism as if it were inherited money and he was an irresponsible wag of an heir. He gave it to everyone.

— Harry, *believe* me, the Greeks were pretty amazing. *Absolutely.* The Japanese are doing splendidly now. And you Americans have been quite sharp. But take the Chinese, for instance.
I like *them.* I think *they're* the best. Smartest there are. Look what
they've got. For one, they've got tons of history. Hundreds of
dynasties. Many of them, at least. Their culture goes way back.
How far back? Far! And art? The stuff's gorgeous. They'll beat
out the snooty two-shoes in Europe *any* day. They were painting thousands of years before your Picasso or your Monet was
in diapers. And their writing? Gorgeous stuff. A visual marvel.
I mean, compare it to ours . . . Can you see a picture in *our*
words? No, it's sad to say. No matter how much you stare at
a page of English, you'll see only cramped little squiggles. But
the Chinese? There's a bloody picture in every fucking word
they've got. You read "man," there it is! A picture of a man,
right there in the word. You read "tower," whammo, your vis-

ual reference is in front of your nose, inside the goddamned word! *Amazing.*

I must admit, against my will, I occasionally learned things from Roger. But however loquacious he was, he was also extremely hard to find, except by mistake. He'd disappear for days. You were likely to bump into him only at Hsimending, the big shopping district, near the movie theaters with their huge signs picturing gigantic actors kissing or jumping through barbed wire or looking upward. I couldn't figure out why he was always there, walking about dragging on his cigarettes. When he saw me in the crowd he'd grin and his teeth would open up into a beautiful smile, and he'd come over and slap me on the back with his tan hand.

— Harry!

He was the kind of avid smoker who looked healthier than everyone else.

Then one day I bumped into him, as usual right by the movie theaters, under a tremendous billboard of Henry Fonda looking up, wearing a fishing cap. It was on Hsinsheng Bei Lu, at midday.

— Harry, I'm going to recommend you to someone who needs an English teacher. Someone very, very important. He's high up in the Taiwanese government. I've talked about you. He's interested. They like Americans. No kidding. I'm serious. They *really* do.

A black car came to pick me up on the appointed day. Our doorbell rang. Just before bolting downstairs, a tie on and my shoes polished, I faced Kate across the room. She was in shorts and a yellow shirt, and was watching me keenly. She grabbed both of my arms and pulled me around so that she got to speak to me while looking in my eyes.

— Harry, slow down. They'll wait.

We stood there, wobbling, and she started to say something. But she veered away from it.

— Good luck, she said.

— I'll see you when I get back, I said, and rushed down the stairs and out the red door.

A man in a gray uniform showed me to the car and shut the door behind me. It was quiet inside, and the darkened windows provided a dim view of the pedestrians and the streets. The air conditioner hissed and the doors were so well sealed that I could barely hear the sounds of the city.

After a long drive to a part of Taipei I'd never seen, the car passed through two great iron gates. We drove up a sloping driveway with trees and azaleas. Strangely, an occasional soldier could be seen standing in the wet green shrubbery, his helmet reflecting the late day sun and his white gloves clamped around a rifle, at relaxed attention.

The car stopped, the door opened, and I got out. A man was waiting for me at the end of the walkway to the house. He wore a dark suit with a lifeless blue tie that looked like the discarded skin of a snake, and with a slightly sour expression he watched me get out of the car.

It was a large, decidedly American-style stone house, with white shutters and flowerpots on the porch.

— Hello, said the man, and a smile appeared instantaneously on his face. Then, in Chinese, he asked, Hao bu hao? Which means, essentially, are you fine or not fine?

— Hao, I said.

We shook hands and he steered me up the walk with a polite but firm guiding of my elbow, all the time smiling, as if we were suddenly great friends. Up ahead, I could see two soldiers flanking the front door, staring out blandly into the distance. The wet walkway was made of slate, and the stone house rose up to a roof with slate shingles. The white shutters were newly painted and dripped water, from a rain that I had missed or had not noticed, and way up top there was a stone chimney that sent a thin wisp of smoke into the white sky. It was chilly, like early October in America. In fact, it was all very much like America.

For a moment I thought of Kate, and wondered what it was she had wanted to say to me. My mind drifted aimlessly to kissing her in bed the night before, and to the feeling of holding her and breathing against her neck in the darkness. I had felt a strange fury inside me as I kissed her, a desire finally to get at it, to find that part of her I didn't know. I had hung back in the darkness to watch her, but when I drew away from her face, more than a few inches from her lips, I couldn't see her. It was too dark. I only heard her breathing. And, just for a moment, I found myself fantasizing about her. But I didn't imagine some other woman below me in the pitch dark; I found myself fantasizing about making love to Kate. Even though she was with me, even though she was close to me and I was holding her, I found myself imagining it anyway.

Then I split this fantasy off to create an imaginary second Kate — an exact twin, distinct from the woman with whom I made love. The two of them, I imagined, were connected in the darkness by an arc that flowed out of their feet. In the blackness above me this second Kate curved over my back and almost completed the circle by staring over my shoulder into the face of the real Kate below me. I was riding on the inside of a ring, an eternal loved woman, my Kate, divided into real and imaginary.

After we made love, this fantasy dissipated quickly, and I lay beside her, my hand stroking her stomach, and quickly forgot the second Kate. But approaching the American-style house, this "vision" came to me again. Admittedly, I had found the fantasy deeply erotic, so it was exciting to think of it once more.

But beyond that I knew there was a message for me in that image; and I resolved to look into my heart and find out exactly where the two Kates met, and discover what it was I was searching for in her.

The faces of the soldiers were expressionless when I finally arrived at the door. There were insignia on their breasts and on their sleeves, and both men were short. When I walked by I could see the tops of their helmets.

The house inside was austere. A large portrait of General Chiang Kai-shek smiled down from the facing wall, his breast puffed out, and his uniform, green and covered with medals, like a thick, impenetrable field of wildflowers. But the extravagance of the painting was tightly confined in a severe black frame. The whole house, in fact, had a spare, almost Puritan feel to it. The floors were wood and rugless, and there was little furniture.

We took off our shoes and put on slippers. The man with the dull tie went off into the next room. He returned almost immediately behind the tallest Chinese man I had ever seen. He was well into middle age but had a look of childish amusement, particularly because of his pouting, cherubic mouth. We were introduced in Chinese.

— Hello, I said. My name is Harry.

— Pleased to meet you, he said, enveloping my hand in his. My name is Chen. Come.

He put his hand on my back and we walked together into the next room, where we sat down facing each other in two black lacquered chairs, stiff-backed and hard.

The room was white, but there were so many scrolls and paintings on the walls that it was like a small, immaculate museum. Pictures of ghostlike cranes mincing through a stream, with delicate legs and beaks, stood on the wall beside several grave portraits of Manchu royalty. Beside them were yellowed scrolls of calligraphy, and beside the scrolls there were ink drawings, some of little bearded men creeping about beneath mossy cliffs.

At the end of the room were two big french windows, and I could see a path of grass and a row of low, well-clipped hedges on either side.

— You have been highly reck-mended by Mister Teef, as a tutor.

— You seem to speak English fairly well already, I said.

— Yes, yes, but I must learn to speak better. I must give speeches soon, to the German bussa-nussmen. We have many forah-nors come for business to Taiwan now. I am in the government.

— Why not learn German?

— Because no one speaks German in Asia. Everyone wants to be speaking Eng-ish, he said with a smile.

Tea was brought in and placed on a low table between us.

— How many years are you? said Mr. Chen, eyeing me closely.

— Twenty-two.

— Two, two?

— Yes.

He nodded and held the tea to his nose. Then he sipped loudly and surveyed me with a blank expression.

— You have read too much?

— What?

— You have read too much?

— Not that I know of.

He looked back down at his tea. A small man came in, neatly dressed, with glasses, and whispered into Mr. Chen's ear. Chen's eyes did a dance around the room while he listened. The man left.

Almost as an afterthought, Chen reached into his pocket and

pulled out a small carved jade figure. It was a statue of a dragon. He placed it on the table. It seemed incredible that such a thing could have been in his pocket and not got broken. Each scale on its body was carved in fine detail. It had flaring nostrils and a long curved tail that swirled back and rested on its spine. And it had tiny, spiky teeth.

— This is my pet, said Chen, smiling affectionately at the figure.

— It's always in your pocket?

— Yes, he said. It prow-teck me. It eats the bad things only. How do you say? The ee-vall? Yes. When ee-vall is around I bring it out to eat, he said with a chuckle.

I must have looked surprised, because Mr. Chen spoke up immediately.

— No, no, no . . . I mean . . . No, do not worry . . . it is a joke. Not you. Of course.

We both looked at the dragon on the table. The jade absorbed the light from the windows and reflected it on the table in soft, green patterns.

— I think you are young. But I need a tutor. Maybe you come and speak Eng-ish with me?

— All right.

— Monday?

— Yes, that's fine.

The spectacled man came in once again, but this time he quietly placed a black box on the table in front of Mr. Chen. It was an electronic device of some kind, with eight or nine buttons on its surface, and a gray screen.

— So, you come next week?

— Yes.

Mr. Chen reached forward and pushed one of the buttons on the box. Several symbols, not numbers, flashed on the screen.

The man who had first greeted me came in once again and nodded to me.

Plucking the dragon off the table, Mr. Chen stood and shook my hand, and dropped the statue back into his pocket. The screen on the black box had stopped flashing, and several symbols were displayed, as if the solution to a problem just calculated. As I turned to leave I noticed Mr. Chen glance at it and take note of what he saw.

Outside, it had started to rain. The black car eased up to the end of the walk, and through the doorway and between the two soldiers I walked with my escort. Our heels *crick-cracked* on the pavement out toward the car, with its plume of idling exhaust and the rain hanging in beads on its black surface. The driver and the man talked quickly, and the driver looked at me with an expression of bored novelty.

The peculiarity of the meeting with Mr. Chen didn't impress itself on me until we got to the bottom of the driveway. Then, as if I were just remembering an odd dream, I thought of the soldiers in the garden, and how queer that was. And the sugary expression on Chen's face kept coming up in my mind, the way his mouth pouted like that of a fat child who'd just eaten a lollipop. His lips were red and shiny too, as if he were constantly licking them. There was something in his strong face that was eerie, and although he was handsome, he seemed distantly grotesque, especially when he brought out the little dragon. God knows why, but the image of him smiling at that little thing frightened me.

7

Sometimes, looking back, I remember Kate in a series of charging poses. She's charging across a beach on the east coast of Taiwan, or bolting along the sidewalk at night bathed in the white glow of the street lamps, her head thrust forward and her eyes set on an indeterminate end point several miles away. Even when she laughed it was short and direct with a blunt surge of energy that would ruffle up in an enticing curl of sound and fan out for just a moment, then end abruptly, leaving the impression that she hadn't yet laughed enough.

She was not tall, maybe five-five, but she gave the impression of height. She had a smooth oval face with blue eyes and a sharp nose that had discreet, streamlined nostrils. There was a point at the center of her upper lip, and sometimes, when she was incensed about something, it made her look hawklike. But then again, it was one of those characteristics you notice only after knowing somebody a while.

I've heard other men describe women, and it has often bothered me that I learned so little from what they've said. At those moments, listening to descriptions of loved women, I have panicked. Part of me was satisfied that I was capable of true love, and from their descriptions, it was evident most other men were not. Yet when I met a man I thought had truly been in love (with his wife or, in that pained and obvious way, with a girlfriend), I would suddenly drop into sadness and envy. Then, when I saw them together, I would find myself watching for the inevitable weaknesses in their bond, the glances, the tense posture, the awkward movements. Part of me, a well-hidden part, hated the idea of a man who could love a woman more deeply than I. But part of me admired it more than anything. And yet even these men, the ones I secretly admired, had nothing genuine to teach me in their descriptions of what they felt. They sank to the same monotonous words as everyone else, and I would despair of getting to what it was that made their emotions different.

Hearing "she's really wonderful" for the thousandth time would cause paroxysms in my gut. I was hoping to hear the final, real thing. But we'd end up, the describer and I, listening to him talk about the way there was a mole on her ear, or about the unusual way she ate cereal in the morning. It always came down to something almost aggressively normal that he had succumbed to and was elevating to the level of beauty. And all the while, there would be that nagging fear in me that it was a lie, this loving of people. All of it sounded so similar, so uniform. How could it be unique, sublime, if it was described every time in exactly the same way?

Inevitably, it seemed, this uniformity would take its toll in its darker form. One day the guy would be extolling the virtues of his love, and then, somewhere along the line, several months later, or several years later, I'd hear how the noisy cereal eating had always, secretly, driven him mad. He had been seething at every crunch. But at the time, the anger had been overridden by a delightful rush of love (which does in fact make love sound like some internally secreted drug that overcomes the banality of other people).

Well, if it was a secret that he deplored her quirks, it was a secret from his most private self as well. At the end of it, he would discover that he didn't love her at all, the way people discover a body in a lake months after someone has been lost in a fishing accident. Suddenly, the whole truth just floats to the top, for no particular reason. She wasn't what he had originally thought, he'd say. Her cereal eating was just that: the consuming of cereals. The mole on her face was just that: a mole. It was not a "birthmark."

And if you are a good friend, you are supposed to change stride with the describer without any evidence of the sharing of hypocrisy.

So, what about Kate?

Physically she was small, as I've said. Her skin was rosy, but paler and brighter because, I suppose, of the open and illuminating color of her hair. It was true blond. The color that looks white in the sun. She had rounded thin shoulders and a small bust. Her breasts were shaped, in profile, like small, sharp waves heading toward her face. Straight on they were white and shadowless, with quiet interludes of pink in the center. Her ribs were often visible, but in a defiant, healthy way. She was a strong woman, and although she was tentative about touching people, when she fought physically, as I saw her do only once, she was a formidable opponent.

In Taipei, she had the demeanor of an honorable, unvarnished, yet attractive woman. She prided herself on being straightforward, someone with respectable goals backed up by a sense of duty. When she spoke Chinese it was without grace, but knowingly so, and it was always correct, like the speech of somebody who'd learned the language during a war. I stood by, invariably ignorant of most of what was being said, yet always seeing her, from outside the conversation, with reverence for her rough mastery.

She made a point of displaying a grip on conversations, showing her ability to control the present moment. She always handled consultations with people, about directions and money, and the practical minutiae of the day, and she seemed pleased, almost too pleased, when she had managed these things correctly. She would smile to herself when she had wheedled information out of someone, or had determined that the price of something had been inflated because we were foreigners. She took great pleasure in confounding the Chinese with her ability in the language. She liked to be underestimated, and then strike.

Her desire to master the present extended to her ideas of how to handle the future, and this is where we began to argue. Kate said I was a mentally disorganized person. When we visited people, she'd squirm if they asked me what I intended to do with the rest of my life, what sort of career I wanted. She knew that I hadn't the faintest idea. In contrast, she knew exactly what she wanted to do, how she was going to do it, and so forth. She wanted to be a lawyer. And she knew precisely what kind of lawyer she wanted to be.

When my career came up in a conversation, we got into the habit of pulling an acrobatic turn back to Kate, and she would talk about her plans in very general terms, and we would pretend that her ambitions were sort of mine as well.

— Men in America don't ever know what they are going to do, she once said to a female Chinese friend. Generally they fake it until they find themselves doing something. And then, when the coast is clear, they announce that they always wanted to do something else, and then they sulk for several years.

One night, as we were lying next to each other, just before we fell asleep, I told her about an idea that had come to me. I had read about something that ignited my interest in a possible profession.

I'd begun to be fascinated with the idea of computers. For directionless people, computers ushered up thoughts of a sensible and purposeful life. In the larger, historical perspective of things it was an infant profession that most of the world was still ignorant of, so you could join in and be assured beginner status with millions of others.

It all started after I'd read an article in *The International Herald Tribune* about a huge supercomputer called the Ouroboros Series 1. It was a new kind of computer, the article said, and many scientists in the United States hailed its intriguing capabilities.

As I understood it, a normal computer approached each piece of a problem sequentially, as if the data were lined up in a queue, and assigned the same importance to each piece of information, like an eye looking at a picture through a keyhole. Put all the information about an elephant in, for instance, and in order to figure out what it was, a normal computer would take each piece of information and methodically identify it — eyes, mouth, wrinkled skin, toenails, tusks, and so on, one after another — until it had enough information to categorize the thing as an elephant. The Ouroboros Series 1, however, was different. It was a massive neural network, a new breed of supercomputer that attempted to mimic the way a brain actually thinks. It was structured to look at all the data at once, the way the brain would. Its inventor had combined two parts of the traditional computer, the memory and the processor, into one entity, creating a tiny electronic unit that resembled a cluster of brain cells. When this unit was connected to thousands of others like it, they resembled a huge model of the human brain. Unlike ordinary computers, the new one really was a "thinking machine."

According to the article (which I read one morning sitting at the bamboo table, completely riveted), this radical structure enabled the Ouroboros Series 1 to do something miraculous, something that no other computer had been able to achieve. Every problem it solved became an integral part of its thinking composition, much like the mind of a learning individual.

The way it did this was to create a symbolic silhouette of the path (or algorithm) that it followed to arrive at a particular solution. This would be stored in its vast memory. Later, while figuring a new problem, it would compare the emerging algorithm with any similar algorithm it could find in its library of correct solutions. If a pattern resembled one already stored, the Ouroboros would track the similarities and record them.

Over time, the Ouroboros became more and more familiar with its own web of knowledge. It was the one machine, probably in the history of mankind, that would work more efficiently and more powerfully a decade, or several decades, after it was first switched on. It had the ability to attain a rich, malleable, and useful past. It thought about the world, devoured what it thought, and devoured itself in order to understand the world again.

For this odd characteristic it was named the Ouroboros, after an ancient symbol from alchemy that dates back to Greece in the first century A.D. The Ouroboros was a tremendous snake curled in a perfect circle, devouring its own tail. The early Greek alchemists drew the picture of the Ouroboros to represent the final stage that two opposites have to go through in order to become one. The opposites, the head and the tail, represent light and darkness, or the desire to know feeding upon what is already known, as in the case of the Ouroboros Series 1. With a certain satisfaction, I realized this thing was a Western version of the Chinese yin and yang.

This caught something in me. There was an untethered rope in my imagination that was flapping around, and when it found this thing, this idea of a machine that could develop something akin to wisdom, that could possibly many, many years hence develop its own system of values, and conceivably ethics and morals at some point . . . when my imagination fell on this thing, it awoke.

I looked down Wei Chi Street, at a lone bicycler pedaling along, a white package tied to the back of his bike, the spokes glittering in the sun, and I felt released. This was something to which I could devote my life. This fascinating computer. This could be my career, I thought. My profession. But the Ouroboros seemed to be the answer for all sorts of doubts. This was a machine that could eventually unfog a thousand foggy issues. We'd finally get a tremendous intelligence, a huge visionary being, in our midst that would not be sullied by the awkwardness of being human. It might look objectively into emotions, and it might one day explain to us the foggiest of all things: love.

— I want to work with the Ouroboros, I said to Kate that night as we were both drifting off to sleep. It's a supercomputer.

— But, Harry, said Kate in the dark, you don't know anything about computers.

— I'll find out.

— You'll need math, you'll need to go back to school and learn acres of complicated math.

— I'll take summer courses.

There was a long cold silence next to me.

— Don't forget Mister Chen, she said.

In the morning I went to the American Cultural Center. It had a library. Frederick took me there. He swayed above the crowd, in his long baggy pants, a white man like a lighthouse with a mustache.

We tacked back and forth through the crowd. Frederick was looking for familiar things. He only half remembered the way. He hadn't been to the American Cultural Center for quite a while. At last his face brightened up.

— There it is, he said pointing with a long arm. That's the street.

We walked past a row of dented soy milk carts with the steam rising and one woman tending them all, ladling soy milk with a battered black spoon. Through the sweet steam I could see the drowsy Stars and Stripes drooping over the street in the sun. A clatter of motorized tricycle taxis went by with their engines shuddering.

— Go into the library there, said Frederick. There's got to be some kind of a computer section.

He patted me on the back and headed off into the crowd. From behind, I could see his mustache poking out like pieces of twine on either side of his head.

Inside, a woman at the desk pointed me toward the science section. After drifting through a whole shelf devoted to spiders of the Pacific islands, and browsing through a book entitled *Angry Soundwaves: The Acoustics of Yelling,* I found a book about neural networks.

Nowhere in the table of contents was the Ouroboros mentioned; the book had come out a year before it was invented. But I began to read anyway, because the work was about some of the underlying principles that led to the Ouroboros, and since I knew nothing about computers beyond elementary concepts, I had to start somewhere.

The library was dominated by the downward glances of readers. Far away, on the other side of the reading room was a huge replica of *The Signing of the Declaration of Independence.* Thomas Jefferson, up front and facing right, was the most prominent figure. His red hair was tied behind his head in a ponytail. He was a tall, gawky man with a kind of severe precision in his eyes. His face was anxious. No one had signed yet. They were still arguing. The older ones, men probably born in the early years of the eighteenth century, stood in the back and looked on with joyless expressions. They knew what they were doing and hated it, it seemed; hated that it had to be done. War was ahead. They saw no alternative.

Among the young bucks there, the lily-white sardonic rogues with their eyes on history, only Jefferson seemed to grasp the weight of the sweaty assembly. Many of the others looked as if they had enthusiasm enough for signing anything, even their own death warrants, had they been guaranteed a role in some sort of mob ritual, with torches, gunpowder, and the fancy clothes you get to wear when you go to battle.

I opened the book. Detailed formulas covered each page. There were diagrams of processing "nodes" composed of "chips." I knew what chips were. They stored information. We all know that; I mean everybody does. So far, so good, I thought. At least at first glance it was stuff that I could handle.

Then I began to read, and I didn't stop for a couple of hours. I made a mental note of what I didn't understand, which was a fair amount. But much of it I understood, and this I devoured with a feeling of excitement. I was on to something.

After a long while lost in descriptions of "collective decision circuits" and "associative memory circuits," I raised my head and looked about the room to rest my eyes. Over at the other side of the room, below *The Signing of the Declaration of Independence,* right below it, directly in the center of that stretch of wall, was an old bearded man, sitting alone at a table, reading. He was reading a book by Zane Grey, in Chinese. Oriental characters stood above the English words on the cover, where there was a brown-tinted picture of a cowboy on a horse. The book was called *Rogue River Feud,* and the old man read it quietly, somberly, and with an expression of reverence. He looked very much like one of the white-haired codgers in the mossy grottoes on Mr. Chen's wall of scrolls. I knew that those ink drawings represented Taoist masters — philosophers and wise men — and it seemed odd to me that these men were represented as wrinkled men, often half naked because their clothes appeared to be falling off; and they were sometimes in tiny water-logged boats, or making their way with crooked canes through forests, hardly visible in the drawings because they were rendered as little bearded beings amidst the huge mountains, the misty lakes. And here was one of those guys reading an American cowboy adventure story. This was an amusing idea and it bounced around in my head for a few seconds. But as I smiled to myself about the idea of one of Mr. Chen's hallowed Chinese sages stealing away to read about saloon fights and horse rustling, I thought, Well, what if it's true, what if this guy was one of those philosophers once? How sad that these great teachers (much like the apotheoses of what my friends were all looking for back in college), these philosophers in their ragged clothes and their wizened bodies, were now coming to the American Cultural Center to read Zane Grey.

I glanced back at my book on neural networks. There was a long formula underneath the diagram illustrating the "collective decision circuits." X did an aggressive dance through a variety of letters and arrived at the end looking not much different, except that it had a tiny number 10 attached to its forehead.

But I closed the book. I had read enough for one day, and it was getting harder to concentrate. I kept looking up at the little man with the white hair and he was beginning to bother me. Whenever I bent down to read I could see this white spot out of the corner of my eye, and every so often a flutter of his hand turning the page of his cowboy book.

So I got up, put the book back in its shelf, and walked outside. The sun was blazing. Hundreds of people swarmed down the sidewalk. For some reason I was busy ruminating about the mural in the library, and the fact of being American, and how vague it sometimes all seemed. Those stolid figures on the wall in this foreign city felt separated from me by a great chasm. I thought back to college and about the feeling of being guideless, and I remembered first seeing Kate in all her fiery moment, dancing like a demon. She was in class now, teaching. I imagined her hand lifting the chalk to the dark expanse of blackboard. I thought of her lips.

A loud funeral procession was going by on Nanhai Road, and the cars were honking with that fury of traffic in hot weather. They were covered with flowers. A woman walked by, her face blank with errands. A skinny young man passed, swinging his arms, carrying in his hand an oily part for an engine. Then came a group of children, all in blue uniforms. Then the teacher. Then four businessmen with briefcases, all talking and smiling, and sometimes nodding quickly to one another.

A dilapidated truck passing on Nanhai Road, loaded with melons, dropped two of its cargo as it jerked through the traffic. One exploded with a smart, muffled crunch. The other dented and rolled lopsidedly for a few feet until it bumped up against the curb. The students screamed with delight in chorus, and one of the businessmen, arriving at the dented melon, kicked it lightly with the shiny toe of his shoe, much to the amusement of his colleagues, and walked on, talking louder and looking back over his shoulder at the wet, brilliant green remains of the exploded melon, way out in the middle of Nanhai Road, now being slid through and scattered by the rushing traffic.

Sitting stubbornly in the midst of all this was an old fat dog right outside the American Cultural Center. His bottom firmly planted on the sidewalk, he sat as if he had fallen there. Unrepentant, he watched the crowd detour around him, one bright eye poking out of his scarred, short-haired head like a tiny window peeking out of a small black ash heap. His other eye was squeezed shut, either by the failure of the nerves around it, or because of some obdurate canine mood. His muzzle was like a short battering ram, and one of his teeth was revealed, uncovered by the upward rumple of his lip.

Although to children he might have seemed a menacing presence, to the adults who passed he was but an obstacle, and was ignored with the same bored dignity with which he ignored them. Suddenly, though, his whole body jerked. Trembling, the loose skin around his mouth curled up in ripples, revealing his yellow teeth. He kept peeking backward over his shoulder, agitated by something in the crowd. His nose jittered, and the nostrils dilated into round black holes. The old paws shivered on the pavement, and then, abruptly, he jumped. His mouth opened and with a howl of old lungs he swung around and viciously bit at a passing leg. I looked up. It was Frederick's.

He gave a yelp and leaped dramatically sideways, and with a grace arrived at through many hours of sword dancing, he tumbled, smacking his shin, over the small white stone wall that marked the border of the scant lawn of the American Cultural Center.

The dog did not follow. He looked absently out into the traffic.

— Frederick! I said, stepping over the wall. Are you all right?

— Schweinhund! he yelled at the dog.

He got up, holding his shin, and limped around in a circle. The dog had completely forgotten about the incident; he looked momentarily back at Frederick with cocked ears and licked his nose. After a few curses Frederick managed to get back on the sidewalk, and we turned the corner and both started down Chungching Nan Lu together, Frederick bobbing up and down with a limp.

— Did you get your fucking computer books? he said, still stooping every few steps to rub his leg.

— Yes, I found one on neural networks. They're computers structured like our brains, and they're supposed to think the way we think . . .

— Harree, he said, interrupting me, I came back because I saw that fool at the Chiang Kai-shek Memorial. I didn't want to run into him. You know, the one I pointed out to you that day.

— You mean the red-haired guy?

— Ya. I know him from long ago. He is from Germany. You know how it is, seeing people you know from the past. This one I deespize. He has all sorts of ideas about me. People who know you from before always have ideas. But they don't get it. They want you to be the same as before, even, you know, even if you are compleee-tly different. And every time I see him something bad happens . . . Fucking dog!

We walked down Nanhai Lu. Every few seconds Frederick would bend down and rub his shin, but he'd keep talking, and his head, caught midway, would end up talking to the sidewalk. He reminded me of the woman who yelled at the lake during that argument I got involved in back in the States. I got hit for that. And I thought of the "bottomless" lake with nostalgia.

There was a lot of mud there. But the stupid myth about the lake, and all the generations of stodgy alumni calling it bottomless, for some reason made me wistful. I was disgusted with myself for a moment.

We passed under a row of lanterns hanging from the awning of a medicine shop. Behind the window were laid out on a green cloth the mummified parts of animals, herbs, boxes of cicada skins (like empty crystals), twigs, and bones. We paused and looked in the window while Frederick talked, even though he peered closely at the objects behind the window. He fancied himself an advanced amateur in Chinese medicine. The kitchen at home was filled with jars of foul-smelling powders that Frederick had brought back to cure a series of real and imagined ailments.

A small woman with an oblong mass of black hair watched us from behind a statue of Buddha deeper in the shop.

— So my mind was on that fool. When he sees me he always rushes up. *(Look at that goat-horn powder.)* He has no soul. He is always too glad to see me. And then that damned dog. *(I wonder how much they're selling that albumate for? Tastes like marzipan dipped in urine. But it cures warts. What do you think they have for bruises? Ginkgo paste?)* So I thought I'd try to find you. That's why I came back . . . He's now always at the Chiang Kai-shek. And also he has a blasted tattoo . . . I can't stand that tattoo. It reminds me of all the times I wasted in my youth with people like him, smoking the pot, doing nothing, wanting to go to Amereeka. And now he's here. It's enough to anger me, that he's followed me here. *(Ah! And there's a garnet wrapped in tea leaves . . . you know, you rub it on your forehead for the headaches.)*

Frederick speared his cheek with an index finger. He stopped abruptly, and the tone of his voice became a low monotone.

— It's right there.

— What? I said.

— The damned tattoo. It's right there on his face. It's a snake. It's in a curve, you know, like in an S. The curve of it.

— The tattoo?

— Ya.

Immediately I thought of the Ouroboros. The snake again. But this time on somebody's face. It's uncanny how when you become interested in something, it begins to turn up in all sorts of places. With a sense of the approach to my budding destiny, as if I were now seeing all the right signs on my life path, and I was secretly being shown that I was moving in the right direction, I marked this off to myself as a good omen. I smiled, and thought of the Ouroboros sitting in an immaculate white laboratory, a huge black box of a machine, its lights winking softly, and the precise whir and almost silent flutter of its massive thoughts dissecting some impossible problem.

We had just crossed Kung-yuan Lu and were walking across a quiet park. The din of traffic subsided behind us. Frederick's billowy black pants fluttered around his legs over the grass. A group of wrinkled men sat around a stone table playing dominoes. We made a shortcut through a grove of trees.

— Yes, it's not large, but it is a snake. I hate it. It's annoying. You can't talk to him without staring at it, said Frederick, fending off a branch.

Through the wet branches I saw a spark of color across the park. The petals on the trees were a soft pink, but there was a bright yellow object up ahead, through the trees, moving along through the park. At first I thought it was a balloon or somebody's shirt. But then I recognized it as a person with yellow hair. It was a young boy, probably a European. But then, no, then again, it wasn't. It was a woman, not tall. And although it was hard to distinguish from my distance, after much squinting and pulling away of twigs, I was able to identify the head of hair. There was no doubt about it. It was Kate.

— I almost got a tattoo, said Frederick. Back then, we were all doing stoo-pid things. It was the way to blend with everyone else . . .

— That's Kate, I said.

— Where?

— Over there.

— But Harree, that's not Kate. She's got her class today. She's teaching.

I headed out of the trees and onto the path, and Frederick followed. We walked swiftly across the park after the blond head. But the closer we got, the more another figure became visible, harder to see through the leaves because of its smart green military uniform.

— Who's that with her? said Frederick.

— I don't know, I said. He looks like an officer.

We strode quickly down a knoll and across a shallow field, but before we were within yelling distance she had gotten to the edge of the park and had started across the traffic of Kung-yuan Lu.

She quickly disappeared across the street into the labyrinthine passageways of the Shiang Shinn market. For a moment I considered chasing her. But suddenly I decided not to, halted by an image of myself kicking helpless chickens and tipping over large ice-filled boxes of mackerel on my way after my girlfriend and her unknown acquaintance.

8

It took a long time to get home. Frederick stopped at a medicine shop on Shiang Shinn Street, since we happened to be there, to pick up a bottle of an obscure moss that he'd heard gave you a surge of energy when soaked in hot water and drunk as tea. I tapped my foot impatiently while he struggled to describe what he wanted to an ancient man behind the counter. Then we missed the Ling Nan bus and had to walk, and got lost for an hour in an unrecognizable district of tiny, nameless streets. Getting lost with Frederick was infuriating, because he seemed to enjoy it, and tended to walk slower and look about him, breathing deeply. The entire time I thought of Kate, and who she was with, if that was indeed her, and I rummaged through my memories of our conversations to see if I could turn up any mention of a military friend. For a while, following Frederick down a back street where the only signs of life were occasional views into garishly lit basements in which men played mahjong, I finally figured out that it couldn't have been Kate. She was teaching. But dozens of doubts rose in me. Why had I become so crazed at the sight of someone who looked like her? Why so desperate? A surge of panic had gone through me as I ran across that park, a heightened, childish nervousness. If it was Kate, then she was with another person, a man whom I didn't know . . . I calmed myself, and watched Frederick's back as he turned the corner.

— Let's take a cab, for God's sake, I said to him with renewed anger at his joy at being lost.

I was sick of wandering around Taipei, looking for the long way to get home. It was after dusk. Frederick shrugged and nodded, and at the next street we hailed a cab and got home, to find the apartment dark and Kate asleep in bed.

I was comforted, because she often went to bed early when she'd had a long day of teaching. I closed the door to our room, undressed, and got into bed. In the darkness, I heard Frederick cough a few times out in the living room. There was the *tink-tink* of his spoon stirring a cup of tea. The Ouroboros Series 1 appeared in my head when I closed my eyes. I saw myself typing in an equation to be solved on its keyboard. A pattern of lines appeared on a black screen, bound together at the ends, but waving outward into a skeletal spiral. Kate took a deep breath, her back expanded against my chest, and I fell asleep.

In the morning, with the sun coming down against the walls, Kate sighed softly, asleep next to me, without twitching, without raspy catches in her throat, so that all complete, with her soft hair and pinkish face, her sighing and her face next to mine, she was peaceful in the fashion of good people recollected from some corner of one's childhood. I suppose the proximity of her face next to mine on the pillow made her appear much larger than she actually was. She was like a boulder above me on the pillow. And right there, with her asleep, I started to think about our short time together.

In the giddiness of the past few months I'd begun to lose perspective on her. I could tell. Just a shade of my understanding of her, just a shade, seemed to have shifted. In fact, I'd almost forgotten that this woman I was with so much was my girlfriend. She was more a hovering female presence than anything else. Her face on the pillow at that moment was an example. She breathed in and out, and her mouth was open just a fraction, and her eyes were delicately closed. She was very much there. Her breathing was very real. But the overall feeling I had was of a strong apparition, not a real woman. She had the quality of a cloud floating steadily over a field, moving with methodical weight and presence, yet mysterious and light in its composition, so that you feel, looking up at it, that if you had not been taught differently, if you were seeing it for only the first time, you would mistake it for something dangerously balanced in the sky.

That's when I began to think of seeing her in the park the day before. But then, unable to resolve that, I began to steal off to an adjacent subject. Wondering about whether it was her or not her, and what she'd say, and about secrets in other people's love affairs, and what they meant, I began thinking about lying.

When I was little I had lied a lot. Even for things I didn't have to lie about, I'd make up a story, just to extricate myself from the mundane world of the truth. It seemed to me then that lying made for a better sort of reality, although I was ashamed of knowing this. I also noticed that the best liars were generally the people who were so accustomed to hiding the truth that to them everything was potentially a fabricated story, so they lied about everything, just to be safe, because they didn't have the time to recall what they'd lied about, or to whom. For that sort, the world is completely reconstructed. The facts are fluid, slippery contrivances.

And yet that sort of lying was the only kind I knew about at first hand. I'd done that. It was pretty quiet stuff. But what I was beginning to worry about had nothing to do with this kind of lying. It was darker. It concerned deception of those who were most vulnerable to it. In this second form of lying, the facts were black and white, solid, rock hard. The liar knew that. This second sort of liar was an expert on the truth. That was the problem.

But there was no reason to believe that Kate would lie to me. It wasn't that I was suspicious of her. I couldn't be sure it was even her I saw in the park.

— Harry, would you get up and put the water on for coffee? she said, blinking from the pillow.

— Sure.

I put on my pants, went into the kitchen, and set the battered blue kettle on the stove.

Kate passed from the bedroom into the bathroom. Frederick had already gone to sword practice. His bedroom door was open and the sun poured in. From the dingy kitchen it appeared as if an incandescent explosion were taking place in there. It was an east-facing room, and on the wall, where it could be seen from the kitchen, was a scroll on which was painted a tiger. Coming down from a bamboo-covered mountain, the animal was peeking through the leaves. I looked at it sleepily, wondering about predators and the silence of the paws in the forest.

Kate came into the kitchen and sat on a chair and rubbed her face, yawning.

— I saw you yesterday. At least I think I did. Near Kung-yuan Lu, in the park.

— Yesterday? Are you sure?

— Yes, I'm sure. How many blondes are there in Taipei, anyway? I said jokingly. It's like a sea of black hair.

— That's a racist comment, Harry, she said.

— Why?

— It just is, I don't know why, she said testily.

I thought about it.

— I don't see why.

— I couldn't have been there. I was teaching.

— Oh. I know. That's what I thought. Some other blond head. The Europeans are invading.

— No kidding, said Kate.

I picked the kettle off the stove.

— You want coffee? I said.

She glared at me.

— I assume that means yes. Where's your cup?

She pointed to it, upside down in the sink.

— It's funny, because I was positive, I said, shoveling freeze-dried coffee into her cup. I was positive . . . and so was Frederick . . . that it was you. It's weird when you think you know what someone looks like, and then you realize you don't.

— You wanted it to be me. It makes things more mysterious. You want Taipei to be mysterious.

— I want Taipei to be mysterious? No, I don't.

— Yes, you do, Harry. You want everything to be mysterious.

She was not in a great mood. There was a long silence while we sipped our coffee and I thought about what she'd said. I must admit I felt a little bruised, but also ridiculous for feeling bruised. I was unprepared for the comment, and it was still too early in the morning to know whether or not she had a valid point.

— Anyway, Kate, I was convinced it was you. It looked like you.

She abruptly stopped sipping her coffee, and looked up.

— Wait a second. What time was this? she said all of a sudden.

— Late afternoon. About five o'clock.

— Was there somebody with me? A Chinese guy?

— Yes, I said, startled. Some guy in a uniform.

— In the park? . . . Yeah, that park. Oh yes, that probably was me, she said blandly, and went back to sipping her coffee.

Dumbfounded, I stared at her.

— Harry, I'm sorry. I forgot. That was Corporal Wu.

— Who is Corporal Wu? I said, incredulously.

— He's one of my students. He took me to see the park.

— That was nice of him.

She said it so placidly. I was right. I couldn't believe it, I was right. What was going on? I was suddenly furious, but my anger was blowing around inside me without much force. It was stymied, and was not prepared to come out yet. I had to assess this stuff. I had to assess what had happened.

I was aware that there was a part of me that was suspicious of a part of her. Or, more accurately, the untouchable part of her was suddenly threatening, something unseen, as opposed to something just unattainable. There was a sour, ugly, and familiar feeling flitting about inside my ribs, and it had somehow jumped between us like a crooked bolt of lightning, and had identified and very briefly merged with a sour and ugly thing flitting about inside her. But then it passed.

— Here, I said unnecessarily, giving her more coffee.

She sipped. Then her eyes followed me, her eyebrows raised.

— What? Don't tell me you're upset?

— About what?

— About Wu?

— No.

— Harry, you are. You're upset. You're preparing to get jealous.

— No goddammit, I don't give a shit about Corporal Wu. It just was odd, *is* odd, that's all; seeing you walking somewhere I don't expect to see you with a man I don't know. And no doubt you two were blabbing away in Chinese to each other.

— What's Chinese got to do with it?

— I don't know. It feels funny. He's probably got the hots for you.

— Christ, Harry, we just talk . . . He's a corporal.

I started to quell my anger, and tilted my chair until my back leaned against the wall, and then thoughtfully took several large gulps of coffee.

— Come on, honey, she said in a warm voice, reaching out and touching my arm. Don't get so upset.

She called me honey. God, how I hated that word, particularly when I was angry. It meant, Stop being an outside person, a person who sees us from some other point of view.

— Anyway, I said, ignoring her tone, but letting the edge in my voice slip away in deference to being called honey. What's the fact that he's a corporal have to do with whether or not it upsets me?

The door slammed.

— Helloooo! Anyone home? called out Frederick in a loud singsong.

— Harry, said Kate, a little unsettled, her voice lowered. You know I have no interest in anyone but you. You know that.

We looked at each other for one or two seconds of measured silence. And in her face there was a soft, sensual color, and her eyes looked at me darkly, with warmth. Maybe, I thought, maybe she truly loves me. Maybe *I* am being the unreachable one.

But in the middle of this thought Frederick's head came around the corner.

— Oh, so here you are. Good morning. Ulla . . . Ulla . . .

come over here, he said into the other room. Come meet Harree and Kate.

A woman walked into the kitchen, and without regarding her surroundings at all she looked me straight in the eye. I was startled. Even though I was no longer looking at Kate, I was still thinking about what she had said and how I felt about it. And then this unknown woman was also staring into my eyes.

She had a voluptuous body and a stony, geometric face. And she was very tan, except for a red patch of oversunned skin on her nose. Almost as an afterthought, with a kindly but slightly lazy expression, she looked at Kate.

— Hello, she said with an accent, and shook Kate's hand politely, then nodded toward me, almost demurely.

— Kate . . . Ulla is also studying Chinese, said Frederick, rummaging around near the stove. He peered down into the kettle.

— Is this tea? he said, sniffing.

— No, that's just water for coffee, I said.

Frederick sniffed it again.

— Are you from Germany? asked Kate.

— No, from Italy, said Ulla. Bergamo. In the north. You are from the States?

We both nodded. She was an imposing figure. Every part of her was accentuated. Her hips were round and full, and her breasts seemed to be trying desperately to get out of her shirt.

— I come here a year ago, maybe a little less, she said, putting a cigarette into her mouth. As she spoke, the cigarette bobbed up and down.

— Didn't you just move in to here with Frederick? she added, lighting the cigarette and squinting at the flame. She rolled the *r*'s in Frederick, as if the name were an exotic dessert.

— Yes, said Kate. I've been here for nine months, but Harry just got here two months ago.

Ulla smiled. It was a small, strangely shy smile.

— I wanted to go to the communist China, she said. But they wouldn't . . . they don't want me in. They don't like the foreigners now.

She looked at me with her lip curled up around the cigarette.

— Yes, I heard that, said Kate.

— So. You like Taiwan? Ulla said, looking at me.

— Yes, but I've only been here a short time, I said, watching her lips.

— Where's the coffee? said Frederick.

I pointed to it. Frederick had a small bandage on his leg. It was so neatly done that it had the look of something in an advertisement: all white and clean and symmetrically taped.

— Frederick tells me you are into computers? Ulla said brightly.

— Well, I'm interested in a certain kind of computer. But I'm not quite . . . I'm still looking into the subject.

Kate raised her eyebrows at me.

— He's not quite "into it" yet, she said.

— Technically, no, I said. But I hope, sometime in the future.

— So you are studying? said Ulla.

— Sort of.

Kate pursed her lips and sipped her coffee. The point in the middle of her upper lip looked hawklike as it touched the cup.

— This is such an interesting thing, said Ulla, exhaling smoke. The computers are everywhere now. Soon everything is connected. Yes? You know? Like . . . *whoosh* . . . you can send to here . . . or *whoosh* . . . over to here . . .

She was using her hands to demonstrate whooshing, and her bracelets clattered on her wrists.

— Are you studying Chinese? asked Kate abruptly.

— Yes, said Ulla, but smiling at me.

It was one of those smiles where one corner of the mouth lags lazily behind. She was coming on to me in a clumsy way, and although it seemed perfectly innocent, I wasn't in the mood to trade glances with her, because Kate and the day before in the park and my jealousy and other things were on my mind. I got up and, excusing myself, left the kitchen. I had an idea that I'd go for a walk, so I made my way to the bedroom to put on my sneakers.

From the bedroom I could hear Kate and Ulla begin to talk to each other in Chinese. Ulla spoke Mandarin with a distinct Italian accent. I heard her husky voice saying, "Hao . . . hao . . . hen hao," as she listened to Kate. I thought about her face. It was a Roman face right off one of those busts at the Metropolitan Museum. Yet at the same time it was a thinking-about-sex face. She actively imagined things, erotic ideas; you could see it in her eyes, it was like a hobby, maybe the way a chessplayer thinks about games or chess positions when he's not playing.

I went toward the door, but first I looked into the kitchen. Kate had warmed up my coffee and was drinking it, having finished hers. Ulla was sitting down with one leg up on the table. Frederick had wandered into the main room and had begun to polish his sword. He was whistling softly.

— Nice meeting you, I said.

— Oh, yes, said Ulla. Ciao, Harry.

— Goodbye, my dear, said Kate, turning to catch my eye with a solid stare.

That evening the black car came to take me to Mr. Chen's. Behind the darkened windows I looked out on the evening as it descended on Taipei. We passed markets and sped through the smoggy squares filled with honking cars and the crowds of persistent people walking, yelling, murmuring, and moving against one another. We drove out of the center of Taipei and over the green Keelung River into the outer districts. Soon we passed through the gate and up the long drive with its azaleas and its soldiers, and stopped, with a clicking of cinders under the wheels, at the end of the slate walk.

It wasn't raining. It was a dry, windless evening. The man who had worn the lifeless tie opened the door, smiling, tieless, but quite formal nonetheless. The two soldiers guarding the door still scowled, their helmets glistening palely in the dusk. Through the cool shadows of the open door I could make out two legs in a defiant stance just beyond the threshold.

— Mister Harry, said Chen, and his hand came out to shake mine.

Together we walked past the portrait of General Chiang Kai-shek and then into the parlor. A clock ticked. The tieless man came in carrying a tray of tea, a clean white note pad, two pencils, and an eraser. He placed each object before us carefully and retreated.

I could see that on a little wooden table in the middle of the room there was yet another likeness of General Chiang Kai-shek, a bronze miniature that I hadn't seen before. It was a replica of the statue that sat, an ominous gold giant, inside the Chiang Kai-shek Memorial.

All around Taipei there were statues of the General. They seemed to reach a critical mass in certain parts of town, and I decided that Chen's house was one of those places. The General was, I had realized over time, a combination of George Washington and an Egyptian pharaoh. He was almost a half god. And although there was supposedly political upheaval in Taiwan as people sought greater democracy, and although they seemed less in awe of Chiang, there was the feeling that he watched sternly, from beyond the grave, with great apprehension at all that was going on. Behind the burgeoning economic success, and behind the new political developments, the old guard of the Kuomintang, Chiang's party, the Nationalists who led the retreat to Taiwan from mainland China forty years before, were still very much in power. There were indeed posters advertising student political rallies and speeches, and there were several candidates to choose from for the legislature, and I heard that all this was amazing, compared with a few years earlier. But there was great uneasiness, and people wondered how far the government would let things change.

Frederick had told me about many of these things. But at Chen's I had the impression that Chiang Kai-shek was still alive and still worshiped. And with the guards in the garden there was a tense, military, and almost paranoid feeling that was palpable in the air. Chen's house, so American and casually wealthy in its style, was a fortress behind the rambling gardens and pretty flower boxes. I wondered who he was exactly.

— Let's talk, said Mr. Chen. It is good to hear Eng-ish. I need to praahk-tiss.

— Practice. Yes, let's, I said, trying to speak clearly and distinctly. Do you have anything in particular that you would be interested in talking about?

— Let's talk about America, he said. About Caryfornia.

— California?

— I have seen many American movies. I'm sure you have been there. It is very pretty?

— I've never been there, I said, embarrassed.

— No? What about Los Angeress? I hear about Los Angeress . . . and Hurry-wooed.

— Hollywood?

— Yes. You've been there?

I felt I was failing my first test as an English teacher. I was the American teacher who had not been to California.

— Well, actually, yes, I have been to Hollywood, once or twice, I said, wincing internally.

The beginning of a lie is always a little painful.

Mr. Chen's face lit up.

— Ah. Tell me about it.

— Well, I said, there are many swimming pools. All over.

He smiled, nodding. I stopped for a moment. I was feeling ill. I remembered thinking about lying the night before, and I saw just a flash of blond moving through the park.

Even so, I'd already said I'd been there, and it was important to give my teaching some interesting images. So I hadn't been there. Big deal. I'd seen it in a thousand television shows.

— There are swimming pools everywhere you go. And in Hollywood, everything is like a movie set. You know what a movie set is? All the props, the costumes, they're all being worn by the people there. No kidding. And the stars live there. They just step right out of their houses and walk down the street.

— Really? said Chen. Did you see any?

— Yes, some.

He tilted his head with a smile, waiting to hear. I gritted my teeth at the agony of listening to my own tawdry imagination. I kept seeing Henry Fonda on the billboard at Hsimending, looking upward. There were other things. I had to think of the other things in California. Why was it that I could think only of clichés? It had to sound more realistic, or at least more interesting. Chen had a faraway look in his eyes, and his smile, while he listened to me, was getting vague, like a slightly wilted flower. I was losing my audience. I had gotten myself in; now I had to make it sound as if it had really happened, give him a sense of the place, and then get off the subject quickly.

— I have a friend in Hollywood, I said. He works in the movies. He's got a house in Beverly Hills. That's just off Sunset Boulevard. Do you know where that is?

Chen shook his head.

— Well, it's a very exciting part of town. Very sunny there too, at Sunset Boulevard. You can see the sun go down from there . . . on the street, that is.

He listened carefully.

— There's a very relaxed feeling. That's what I like about California. People come out to watch the sunset and they all stand in the middle of the boulevard. This is an old custom, much like the dancing at the Chiang Kai-shek Memorial. The sunset is beautiful there, because, you know, they are facing west, out across the Pacific. Sometimes it stops the traffic on Sunset Boulevard. They have terrible traffic jams in California, so they drive on freeways. Do you know that word? Freeway? Why don't we look it up? Do you have your English dictionary? Ah, here it is.

I reached for the dictionary and started flipping swiftly through the F section. Mr. Chen was silent. I had caught myself at the last moment, before I plunged into the colorful abyss of what I didn't know about California.

— Ah, here we are. "A toll-free highway." You know . . . a big road, long and flat.

— What is this word "toll"? said Mr. Chen. Is this the little man with the beard who is under the bridge?

I couldn't figure out what he was talking about. But I was glad to be off California.

— No, I said, feeling once more in control. It's a payment of money on a road. You give money, usually at a little booth. You know what a booth is? A very small house on the road, right in the middle.

Chen was perplexed.

— You're driving down the road, and suddenly you get to a little house, with a man inside.

— Ah, yes, he said with a grin. This is the toll. I have read about tolls in stories. The toll lives on the road?

— No, I said. The toll does not live in anything. You *pay* the toll.

He realized I was serious, and now was fascinated.

— Ah, he said. You give moan-ey to the toll.

— Well, sort of.

It seemed that he was getting the point.

— This toll, he said in a harsh whisper. How tall?

I massaged my forehead.

— Well, it depends. Twelve, fourteen feet high.

He was shocked, and his cherubic mouth dropped open slightly.

— But there are signs, I said quickly. You have to understand, there are signs that tell you about the tolls. They tell you how much you will have to pay. They'll say, for instance, "Toll ahead. Pay one dollar."

It seemed odd that he should be so upset about this stuff.

— But remember, we're talking about freeways, in California.

— There are no tolls on the freeah-ways?

— That's right.

This seemed to make him feel a little better, but he was still confused. So I thought it was best to move on to something else.

— Why don't we read out loud from *The International Herald Tribune?*

Chen wasn't listening. He was thoughtfully turning around in his hand the little statue of the dragon, which he had just taken from his pocket. He seemed to have fallen into a world of his own, seriously pondering the nature of tolls and the peculiarities of America, and was ignoring me. At that point the man with the spectacles came in and, bowing to both of us, placed on the table in front of Chen the small black box.

— Shieh-shieh, said Mr. Chen, and the man departed.

On closer inspection, it looked like one of those boxes which are designed to appear high-tech and impressive but actually do nothing.

— Let's read from this sentence on, I said.

Mr. Chen bent over and began to read out loud, still rubbing the statue in his hand.

— "The sed-dial-men was agreed to by the two minee-sters . . ."

— Try again. What's this word?

— Sed-dial-men.

— Settlement. Do you know the word settlement?

— This is like a meeting?

— Sort of. But not quite. The difference is that . . .

He slid the black box along the table so that it was in front of him. Then, as he was looking at "settlement," to which I was pointing, he pushed one of the buttons, and symbols began to flash on the little screen.

— What is that? I asked.

— Oh, this? he said. This is an electric.

— It's electric?

— Yes.

— Electronic?

— Yes, he nodded and pulled the *Tribune* closer, rustling the pages.

He peered closely once again at the sentence, his fingers still stroking the little statue on the table in front of him.

— "The sed-dial-men was agreed . . . "

But I was concentrating on the black box. His eyes drifted up and looked at me.

— It makes you curi-ooz. This is the word? Curi-ooz?

— Yes, I said. What is it?

— Tang dynasty, he said, opening his hand and looking admiringly at the statue.

I looked briefly at the dragon.

— And the box?

He raised his eyebrows and looked at the gadget, as if he had just noticed it.

— Oh, he said. It is from Panasonic. It is the *I Ching*. A book. It is an ancient book of wisdom. But now — he waved at it — it is inside the lee-tle box. On the compoo-ter in there. You push the buttons, here, and it oh-tow-matically . . . ah . . . how you say . . . it finds the answer. And shows it here — he pointed to the small screen — It helps with kwesh-tons.

— What sort of questions?

He looked at me with an expression of infinite boredom.

— Many kwesh-tons, he said. Things in your head. You don't have to speak them, he said, pointing at his head.

I was reminded of Frederick on my first day in Taipei, pointing at his head, just as Chen was doing now, saying, "Too much this. Too many books." He'd been describing his search for symmetry.

I looked at the gadget, very much wanting to pick it up and play with it, see what it was and what it did, but I realized that Chen was impatient and wanted to get on with the lesson. There was something about the computer book that Chen found extremely tedious, and I could see that dwelling on it any longer would cause him untold amounts of weariness. But the idea of a book of wisdom compacted into a desk calculator nauseated yet still interested me. Supposedly the Bible had recently been put into a portable pocket computer. And it amused me, since I considered myself an atheist, that this grand text, this supposed word of the supreme being, had been made user-friendly, something modern and almost effortlessly convenient. I'd never thought of such a thing as offering itself up to convenience. And here was Chen, blithely, almost blandly, consulting his ancient book of wisdom by pushing a button with his pinky.

The Ouroboros

— Let's start here again, I said, drawing my eyes away from the box to assure him of my commitment to the lesson.

— Yes, he said, peering at the page.

And, knitting his brow, he began to read again.

— "The sed-dial-men was agreed to by the two minee-sters, but only after many days of neggo-shee-ayah . . . neggo-she-ayah . . . *shuns*."

9

While most people compromise, or completely kill off their original ideals, the ones from childhood, out of practicality, Kate was able to keep them alive in herself even though she was a down-to-earth and unromantic woman. She tried to view other people without sentimentality, made a point of it, and yet I had the feeling that she had a deep sense of herself as a heroine. I know this sounds implausible. But let me explain.

Kate didn't believe in God, or in any supernatural power in the universe whatsoever. She was a proponent of the opiate theory of religion, although it was not something that she thought about much at all. If you asked her, she'd probably say, "It would be nice if there were a God." But if you pried a little further you might find out that she believed, in fact, in something that was akin to a god, but she kept this belief fairly well hidden and never talked about it.

The world, for Kate, was a place where rewards came to those who did good works. There was no direct explanation for this, she thought, but it happened. Yet there was misery everywhere and she was able to see it without self-deception. She was acutely aware of unfairness, of desperate, unearned unhappiness, and of things that happened to people that were horrible and beyond comprehension. She accepted the cruelty of chance, of being born with everything against you. There were many people in Asia and Africa who were starving or were massacred by one another while, inexplicably, we were able to be happy. There were also millions of people in America who were destitute, dirt poor, sick, and abandoned. It was happening. We had both seen it. If not in our own lives, then through others', or in the newspapers and on television.

But, for all that, happiness did exist. There'd been a lot of it, and we had both been lucky, almost superlucky, if you discounted the normal day-to-day depressions and doubts of people in their twenties. And health did exist, and you could maintain it pretty easily if you wanted to; there were ways available, and you could make a choice and do things for yourself — eat well, run, that sort of thing — and not all of us, but many of us, could attain health just by deciding that we wanted it. It was that easy; you just had to decide. And regardless of the difficulties in Kate's family and her time at college, and the problems in our affair, love existed as well.

When Kate thought about it, she knew that somewhere there was someone or something very powerful that liked her. Out there God did not exist. In most people's lives there was no God. There may have been no God out there in the blackness of the universe, out around the airless planets. But for Kate, secretly, there was. She saw it and she felt it. God did exist, but probably, and sadly, only for very, very few.

There is, for example, the sunny street in Pennsylvania where she grew up, and the modern house overlooking the long, dandelion-speckled field. There is a large, flat wall of windows that faces the field; and in the distance, from the house, you can see a line of blue pine trees. Sticking up over the trees there is a spindly steel tower through which the telephone wires pass. It's quiet inside in the morning, and her father is humming to himself as he walks around downstairs, over the sanded wooden floors, and then, with a muffled step, over the cool flagstones in the hall, then through the pantry and onto the waxed tiles in the kitchen. In the kitchen he makes coffee. He also feeds the cat, Archie, but first whistles for him. When Archie doesn't come, Kate's father makes a *sh-sh-sh* sound with his lips until the animal enters, soundlessly, blinking, into the sunlight that slants in from the tall windows over the sink.

He remembers Kate when she was small. He remembers her squealing as she tried to swim when he held her in the pool down the street, just above the water line, while she practiced. She was like some wriggling creature between his hands. A small thing shaking with squeals.

Kate's mother gets up and comes down. She's got her glasses askew on her nose and is wearing her ragged slippers. Everything is so clean in the house that the slippers look like tattered relics from another era. And they are, in a way, and have been kept, much like Archie, for the subdued assurance they give. The slippers and the cat are related. The cat moves along the kitchen floor, keeping close to the cabinets, and finally sits, curling up against Kate's mother's slippers on the warm floor while Kate's mother makes orange juice.

There is giggling between Kate and her mother at something Kate's father did just now, unconsciously, like throwing out the plastic funnel from the coffee maker along with the coffee grounds.

Outside in the driveway there is a two-car garage that sits apart from the house, with bushes around it. When you walk inside the garage it is cooler than outside, and there's the smell of metal and oil, and the pleasing musty odor of things that were once wet but aren't anymore. It's very quiet and peaceful, and the cars seem like large domesticated animals asleep beside each other in a cool cave. This is where you go if you are exasperated by something in the house. You go to the other side of the driveway. You can escape to the garage and you can cry on the shoulders of the sleeping, bovine automobiles. And then you can sit in the corner and look up at the wall, at all the garden tools hung there, and the bicycles, also hung on the wall, and you can pick off the grass from the blades of the lawn mower.

In this way you can come to a kind of peace with your own prosperity. You can love it because of the poetic and often comfortable sadnesses it offers. Kate felt that, deeply, I think. There was sanctity in comfort. I don't mean to look askance at this. If I sound a little suspicious of it, it is only because this is the way I too was brought up. Health and comfort were Kate's main avenue, through nostalgia, to her idea that there was a spiritual force in the world. But she didn't believe she believed in god, any traditional god, at least; whatever that is.

There is a darkness or, rather, a lack of complete light that hangs over Taipei at all times, and I realize that I have not conveyed that fact. I had a dream a couple of years ago (a dream that bothered me for a while) in which there was a highway through a lush countryside, but there was one thing missing, and it was a full spectrum of light. It was as if someone had draped a muslin cloth over the sun, and everything I saw, although alive and in full bloom, was shrouded by an irritating dullness. Taipei had that quality. Halfway through my dream an old woman appeared, driving down the highway, being chauffeured in a big limousine. It was a silvery white car. She was driven past expanses of fields lined with fences. For some reason the fences were made of driftwood, the bleached white kind you find on the beach way up in the high sand, dried out in the heat. These were beautiful weatherbeaten fences. They had a dazzling, toothy appearance against the green fields, and the old woman whooshed by looking out the window at the fences going *zippity-zip* past the car.

Still, and this is the connection to Taipei, there was a sense of a dull light, and it bothered me. Everything was all right except for that. There are some foggy images from the end of the dream, but they were disturbing, so I think I unintentionally forgot most of them. What I do remember is that the old lady's car drove over a hill and into a very poor section of town. She went over the hill, and as the car went down, the foggy daylight gave way to night, as if just by going down the hill you could enter nighttime. It was a ghetto down there, and the streets were filled with trash, and there were many people who seemed lost and were wandering about blank-faced, like somnambulists in the dark streets.

But I'm getting away from the main point here, which was that the sunny part of the dream (the earlier part, when the old woman was being driven past the fields) was still shadowy and disturbing. You were supposed to be happy in the first part of the dream, but you couldn't, because though it was the sunniest of days, there wasn't enough light.

So that's the sky over Taipei. There are many explanations for this, one being the mood of the city, its decorated and economically secure present shaded by a fear of both the past and the future. There was the sense that everything was watched over, regulated, observed. The government seemed afraid of the people. Even though martial law had been lifted, and the economy was booming, and signs of wealth could be seen everywhere, there were always policemen and soldiers on the streets, sometimes just laughing and walking. But they were all the more threatening because of their assurance. I didn't pay much attention to politics in Taipei. I couldn't read the papers, and if I could, I wouldn't have been interested. But I felt the place. There was something withheld. And the mood was only one explanation for this phenomenon.

There was of course the other, more obvious fact that Taipei is a city covered by a sky thick with dense, choking smog.

But I had a job, and a good job at that, talking my own language with a peculiar but well-paying Taiwanese official. After four months, Kate and I had settled into the secure life of working foreigners, buying our groceries at the Wen Chow market, teaching, and socializing with our small group of friends. We had some Chinese friends, but mostly we spent time with the expatriate Westerners with whom we identified most strongly.

There was Ulla, who had become, oddly, good friends with Kate. Apparently she'd gotten a divorce from a man in Italy whom she described as a "big baby." She chewed gum and walked around Taipei with earphones, listening to American rap music, which emanated from her with a tinny, barely audible mosquito sound and a thumping of drums that seemed to come from her chest.

Her tan, angular face was always tilted slightly upward. I would see her coming toward me on the street, and would watch as Chinese men stared at her, with her rounded, baroque Italian movements, her shoulders and her hips swaying with each other's influence, and her eyes gleaming with some inchoate plan to make love in the future.

She was the kind of woman who made men jealous in the

company of other males, even animals, like horses or large dogs, just because of the competition. She made everyone feel inadequate to the task. That was her appeal. Normal men were not enough, so if you happened to be normal, she would sigh and be bored just thinking about you. And so you'd have to prove that you were abnormal. Even men who didn't want her, or could never imagine it at first, even they would ultimately be caught up in the competitive dance to get her aroused: a lewd smile, a hand on the shoulder, a nudge from her hip in the kitchen during a party. Men, particularly the gothic kind, the ones who stare at everything from beneath a lowered brow, these were the most vulnerable. The guys who stay aloof at social gatherings, who go into another room and stare forcefully out through the darkened windows, or who sit at the edge of conversations with their arms folded tightly over their breasts; these were the ones. They'd start out scoffing at her, even despising her, but they'd invariably end up putting forth the greatest effort of all, to the point of making total fools of themselves, to the point of coming out of their shells and blabbing nervously, revealing themselves as total idiots at some level (which may be the reason they were so reticent all along). These were the men who were the most easily undone by Ulla.

Given the fact that there are few people nowadays who'll leave their own country and go to an unknown and polluted city without something against themselves, some boiling anger, given that fact, you can understand why Ulla thrived in Taipei. The majority of the male Westerners there were definitely of the gothic variety and were easily unraveled. And so she looked well all the time, as if she were constantly arriving from a small but expensive party thrown in her honor.

Then, of course, there was Frederick. We need not go into his case too deeply here.

There was also a couple named Klaus and Sally. Klaus was

half Chinese, half Dutch. He had a long thin body and a mild face that never seemed to think of anything upsetting. You couldn't figure his feelings, because his face floated in a limbo of moodlessness. And although he was definitely Oriental, he wore such chic European clothes, and spoke English with such a beautiful accent, that it completely slipped your mind that he was Chinese.

Sally, his girlfriend, was an American. She was mulatto and spoke Chinese very well. She was shy. They lived in the industrial district near the Keelung River, in a large apartment with floors covered by bamboo mats, and a lot of low furniture and flat pillows. Sally was a painter, but she was so embarrassed by her paintings that she hid them in a back room. I saw one once in their kitchen. It was green with speckled orange fish all over it. I didn't like it. And I felt a little sorry for the rest of the garish paintings hidden back there in corners. Yet there was something about Sally, a fragile sense of things, that made the bad paintings all right. One couldn't help feeling that there was some wisdom in her, some graceful sense of the badness of her paintings, that made her hide them.

Then there was the Australian, Roger Theef. He was, as I've said, an incorrigible optimist and would always say the wrong thing at the wrong time, such as "Well, it isn't all that bad, is it? I mean you've still got your well-being" — things that made him invariably despised by Ulla and Frederick, inveterate realists of the European school. Frederick would scowl and pull on his mustache when he was forced to listen to Roger.

There was also a British guy everyone called Wilcox, though his real name was something else. He was a self-styled hothead who took himself quite seriously (and hence came under the spell of Ulla) and studied Chinese in Kate's class. He was often morose. When Ulla was around, he was more morose.

We'd invite him over for dinner because he was interesting to talk to, but he'd get into arguments with me, continually making jabs at America, and for some reason I'd always take offense. I would point out to him that his singular dislike of my country was a little out of date, given that we now had a million problems of our own, and the world no longer could be divided into the spheres of two heavy-footed, imperialistic monsters.

— Come on, Wilcox. There are other menaces now on the horizon. America is nowhere near as powerful as it used to be.

He'd agree grudgingly, and then he'd switch to talking about the "bloody" Kuomintang. He had been involved in left-wing politics in England, had briefly been a member of an anarchist group, then taken an interest in the Green Party. But he'd lost interest in politics and Europe altogether and had come to Taiwan to study ink drawing.

Once in Taipei, though, he became disenchanted all over again, seeing the rampant pollution and the veiled totalitarianism of the Taiwanese government. So he again became a disinterested and disgusted expert on politics. This time, however, he was an expatriate and an outsider, and saw things with a measure of clarity and arrogance. He was quite certain about where I stood and had a habit of bringing up, during the last few minutes of dinner, my involvement with Chen. He would make sure, as we sipped our coffee, to get in a few stabs at what he called my "polite apathy." He always used that term.

— Harry, you have no excuse. You're teaching one of them, he said, clearing the dishes off the table, and walking into the kitchen.

Kate looked at me to gauge my response.

— Chen? But how do you know that he's one of the Kuomintang? I said, looking at Kate.

She peered at me over her mug, and I felt a twinge of anger because I saw that she wasn't going to say anything. She was looking at me critically, distantly, and I had the clear impression that she agreed with him.

— All of them are! Shit, Harry. Every last one of them in the government is a stinking Kuomintang, he said, coming back into the big room and sitting in his chair to face me.

He had a pointed, pale face and dark eyes, and the tendency to chop his hands while he talked.

— The Kuomintang *is* the government. The government *is* the Kuomintang. They say this is a democracy, but everyone knows that the Kuomintang is secretly keeping an iron grip on everything. They make concessions, sure. They say they'll let the opposition run for office, but just wait. Just wait. See how many get arrested when they *do* run for office. See how many get bashed in the head or disappear.

— That's just speculation.

— And you're sitting there, he continued without listening, a polite, apathetic American . . .

— There you go again . . .

— No, it's relevant. An apathetic American, helping one of the most repressive regimes on this earth. Yes, one of the most repressive. Just as in Beijing, except they can get away with it here because they have a booming economy . . .

— Give me a break, Wilcox, I said with a sneer.

But after I said this, the expression of scorn felt stony and false on my face, and when I relaxed my mouth, I felt embarrassed.

Wilcox went home soon after that, and I found myself moping around the dark apartment in my underwear after Kate had gone to bed. I was deeply uneasy. It wasn't the political stuff, really. It was the feeling of being accused. Why had he accused me like that? What had I done? But in the back of my mind I was actually thinking about Kate. Was something unseen taking place between us?

The next day, riding to Mr. Chen's, I considered Wilcox's speech again, and for a long time, driving along the outskirts of Taipei, my doubt in myself became hard, almost crystalline in its sharpness in my chest. How blind was I, really?

However, as we passed over the Keelung River, and the bars on the railing shot by with a muffled sound, white lines going *zippity-zip* past the window, and the green river wove slowly below, suddenly my feelings shifted, and I began to feel angry because of Kate's expression as Wilcox talked, that look of secret approval. Her opinion had been quite clearly against me. She thought about me negatively. I had seen her watching me as if from a distance.

As the car went up the long drive, I saw some people milling about in the garden. It seemed that the soldiers had caught somebody on the grounds of Chen's estate. There was activity beyond the fountain at the end of the garden near the high brick wall bordering the property. Both the driver and I craned our necks to see. They were leading a young man away from the wall. The man wore a headband with Chinese characters on it. He looked rumpled, as if there had been a scuffle. All in all, though, it was a tame scene, which appeared under control. I wondered whether he was a protester or whether he'd been stealing something or trespassing. All of those involved, the man and the soldiers, looked quite serious as they led him away. The driver was very curious, but we continued up the drive until we stopped, as usual, at the end of the long slate walk. Everything else was peaceful and normal at the big house.

Inside, Chen was waiting in the study, as usual. But this time, sitting next to him in a third lacquered chair, was a pale, serious woman of indeterminate age. Her hands were clasped in her lap, but she seemed to be staring at the edge of the table and did not look up when I came in.

— This is Mai Kai-lin, said Chen, introducing us.

Mai Kai-lin nodded in greeting and shook my hand briefly, but she still watched the table and did not look me in the eye.

— Mai Kai-lin is with our Departa-ment of Education, said Chen. She is interested in your teaching tekka-niques.

— My teaching techniques? I said nervously, sitting down.

— Yes. I have told her of my progress, said Chen.

I saw him reach mechanically into his pocket and pull out the dragon. It peeked from between his fat fingers. With a small tapping sound of jade touching wood, he put it down in front of him on the table.

I stared at it as if it were my nemesis. I had one of those moments when everything seems stuck in your head between two notions, and all you can do is stare. On one side was the dragon and on the other was the woman. For some reason I felt that she was not from the Department of Education at all, and I had by now begun to hate the dastardly little dragon. From the beginning, when Chen mentioned that he took it out to ward off evil, I had associated it with evil, and eventually thought of it as a sign of the presence of something sinister. Consequently, I had developed a deep resentment toward it, a resentment unparalleled by any anger I remembered feeling toward an inanimate object. Chen knew it annoyed me. I wondered whether he could have done the same thing with just a pebble, if he had repeatedly doted on it in the same way. Could he have antagonized me with something that had no likeness, just by placing it, day after day, on the table in front of me?

I took from my briefcase a battered copy of the *Tribune*.

— We'll read aloud and then we'll discuss it, I said, enunciating carefully for the sake of Mai Kai-lin.

Opening to the middle of the newspaper, I pointed to a paragraph for Chen to read. He began, dutifully.

— "Soo-prizingly, it is not common . . ."

Mai Kai-lin watched as I pushed my finger along the text.

There was not a drop of warmth in her eyes. She's like an automaton, I thought.

— "Troops were dee-proyed" — I'm sorry — "deployed."

— Good.

Chen looked up at me and rubbed the side of his nose.

— What does this word "deployed" mean?

— Well, why don't we look it up? I said, watching Mai Kai-lin out of the corner of my eye.

I smiled at her as Chen and I went through the dictionary. She smiled back, but without any perceptible change in expression, so that her mouth appeared to flicker for an instant and then freeze, once again, into a straight line.

— Oh, I see, said Chen, peering over his reading glasses — they were long slivers of lens and very thin — I see . . . it means . . . hao . . . hao . . . to "spread out into an open for-may-shun."

— That's right.

I could see that he didn't know what "formation" meant, but he wasn't going to ask. He just mumbled and looked at the dictionary, and I didn't want to show him up, so I didn't say anything.

Mai Kai-lin interjected with a question to Chen in rapid Chinese. I waited. Chen answered quickly.

— Go on, she said suddenly. I am sorry to stop you.

— "Many bee-leave that there is a good reason to keep the . . ."

Suddenly, in midsentence, Mai Kai-lin once again interrupted Chen. Chen nodded.

— Mai Kai-lin must leave now, he said.

— That was quick.

We all got up, and Mai Kai-lin and I gave each other a perfunctory handshake.

— How's my teaching technique? I said with a smile. Did I pass?

She nodded faintly.

— Before I leave, may I ask you a kwesh-ton? she said politely but very pointedly, finally looking in the general direction of my eyes.

— Yes, of course.

She wavered for a second, pursing her lips, choosing her words precisely.

— Are you acquainted with a Chinese man named Mister Wu?

— Mister Wu? I said, suddenly nervous.

— Yes, she said. He is a corporal in the Nationalist Taiwanese Army. Are you acquainted with him? Corporal Wu P'ei-fu?

— No, I said immediately. Not that I know of.

I don't know why I was so quick to deny it. I just blurted it out. Then she looked me directly in the eyes. Her gaze was firm and official. Even though there was a trace of warmth in her eyes when at last I saw them, it was directed toward interpreting me, not knowing me.

— He is interested in the English language, she said. You know many English tutors. I thought maybe you'd know him. But maybe you have heard of him?

— Sorry. I haven't.

She gave a strained bob of the head.

Chen motioned that she should go, with a curt nod toward the door, and it was then that I realized she was his subordinate, not the other way around. She turned and headed out of the room with a self-conscious, tight walk. She was aware that I was watching her, and the muscles of her body were tense. Her legs went very fast and she held her hands in front of her so that they weren't visible from behind. On the back of her head was a small comb holding her hair up. It was made of a red enameled wood. She stooped down near the door and picked up a thin briefcase, and then, with efficient little steps, quickly disappeared out the door.

We sat down again, and Chen reached down and thoughtfully began to move the jade figure on the table, looking at it from various angles with a cock of his head, studying its scales and its tiny etched eyes.

— What was all that about? I asked, feigning a relaxed attitude.

— I am sure it is nothing, said Chen. After all, you do not know the man.

— Who is he?

Chen's eyebrows went up at this question.

— There is some interest in him.

— Oh, I said, reaching for the *Tribune*. Shall we start reading where we left off?

— He is from an important family, said Chen, apropos of nothing, but he said it in a low voice, with his gaze on the jade dragon.

10

Frederick was home when I got there. He was sitting at the bamboo table writing a letter. He was unhappy, and wrote with bleary eyes, his body way down in the chair, so that his legs were splayed out across the floor.

— I'm writing to my son, he said morosely.

— I didn't know you had a son.

— Well, I do. He's ten. He lives with his mother in Frankfurt. I have no idea what to say to him.

His sword lay beside him on the table, next to the writing pad, like a backup writing implement. He kept it near him at all times. At night he would place it ceremoniously on the wall over his bed, and sometimes he'd attach a red tassel to its handle and sling it on his belt and walk that way around the apartment all day, like an enlightened pirate.

— I haven't seen him for sev-erall years. Now I hear he is going to turn ten, and I don't know what to write.

— When did you last write him?

— I don't know. Last year? A year and a half ago? I sent him Chinese stamps. But tomorrow is his birthday and, well, even if I mailed it today it wouldn't get to Frankfurt for two weeks. So that's two weeks late already. He'll have to accept that.

— Where's Kate?

— Out, he said, already ignoring me.

Talking about his son drained him, and he seemed to resent me for even listening to his woes. I dropped my tie on a chair, unbuttoned my shirt, and went into the kitchen. Some horrendous medicinal concoction of Frederick's was at the bottom of a pot on the stove. It was burned and hardened. There was a musty smell, like bark.

The door slammed, and Kate whisked through the big room past Frederick, who said mournfully and to no effect, "I'm writing a letter to my son." I heard her say, "I didn't know you had a son," in reply to which Frederick grunted. Then she went into our room, and I heard the *whump* of her falling, exhausted, on the bed. I went out of the kitchen, past Frederick (who was now doodling a series of microscopic, neurotic drawings on the side of his letter), and into our room, where Kate was lying, her face red from the heat, on the bamboo mat. Her hair was sticking to her forehead.

— Hi, she said, out of breath.

I was unsettled when I looked at her. Where had she been? The problem with Kate was that if I didn't get the doubt out of my mind soon, or camouflage it, she would spot it discoloring my eyes. She had a way of pegging me. She'd seek me out even in the privacy of my own thoughts, as if my head were missing a wall.

— Harry, what are you thinking about?

— I guess I was thinking about Chen. There was a peculiar woman he introduced me to today.

— Who?

— Her name was Mai Kai-lin. Some official of the government. He said she was from the Department of Education. But I don't know . . .

For some reason, I couldn't get myself to mention Wu P'ei-fu.

— You don't know what?

— It's odd, that's all, I said, lying down beside her. Why would an official of the Education Department be interested in how I was teaching another official of the government? I mean, they're all part of the same club, aren't they? It's not as if they have to make sure their peers are being taught well.

In the back of my mind, as I talked, was a growing smudge of worry. I felt as if I were beginning to lie to Kate, because I was afraid she was lying to me, and she became less familiar to me as a result. The worry darkened my thoughts. Bluntly, it was the cold and ancient fear of being a cuckold; the worry, dreary in its lurking nature, that what seemed like Kate's distance from me was actually her boredom. Or, worse, her excitement about someone else. I could see no overt evidence of it. But my imagination began to stir up all sorts of things.

— Harry . . .

I refocused on her.

— What?

— Did you hear what I said?

— No.

— I feel we should go out tonight . . . maybe to the opera. They usually pitch their tent outside the market on Saturday nights, she said, reaching up and stroking my cheek. I walked by last week and it looked really fun. This cramped apartment is filling up with the smell of Frederick's new moss tea, and I feel sick here and I want to do something new. Okay?

Under the light bulbs that hung from the wires we walked, watching how they lit the surrounding ground outside the tent. It was just a makeshift ceiling made of canvas. There were no walls. It wasn't fancy at all, but with the lights on it looked like a billowy, enchanted thing. Many people were there, milling about before the show started. There was always a stir around the opera. In the tent everyone was already sitting down along the wooden benches. We found some places in the second row. The lights went down, and after an overture of hooting pipes, the show began.

The faces of the performers were painted in stark white with red lips. Beside that there were sweeping lines of black or red or blue around the cheeks or over the brow. The costumes were elaborate, sewn with bangles and tiny reflecting bits of metal. The singing was in Cantonese, not Mandarin, so Kate could not understand what was being said or sung. Early in the first act a man dressed as a warrior came out on the stage wearing armor that flapped about on his body. The armor was made of thick paper, and was curled slightly by the humidity. He bellowed out several baritone lines and, with his voice plucking and twanging, strode about with great, windy gestures. This was the serious part.

Then came a thin man with high cheekbones who fawned and whimpered. He crouched and waddled across the stage as he sang, sometimes bending his head from side to side with a pursed smile.

Then out came three ladies. It was obvious at first that they were men playing the roles of women, but after a few minutes it was hard to be sure. Kate leaned over and whispered that two of them were men, but one was definitely a woman. They danced in a little circle, preening and fluttering. The tallest (the one Kate thought was a woman) had very long fingernails. She fanned them menacingly. She sang. It must have been a love song, because the other two crooned with great empathy, their hands clutched beside their cheeks. It seemed clear that she was in love with the warrior.

Over the tops of the people in front of us — a family with five children, all squirming on the bench — I was surprised to spy Frederick striding into the tent and looking about for a seat. Behind him was another white man, someone with a sheepish, self-deprecating manner. He walked very closely behind Frederick, seemingly embarrassed by entering the opera, particularly in the middle of a scene. His face passed through the glare of the stage lights and I could see at once that it was the man whom Frederick had pointed out to me that first day at the Chiang Kai-shek Memorial: the redheaded fool, the man Frederick said he despised. Yet they sat down together without any evidence of animosity.

Two men on horses rode onto the stage. The horses were strapped around the actors' midsections, and the horses' heads, garishly painted blocks of wood, bobbed up and down in expressionless enthusiasm. The two men trotted to the center of the stage and began a conversation full of sneers and grins that were met with laughing and one or two hoots from the audience. One of them bent over and showed his backside, which had a tail on it. The audience laughed. Then they rode off, galloping slowly behind the curtain, which bulged for several moments after they'd gone.

Kate leaned over to me.

— It's a love story.

— No kidding, I said.

The sniveling, whimpering man came out again, and began to sing a short song.

— But who's he? I asked.

— He's the villain . . .

— Kate, do you see Frederick over there? I said, interrupting her. He's sitting with that guy.

— Who?

— A guy, a German guy, who's in Frederick's sword-dancing class . . . but the strange thing is . . .

— Oh, she said, there he is.

— The strange thing is, Frederick pointed him out to me once and said that he hated him. I mean, you should have seen him. He was infuriated just by the sight of this guy at the Chiang Kai-shek Memorial.

Kate shrugged and looked back toward the stage.

— So? He doesn't hate him anymore.

The whimpering man on the stage sang in a nauseating, twirling voice. He crept up very close to the footlights and was clenching and wringing his hands. I felt an urge to go up onto the stage and beat him. He was one of those characters everyone hates. But something about him made me certain he really *was* like that, as a person and not just as a character, and I wanted to go up and thrash him for it.

— I think he's talking about his plans to trick that soldier, said Kate.

— You mean the one with the floppy armor?

— Yeah. The soldier is in love with the woman with the long fingernails. He's the good guy. This one is going to do him in, said Kate.

The warrior came back onto the stage, and immediately the whiner straightened up and talked to him with perfect gentility. The story was becoming clear. Their mouths were opening and closing, and as far as I could tell, gibberish was coming out. But this was definitely a story about deception. And then, just as quickly, I thought, No, it's about the gullibility of good people.

The limitations of being good. The warrior was liked by the crowd. You could see it. Even though he wasn't particularly heroic. He was foolish and blustery, and when he raised his sword it sagged a bit to the side, like a badly watered plant. But everyone knew that it wasn't supposed to do that, and everyone pretended that it didn't.

The whiner left the stage.

At that point my attention was caught by a child standing at the foot of the stage who had made his way up from the front row until he was beside the footlights. He was gazing up at the actors and he leaned over the lamps (which were set into the ground in front of the stage) so that his chin was illuminated from below. What interested me was that he had a monkey on a leash. The leash, however, had dropped to the ground, and the monkey, given freedom, rambled about at the boy's feet and along the foot of the stage amidst the lights. It was a squirrel monkey, the kind with short gray hair, about the size of a cat, and one of those typically simian expressions of sustained astonishment, disturbed occasionally by twitches of calm. Every few moments, as the opera continued several feet above its head, the monkey would inspect something on the ground in the darkness, like a discarded bottle, and with teeth gritted and its eyes wide open it would sniff it and fiddle with it. These motions below the stage were not noticed by anyone, and the monkey came into the audience's general awareness only when its tail flicked up and passed by one of the lights, so that it appeared to be moving along the rim of the stage like an animated piece of rope. But that was only for a second.

Once more the warrior plodded onto the stage and belted out a melody. He moved his legs so that his feet got placed very gingerly wherever they landed. He was wearing bright white socks — I guess you could call them socks — and gold sandals with black straps. He did a bow-legged dance in which he always seemed to be sitting down on an invisible stool, and he waved his sword in the air.

Then, out from behind the curtain, came the woman. She looked to me even more like a man this time. There was that powdery look about her that resulted in a disjunction between the man beneath the makeup and the soft woman outside. Her movements were too jerky to be genuine. Her mouth, for example, was exaggeratedly puckered, and was pouting in a badly conceived imitation of femininity. It was an expression formed, I thought, only by a young man who had jealously observed women in every detail during an agonizing adolescence, in dance halls and in glossy magazines, but had had no personal experience of them whatsoever. But, to his credit, even though there was the faintest hint of unshaven whiskers beneath the chalk-white neck, one could almost get it if one squinted one's eyes.

— Kate, there's no way that's a woman.

— Yes, it is, she said, concentrating on the stage.

I snickered audibly, because she didn't want to give in.

— Look how she moves, I said.

Kate said nothing. She put her hand out and grasped my knee. I was wearing blue jeans, and I looked down at her hand over the faded blue. It was at that moment, as I looked back toward the stage, that I happened to see the monkey again. His owner seemed to have completely forgotten about it, and it was ambling about, sometimes sitting down in that self-conscious way monkeys have, placing its bottom very carefully on the ground, and from time to time picking up its tail and furiously gnawing at it for fleas. It sat among the lights like a tiny man beneath a canopy of glowing mushrooms, as the stems of the lights were black and dirty below, but gave way as they went up to a widening blossom of a bulb. It must have been as hot as hell down there. He panted desperately.

There were many bugs below the stage: diaphanous-winged insects whirring around the lights. The monkey snatched at them occasionally with quick jabs of his paw, although, in his heated and exasperated state, he didn't seem agile enough to catch anything. That's when a particularly large moth, the kind you see only in the Far East, came flapping into the scorching little underworld beneath the stage. It was one of those insects which look like small birds when you see them out of the corner of your eye. It had huge gray wings and antennae that were fuzzy, like two doll house feather dusters.

It landed right above the monkey's head, on top of a bulb. But he'd seen it drop. And while the moth ambled along up there, the monkey reached over and felt around delicately, not quite touching the bulb, but searching with its fingers in the air just above it, missing the moth by a few inches. At that moment, when the monkey was completely vexed, the moth's shaggy antennae poked over the edge, and the monkey, aghast at the thing's proximity, brought his hand down sharply on it and the burning bulb.

I was shocked that such a noise could come out of an animal that small. It screamed so loudly that it sounded like a high-pitched winch backstage. Before I could even see it move, it had jumped at a terrific speed up onto the stage, and with one long hop it soared through the air and landed directly on the outwardly thrust chest of the singing heroine.

Immediately the audience leaped off the benches. The monkey had moved so quickly that it seemed to have materialized out of nowhere, clinging like mad to the singer's chest. And for a moment the crowd stood in absolute silence, gaping at the stage, because the monkey had burrowed its face into her breast and appeared to be taking part in a horrible parody of nursing. The woman (or man) screamed and jostled about the stage, trying to shake the monkey from her (or his) bosom.

Screams rose above us, shimmying high on the scale, higher and higher, in terrified soprano trills. It was at this point that I realized, in dazed silence, that she was definitely a woman. There wasn't an ounce of manhood in her voice.

Further evidence emerged. Looking up to the stage I saw the monkey's hand ripping, bit by bit, at every bounce, her dazzling costume, and bit by bit a creamy white breast, full and naked, was revealed to us, undulating in the glare of the lights.

The audience was transfixed, and some who had jumped to their feet were now staring motionless at the dance of the monkey and the woman, and the emerging breast. While the women in the audience, many of them, were genuinely horrified, the men, and even the very small boys, gazed at the stage as if a revelation were taking place before their eyes.

It was then, at the peak of our fascination, that the monkey, crazed by some new fear, jumped from the woman's breast and dove off the stage, over the lights, and into the audience. I saw its silvery body pass below our bench with its tail following behind it like a little, backward-rushing spear.

The crowd erupted in panic. Arms flailed about, and many people, even old men, were taking big, gawky steps over fallen benches, pushing other people to get away from the hairy thing that was rushing angrily beneath them. It resurfaced, screeching, and quickly climbed atop a woman's head, pulling at her hair and hopping about. She yelped and batted her head with her fists until it jumped to the ground, only to dart beneath the benches again, disappearing like a subterranean terrorist.

Suddenly the entire commotion stopped. For a few seconds a man was heard yelling, but not in Chinese. Through the tangle of bodies I saw Frederick at the edge of the crowd. He was fighting with the monkey, swiping at it with his long arms as it ran around him, squealing and flashing its teeth. The monkey lunged at him with a squeak, and then, all at once, as if someone had turned off his switch, Frederick fell flat on the ground.

The monkey skittered off into the market across the street, its tail raised high in the air, its leash flapping behind it, and the little boy, its owner, running after it at a distance. It was but a small object scampering away into the night.

Frederick lay on the ground, moaning. I ran over to him, and Kate did too, but somehow she'd ended up, through the chaos, somewhere else, and she came running from a different direction.

Frederick had been bitten right below his ribs on the fleshy part of his waist. The blue silk shirt he was wearing was ripped open in a small, jagged halfmoon. He was bleeding. His eyes were closed, and he held his side and gritted his teeth.

— My God . . . Frederick are you all right?!

— Frederick! said Kate.

— Fuck! he yelled, startling those who stood around him.

He opened his eyes, and then wrinkled his nose into a snarl. He was lying halfway between the opera grounds and the street, so that to passersby there was some confusion as to whether his injury had anything to do with the opera. The opera was open to the city, and it was so near the market, and there were so few demarcation lines or ropes or gates or anything of the kind, that you could have mistaken it as the location of a temporary camp of nomads.

The crowd gathered around but seemed immediately disappointed that Frederick's wound was not more serious. There were a few boys who began to leap about on the street shouting about what had happened, with emphasis on the monkey, and the waigoren (outsider) who had been bitten. Several groups of curious people came hurrying over to see. But when the extent of Frederick's wound was observed, and it was discovered that the monkey was no longer present, there was a general sighing and sideways glancing, and all those who came to gape eventually wandered back into the far more interesting nighttime streets. Some people were even laughing. And there were several outright guffaws heard when the tall thin white man was seen on the ground bleeding, having been bitten by a squirrel monkey.

Those of us who knew him, however, were not amused. Kate, accompanied by the red-haired man, steadied Frederick's wounded side while I pulled him slowly to his feet by putting his arm around my shoulder. He groaned and got up.

— That little bah-start! He spat.

He turned to the red-haired man, who was trembling.

— Did you see him? He came right at me! shouted Frederick.

At that moment I saw the tattoo on the face of the red-haired man, the one Frederick had described to me. It was a snake, but from even a short distance away it looked like a colorful S-shaped birthmark on his cheek. However, there was such a commotion that I didn't have time to examine it closely.

A woman standing nearby was talking loudly. She said the monkey had dropped off the curtain, and that it had been rolled up in there several weeks ago by mistake. She said, according to Kate, that the curtain unrolled and the monkey had fallen out. This was forcefully denied by a gaunt man with yellow teeth who interjected, once again translated for me by Kate, that this was all wrong and that the monkey had in fact been in the heroine's skirt the whole time, that it was actually a part of the opera but had come on a bit early. The arguing continued, even as we began to hobble slowly away, helping Frederick down the street.

A few of the opera players had come out from behind the stage, annoyed at losing their audience. One of the horsemen had disengaged himself from his horse and was sitting dejectedly on the edge of the stage. The vacant-faced horse sat next to him, legless. The actor was furious that the play had been stopped and pounded his fist on the stage while he debated with an unseen person backstage, whose muffled voice came through the curtain in pessimistic tones.

When we got Frederick home, his bleeding had stopped, but he began to mutter in a vituperative heat about apes, monkeys, animals, and the like. His face was flushed and his eyes bulged. We cleaned his wound, which, though it bled a great deal, did not seem to be serious. Frederick leaned over the bathroom sink and peered down as Kate washed it. He mumbled away, half to us and half to himself, caught in a path of circular reasoning, more furious at having been bitten by an animal than at the pain.

— Bah-start. Fucking *simian*. Der Affe! Der Schlingel! Fucking ape. This little ape, little any-mall comes up from nowhere . . . to bite me . . . what? I mean, the nasty thing! Any-malls, all over. Where did it come from?

— It was under the stage, I said. I saw it.

He looked at me a moment indignantly, lost in angry thoughts. Then he looked back down at Kate's hands cleaning his wound.

—- Hold still.

— *Attacked* me! he said. *Me* again. Again it's *me!*

We bandaged his side. And I noticed the other bandage, the one on his leg, was dirty now, in contrast to the new one on his side. We helped him into his room and lay him down on his bed.

— We'll be in the next room, said Kate, leaving his door open.

We tiptoed into the living room and sat around the bamboo table. Between Kate and me sat the red-haired man.

— So, said Kate, with a sigh. I'm Kate. What's your name?

— Null, said the man in a thick, bland voice.

— Null?

— Ya. Null Geschmack. From Berlin, like Free-derick. I've known Free-derick for many years. We went to school together. Pleez to meet you.

He grinned and held out his meaty hand. We shook all around.

— Library school? I asked.

— No . . . no . . . he said with a smile showing a huge gap between his two middle teeth. Small school, you know.

He held his hand with the palm down to indicate a child's height.

— Grade school? said Kate.

— Ya.

— That's nice, I said.

We all fell silent, and the silence gave way to Frederick's murmuring.

— So, you all live here with Free-derick? said Null, looking around.

— Yeah, we all live here, said Kate as she got up from her seat. Would you like some coffee? Unfortunately it's just freeze-dried.

— Ya, said Null, jumping a bit in his seat.

Real coffee was too expensive in Taiwan. There was only freeze-dried for anybody who wasn't rich. And that in itself was considered an extreme delicacy, because it too was expensive. Null grinned. Then he called over his shoulder.

— Eh, Free-derick . . . they've got coffee. Want some?

Frederick exhaled audibly.

— I know there's coffee, Null. I *live* here.

— Ya, but do you want some? asked Null.

— No.

Frederick could be seen through the half-open door lying on the bed, staring at the ceiling with his arms at his sides, musing at the ceiling in a reverie of pain.

— And why did you come to Taiwan? I asked, searching for something to talk about.

— Sword dahn-sing, like Free-derick, he said, gesturing with a toss of his head toward Frederick's room.

I remembered standing at the edge of the Chiang Kai-shek Memorial, watching the sword dancers. Here in front of me, finally, was the red-haired man.

— Free-derick was always the superman when we were young, said Null with a sentimental smile. He was always the one who could do more . . . you know . . . very tall . . . very strong . . . smart . . . yes, always very smart. But now I am trying to sword dance.

— Null, said Frederick, raising his voice from the other room. Please.

— He gets embarrassed when people talk about him, said Null, lowering his voice. But it is true. He was, you know, everybody's hero. The girls loved him. He was so cool. You know, cool? Smooth, like he don't care. He score a goal and walk away with a frown.

Null nodded to himself. The tattoo on his face was duller and less detailed up close. The whole thing was no larger than a young caterpillar curled in a curve on his cheek. Stubble covered the lower half of his face, and some of it went through the tattoo, so that the snake was dark and hairy in parts, like a true caterpillar. Like many tattoos it blended in perfectly with his face, but in such a way that it gave off the distinct, tawdry feeling of carnivals. It was like a smell. He had the appearance of someone cheerful and kind, but there was something hanging over him or under him, as if there were something small that was rotting in the back of his mind.

— Free-derick is missed at home. There he is a hero, and he is missed, said Null.

— Please shut up, Null, said Frederick, staring at the ceiling.

— No, no, it's true, he said, getting more excited, leaning over the table as he talked. They were all so sad when he left. Why? Because they look high at him. How you say? Look up toward him. No one undoor-stood why he left . . . Sure, they thought he was to travel, but then he didn't come back. But I undoor-stant. I know Free-derick. I watch him now during the sword dance and the way he moves. He dances like a master. And the way he uses the sword . . . have you ever seen him?

— *Null!* bellowed Frederick.

He was standing in the doorway of his room, and his face was red. He held his side.

— It makes me sick! Very. This talk makes me *sick.*

Null lowered his head between his shoulders. He didn't turn around. He seemed afraid that Frederick might hit him on the back of the head.

— I am sorry, he said with trembling lips. But you know me, Free-derick. Sometimes I talk too much.

Frederick winced.

— I know, Null. But please. I have a cut. I am feeling sick. I just don't want to hear any more.

Null looked up at Kate and me with a damaged smile.

— I'm only saying good things, Free-derick. I am not saying bad things. I'm saying *good* things. Is it not all right to say *good* things about someone? Isn't it? If this is bad, then I am quite sorry, and I will not say a word. I didn't know that it was bad to say *good* things about you. People try to care. They do.

Frederick pressed his hands against his temples, massaging them, and watched Null's back.

— Null . . . Null . . . I'm not feeling well. I've been bitten by a goddamn any-mall.

Null raised his hands limply and shrugged.

— I am sorry. I am, no doubt, to blame, he said, looking at us mournfully. I praise him to the skies. He objects. Das bin ich . . .

— Out! shouted Frederick. Please get out!

— What? said Null, finally turning to look at Frederick.

— Get out please, Null! I cannot deal! I've been *bitten.*

Null got up slowly, shuddering, and without turning to look at Frederick again he slunk past us to the door and very quietly opened it. Then, having pulled the door open only a crack, he slipped through it and closed it behind him.·We could hear a whimpering through the door as he ran quickly down the stairs and out of the building.

11

Kate and I went south that weekend. We were settled into our lives in Taipei and it seemed only natural that we should, like everyone else, go on a vacation, even if it was just for a day. We took a bus, which was hot and filled with dead air, and when we came to a rest stop in the country not far outside Taipei, we got out, thinking we'd look for some water. We had stopped just short of a high bridge over a shallow river. The air was filled with the city's smog, but we were far enough out so that all around were trees, and when we looked over the bridge we saw the river running through a cool, shaded glen where dragonflies whizzed above the water. We were in good spirits and very thirsty, and so out of a need to be near water we slid down the cliff and, taking off our shoes, waded into the cool river.

But we couldn't drink, even though it looked fine; it was too close to the city to be pure. So we waded up the river, which moved slowly, or seemed to, except when it passed rocks, where it kicked up low curls of white water that revealed the real current. Yet the water was less than knee-deep. And we were still thirsty.

We carried our shoes and walked through the water, away from the bridge. The farther we walked, the denser the foliage became, and the more junglelike it seemed, except for the grainy haze that sat in the shafts of sun cutting across the shadows.

We came to a large flat rock in the middle of the river, and Kate promptly sat on it. We had started to debate about how far up the river we should go. I had been saying that we should go up as far as possible, maybe even get lost on purpose, because we were on vacation and we should do whatever the hell we wanted. On a vacation, I said, you don't worry about the practicality of something; you just do it. Kate was skeptical. The debate had for some reason turned peevish, and just before we got to the rock I heard in my voice an unmistakable whine. So when she sat on the rock, it was a silent way of saying that she wasn't going any farther.

I didn't want to sit down. To do that, I thought, would imply that she had won the argument. So I paced around the rock counterclockwise, sloshing through the water in long strides, my hands behind my back. The Ouroboros came into my mind briefly, because I saw a very beautiful large stone balanced on another not far away, and I thought of something I had read the day before concerning a supercomputer deducing the exact influences on a pebble by its structure and the patterns of erosion on its surface. The Ouroboros had been briefly mentioned in the article, by a professor at M.I.T. He had pointed out that "universal expert systems," like the Ouroboros, might be able to solve questions about geological time, and other things, that we'd never even thought to ask before. "Hypercomputers of this sort will be the most powerful thinking forces on earth, and will be able to reveal many of the underlying connections between entire histories of human thought and intuition." For a moment I considered what that would be like: to look at something, like that stone, and immediately know every single secret it held, from the elements that went into its creation, to all that it had experienced and had been exposed to until this very last second at which I looked at it. To know it completely and absolutely.

— Sit down, said Kate.

— Nope. I want to keep going up the river.

— Well, I'm staying here. You can go alone.

— I don't want to go alone, I said, watching my legs slosh through the water. We're in the jungle, Kate . . . let's voyage upstream into the jungle.

— This isn't a jungle, Harry. We're only twenty minutes south of Taipei.

— Come on. Get off your ass.

— Sit down.

— No, I'm going onward, I said, pointing up the river.

— Then go, she said.

I continued to pace around the rock. It looked wonderful up ahead. The branches bent over and shrouded parts of the river. It was a shadowy tunnel with spots of sunlight. The water collided luxuriously with the rocks, and sometimes there were rambling patches of white foam. There were boulders, some of them sitting in the middle of the water, rounded and covered with moss. What about that moss? What could the Ouroboros tell me about it, its structure, its history, the path of its genes through time?

— God, it's beautiful up there.

— Then go. Don't let me spoil your adventure.

She'd been testy recently. Little arguments like this had been occurring more often. She refused even to turn when she talked to me, so that as I walked around her I saw her from every angle. And I found myself focusing on her, the woman I loved and tried to understand. I wondered, What could the great Ouroboros Series 1 tell me about Kate?

From behind there was the impression of someone who was passive and dreamy. Her blond head leaned back so that her short hair touched the collar of her shirt, as if her gaze were planted lazily in the trees. I kept walking around her, my feet sinking in the underwater sand.

From her right side her expression was stolid and impassive. Her brow was strong and her cheekbones were illuminated by the sun in such a way that the tiny blond hairs on her cheeks lit up as specks of yellow on her face. Her hands lay in her lap, thin, strong, unclenched but touching each other. I looked at her hands. If I had eyes like electron microscopes, could I deduce everything she had done with them, all the way back to the cradle?

When I came around to the front she let her eyes meet mine with a sarcastic, slightly annoyed expression. She was saying something like: Examining me, are you? Her eyes were bright; her eyelashes were long and white in the sun. Her chest was pushed out so that her back was straight, and her legs, folded on the rock, had a look of relaxed, effortless poise. Where had she learned that? When was the first time in her life that she sat on a rock in the sun that way?

She was like an athlete in repose, someone you would have recognized from afar as being nimble and sure with her body, just by the way she sat. There was physical confidence, but it mostly resided in her legs. Yet farther up, in her arms and

shoulders, there was a nervous tension. I marveled at this, because I'd never seen it before, this division.

Her eyes lingered on me as I passed. She was looking at my
crotch, I thought.

— I think your belt's too loose, she said absently. Or maybe
your pants are too big. Where did you get those pants?

I sloshed by, passing to the right, and ignored the question.
She was leaning forward, and now her straight back made her
look angry and rigid. She didn't turn her head to follow me as
I passed, as if to punish me for not talking about my pants. She
stared ahead.

It was then that I looked at her form. Her ass was accentuated by the curve of her back, and it turned with a certain
precision around and down against the rock. Her pants pressed
tightly against her hips. A warm, heavy silence rose between us.
She felt me looking at her now, and her body was accepting my
gaze, opening up to it.

I had arrived around to where I started, staring at her back.
And I immediately remembered what I'd seen when I last
looked at her back: the head dreamily staring up into the trees.
But this was all overlaid on the other things I'd seen. I felt as if
I were wooing her, like an ardent lover circling below a window.
Wooing her with a mandolin.

It was getting late. All of a sudden I wanted to go up the
damned river.

— Kate. Let's go up, just for a little while. We'll take off our
clothes and swim. We don't have to drink the water. We'll keep
our mouths closed. But let's go up there and swim.

As I said this, I realized the whine had gone from my voice.
And I was secretly elated.

She got off the rock and dusted herself off.

— Okay, she said, with a sigh. But only a little ways up. All
right, Harry? Just a little ways.

The Ouroboros

We started up the river in long, splashing strides. And for some reason, as I listened to the rushing sound of the water being parted by our legs, my mind just fell onto the other thing. So I spoke. Just like that.

— Kate, I said. I want to know. Who the hell is this guy Wu?

12

Wu, for all his genteel exactitude, was not what you would call a polite man. My first impression of him was that he was intensely arrogant and had a large chip on his shoulder. This arrogance mostly resided in his bearing, which was that of someone very smart who'd been wronged and had staked a large part of his soul on the prospect of getting even. Yet for all the scorn inherent in the outward Wu (the one who sat across the table from me in the teashop on the first day I met him), there was obviously someone inside who had deep, unusual emotions. It could be seen in the subtlety of his expressions. Primarily, though, he wanted to be tough. But he struggled with it, unlike truly tough people.

— Tea, he told the waitress.

There was an awkward silence. We faced each other across

the table. Kate was late. She had arranged the meeting so that I could meet Wu, and "set my mind at rest," and now she was late.

— She ought to be here soon, I said.

He nodded, staring across the table at me. He had smooth skin and a glistening, high forehead.

— You are teaching?

— Yes. A man named Chen. He is in the government . . . I think he's in the Ministry of Trade . . .

— No, he's in the legislature, said Wu curtly.

I was surprised. But it explained the guards around Chen's house.

— You know him?

— No. I know *of* him.

I was amazed at the precision of his English. "Of him." How many Chinese would use that distinction?

— You are in the military?

He smiled, but ignored my question.

— Why is it, he said, that you Americans come to Taiwan to teach? Are there no teaching jobs in your country?

— Well, I said, we generally don't come *just* to teach.

— Then why? he said. Just to leave and go somewhere?

— Not just to leave.

— You are gaining experience?

I looked at him and scratched my chin. There was no way I could answer the question without falling into his trap. No matter how I answered, he would laugh at me.

— Yes. Seeing the rest of the world.

— And what do you see? he asked, looking out the window of the teashop with a slight smile.

There were a few battered sheds and a gray street outside. I hesitated for a moment, thinking.

— A different city. Different people.

Wu remained staring out the window, and his smile broadened a little.

— I see a city clogged with traffic. I smell dirty air. You have these things in the States also. What's the difference between your dirty cities and ours? Can it really be worth the distance you've come?

Even though he was smiling, he was quite serious, and he stared at the middle distance above the battered roofs of the shacks.

— Well, I said. I'm from a dirty city as well.

— Where?

— Baltimore. It's in Maryland.

— In the South?

— No. Midway between the North and South.

— Midway, he said, amused for some reason.

There was a pause as he took a raspy sip of tea. His arm crooked in a stiff bend as he put the cup to his lips. He was so clean, and everything about him was so poised, that there were moments when he looked like a statue. He had the quality of a shiny illustration called *The Officer,* or something of that sort, in an old *Life* magazine. Shiny and stiff. And he was conscious, overly conscious, of every gesture he made, so that he looked always poised and precise. I think he had an idea of himself as heroic, and refused to accept a physical presence that was anything less. I could have laughed at that, but there was something about this extreme portrayal of himself that rang true, even though it was forced. And it made me think of Kate. How did it affect her?

— Yes, I'm in the military, he said, answering my question of a minute before. I was just thinking about what you said: "Midway." I'm sure you know of the American sea battle in the Pacific. I studied it. I've studied many American battles. What do you know of America's war history?

— It depends on what war, I said pointedly. I was beginning to get a little angry. It was as if he were interviewing me for an assistant's position.

— Your Civil War?

— What about it?

— Do you know of Grant, Lee, and Sherman? Do you know anything about William Tekki-oom-sah Sherman?

"Do you know anything . . ." He was smug. He was trying to show me how little I knew about my own country's history.

— Tekki-oom-sah? I said incredulously.

He looked embarrassed. His cheeks turned red.

— An American Indian name was the middle name, said Wu. He was a general. I've studied his campaigns. The name, I am not sure how to pronounce it.

— William Tecumseh Sherman? I think it's Tecumseh. You're talking about Sherman's march?

— Yes. He brightened up, as if finally on a happy topic. Sherman's campaign across the South.

— What about it?

His enthusiasm was brimming over, as much as it could, given his handsome, emotionless face and clean, pressed, spotless green uniform.

— A smart man. He chuckled. A very smart man. Sherman was a brilliant general . . . He went on murmuring and he smoothed down his hair with several long, careful strokes of his hand across his head.

— How's that?

— Sherman. He thought how to *make* peace, he added.

— That's a novel way to see it, I said, scouring my memory for shreds of knowledge concerning Sherman.

The only image that came to me was a view of Atlanta, burned almost to the ground, with row upon row of charred houses in the distance. It was from an ancient photograph I'd seen, and there was a pitiful woman in the foreground holding a bundle of clothes, sitting on the burned step of a building. Her face was covered with soot. Smoke dwindled upward on the horizon. She was the only person in the picture. And I also thought of the face of Sherman that I'd seen in a textbook, with a beard, and all I could remember was a quote from him saying something like "I shall make the people so sick of war that for generations they shall . . ." What? Be scarred and miserable? I couldn't remember.

At that moment Kate came bounding through the door, out of breath, with a flurry of apologies. I stood up because Wu did.

— I'm sorry, she said. You've both met, I guess. Harry, this is Corporal Wu. I'm sorry . . . Wu P'ei-fu. That's a famous war-lord, Harry. Did you know that? Wu was named after a warlord who was his great-grandfather.

Wu looked at her as if the day had just begun for him and he was watching the sun rise. He gestured, with a grand sweep of his arm, for her to sit down next to him. After that, both of us sat down and pivoted our attention on Kate, who had so altered the chemistry at the table that Wu and I were once again almost strangers.

She was glowing and beautiful. She drew her hair back to get it off her forehead and smiled at me. At times she looked mas-culine, and this was one of those times, with her short hair and sharp, almost boyish face. I saw that she and Wu were almost exactly the same height. Their bearing, also, was similar at that moment, with straight shoulders and upright posture. Blond, boyish Voltaire and the Chinese corporal. An interesting pair, I thought to myself, but smiled at Kate, because now that she was across from me, I was feeling strong and sure of myself, as I always did in her presence.

She took a crisp white napkin off the table and spread it with a flourish across her legs, which were bare because she was wearing shorts. I saw her beautiful legs around the corner of the table just before they disappeared beneath the napkin.

— I was coming up from Chinese class and I got stuck on the Ling Dong bus, she said.

— I was wondering whether you were late on purpose, I said.

I meant it jokingly, but it annoyed her, and she gave me a quick, angry glance, then drew her eyes away.

— Hello, Wu, she said, turning toward him. It's good to see you. Did you two get to talk at all?

— Yes, said Wu. Harry is very knowledgeable.

— Oh, you talked about computers, said Kate.

— No, said Wu, turning toward me and reassessing me briefly. He is, like myself, interested in history. We talked about your country's Civil War.

Wu's theatrical sense of himself had increased exponentially since Kate's arrival. He struck a pose that reminded me of a photograph I'd seen once of Ernest Hemingway. He leaned toward Kate with his chin resting on his fist and his other hand on his hip, so that his elbow jutted out behind him in a defiant, carefree manner. What amazed me was not his open display of attraction to Kate (my first instinct wasn't anger or jealousy) but rather his wide array of specific, clearly formed postures of heroism. And although he'd choreographed himself quite well, the poses looked agonizing. One moment he'd be the "masculine listener," his brow furrowed just so. Then he'd be the "calm, handsome guy," listening while Kate and I spoke together. When he talked, he used his hands and never opened his mouth too far. He always smiled at the appropriate time, or looked appropriately grave. He used his face and his body very precisely, as if it were a delicate instrument. I watched his hands. They were small and neat, and he took great pleasure in using them while he talked.

— The American Civil War is studied very closely in the War

College, he said, making a little mime of holding a magnifying glass up to his eye, and studying the palm of his other hand as if it were a map.

What a strange man he is, I thought. How unusually he uses his hands. It's almost embarrassing. But there was something impressive about him. And besides the urge to burst out laughing in his face at his little mimes and dramatic contortions, I felt, against my will, a liking for him.

But after admitting this to myself, it dawned on me, watching his face closely, that one couldn't put up with him too long. He was excessive. And I was certain there was something in him that was set against me.

— And you see, Kate, said Wu, snaking his hand through the teacups to illustrate his point, Sherman had a difficult choice. If he stayed, he would be attacked by the Confederate army under General Forrest. If he attempted to protect his supply line, he would be attacked by the other Confederate army to the north. He decided to do something very brave. He marched directly into the South, into the enemy's territory. He cut loose from his lines of supply and marched through Georgia with his army to the sea . . .

— Burning, raping, and pillaging everything in his way, I added.

— But Harry, said Wu, leaning back in his chair and folding his arms across his chest dramatically, he ended the war.

— Yes, a little like the way Hiroshima ended another war. I'm not saying he was wrong. I'm just saying that you can't flatly rejoice over destruction and devastation . . .

— He's not rejoicing, said Kate pointedly. He's admiring.

— Fine with me, I said, feeling the anger rise in my throat at the banding together of the two of them. Admire away. Don't let me stop you.

There was a long silence.

126

— But you do think the Civil War was for a just cause? said Wu.

— Yes, absolutely. But it's just not that simple. You can't see history that one-sidedly. There's bad on both sides.

— There is always bad on both sides, said Wu P'ei-fu, smiling politely. But the bad that good people do is not as bad as the bad that bad people do.

I was stunned. He was a true acrobat in English, and he always pronounced things correctly. It was unnerving. But on top of that he was smug. And here he was lecturing me about right and wrong. He was trying to get me in a corner.

— I don't see things that simply. And I know you don't either, I said, glaring at Kate.

But I realized that this was a fairly flat-footed appeal on my part, and Kate looked at me sardonically.

— I'm not sure that I agree with either of you, she said, touching my arm. But Harry, I do think that you're trying to make things too simple. Wu has a point.

— I think you've got a very romantic view of America, I said.

Suddenly he blushed. Ha, I thought, maybe I've found the unguarded hole in his suit of armor. Is he an unabashed admirer of America? Or was he just embarrassed that I said the word "romantic" when he was so close to Kate? Regardless of my quiet delight in finding a weakness, I was becoming more and more aware, through all these observations, that there was already a bond of friendship, a real one, between him and Kate. And I envied it.

— Harry, said Kate, aggressively changing the subject, I saw Frederick's friend Null on the bus. He was acting very weird, glancing all around while we talked. I don't know what it is about him.

She turned to Wu, who was listening carefully.

— He's a friend of a friend, Wu. An odd sort of guy. A German. Wu nodded, but looked at me with an air of caution.

— He's got a tattoo on his cheek, I said as earnestly as possible to Wu, trying to put my voice back into the sounds of a friendly conversation. It's a snake. You know? A drawing of a snake. On his skin.

I circled a little pattern on my face with my finger.

— It's like a pictogram. You know, a tattoo? said Kate, pretending to draw on her arm.

— Oh, yes, said Wu finally. *Tattoo.* A painting. I thought it was a French word for a second. Yes. On the skin.

— Right. Well, this guy has a tattoo of a snake on his face.

We all shook our heads and chuckled self-consciously. Admittedly, it had started off badly. But for now, at least, I would try to get along with him.

In the back of the teashop we could hear chopsticks and bowls being cleaned in a metal sink. Wu turned to Kate and began to talk slowly in Mandarin, slightly opening his shoulder toward me to imply, I suppose, that he wasn't closing me out. Kate nodded at what he was saying. Occasionally they turned to me to see that I was getting it all, and Wu made a show of going very slowly and then winking at me as if to assure me that this was the best way to learn Chinese. I could pick up only a few things. He was talking about forests or something in China, and then he made a reference to the National Zoo of Taiwan, but all in all I wasn't keeping up with them. Then he sped up, talking faster and faster, until his shoulder had completely turned away from me and he was no longer attempting to bring me along.

He had managed to exclude me successfully. Somehow I felt that I was the interloper, not he. And my mind drifted back to that time in my room at college when Kate was speaking Chinese in her sleep. I'd felt invaded. The language had seemed so primitive then, so full of guttural sparks and looping twangs. It had seemed like a primeval language, as if it were the true, mysterious tongue of her dreams. And I'd been afraid of it.

Here, however, coming with speed and precision out of Wu's mouth, it took on a different meaning. It had the direct, exact quality of mathematics, and I longed to understand it.

While Wu talked, my mind glided to an article I'd read several weeks before in the American Cultural Center while doing research on the Ouroboros. It was in a book on what are called "intrinsically difficult problems." These are mathematical problems that can be solved only in principle, and only with a computing machine that would have to exceed the capacity of the most powerful computers imaginable today. On the face of it, these do not appear to be impossible problems. Yet one mathematician hypothesized that to solve some of the most basic of these intrinsically difficult problems, one would have to construct a computer the size of the universe. I remembered how this mathematician attempted to prove that such a computer (100 light years in diameter), which could not consist of hardware smaller than a proton (10^{-13} centimeters in diameter), transmitting information at the speed of light (3×10^8 meters per second), would take 20 billion years to solve certain mathematical problems that we know are true in principle. These intrinsically difficult problems were the main stumbling block to the success of huge computers like the Ouroboros.

And as I watched Wu talking and Kate listening ever so attentively, her eyes playing on his lips, her pretty face turned upward, I thought about what this particular mathematician had called "the blight of unsolvability."

— Harry, you should hear what Wu says about snakes in southern China. It's fascinating.

— Yes, said Wu, finally looking at me, evidently unwilling to go over it again.

There was an anxious moment between the three of us. I wondered why I was so unhappy. My girlfriend talked with another man for a few minutes in another language, and I felt abandoned. Was that right? Taken on just that level, there was nothing wrong. Yet there was something about Wu, about the way he entranced Kate, that made me very uneasy.

— Snake is a euphemism in English, I said to Wu, while Kate, watching my face, listened nervously.

— Ewe-pha-meezum? said Wu, cocking his head with curiosity. I'm not familiar with that word.

— You know . . . something that means something else. A word that . . .

— Snake is not a euphemism, Harry, said Kate.

— Yes, it is. In my definition, at least. It's a word that covers a whole range of messier meanings that take too long, or are too harsh, to say flat out without offending someone.

— Harry . . . snake, I mean, come on. Snake is not a euphemism.

Wu looked back at me questioningly.

— How is it a euphemism? she said curtly.

— You know what I mean, I said looking at her. Snake. It means someone who is no good . . . a crook.

— A crook? Yes, I know this word, said Wu thoughtfully.

He looked at me and then at Kate.

— A crook. As in "crooked." Like your President Nixon. Right? Yes. I read an article about the Watergate affair and it quoted an American politician who called Mister Nixon this word. Crook, said Wu.

Kate was staring directly at me.

— Yes. There's an example. He was a snake, I said, measuring the antipathy in her eyes.

Wu laughed.

— Oh, that's a ewe-pha-meezum for "crook." Snake. Nixon. A crook. That is funny, he said, and seemed amused by it all.

— Why does that seem funny?

— Mister Nixon, and your seriousness about his being a

crook. I don't know. It struck me as funny. He was a snake, as you say. But he was a snake to us for other reasons than yours. You see, said Wu, getting more serious, he was the first American President to betray Taiwan, when he visited the mainland. But . . . for that the American people don't care. They have their own, I'm afraid smaller, reasons for calling poor old Nixon a snake.

— Well, he was corrupt. He lied to his own people, he broke the laws of the country, he led . . . The man was corrupt, I said.

— Cor-r-r-ruption, pronounced Wu, still smiling, but now not at all amused. I would suggest that we, the Chinese, have a much longer, much older, probably more accurate experience with corruption. The real snakes are not like your Mister Nixon. It is funny that you find it so easy to hate these small snakes. That is, if Mister Nixon is indeed a good example of a snake, as you put it. Yes, he was two-faced. And Taiwan suffered the worst from this. Still, your Richard Nixon was a worm compared to some of the snakes we have seen in our history, he concluded with a shake of his head, throwing back a big gulp of tea.

I was seething. I imagined myself giving him a little holier-than-thou lecture about Mao Tse-tung: *"Hey, he wasn't all that bad, was he? You guys are so paranoid holding out on this island . . . I don't think you Nationalists really were on the right side anyway. Look how much land you gave up . . ."*

Suddenly he spat up some tea. He didn't actually eject it from his mouth; he just sort of sputtered because the tea was evidently halfway down his throat at the moment something amusing occurred to him.

— Ah — cough — Harry, I am sorry, but if you want to find out about *real* snakes, you should talk to your Mister Chen. He will tell you. He is an expert.

He chuckled and took another sip of tea. And then, as if he

no longer had any interest in talking to me about it, he turned to Kate and smiled.

— Kate, you are very pretty today.

— Thanks, said Kate, looking over at me with a wilted smile and raising her eyebrows, as if to say: Sorry, Harry.

I almost jumped over the table and strangled the bastard. My chair even jolted forward a few inches. I clenched my hands. But Wu went along blithely in the same tone.

— There's an old film at Hsimending, an American film, on Monday night. Would you both like to come with me? he said, looking from Kate to me with anticipation. You would be my guests. It is an *American* film.

— I can't come on Monday, I said flatly. I teach Chen on Mondays.

— Sorry, Wu, said Kate, shrugging.

— That's too bad, said Wu, looking, for some reason, at Kate's hands on the table.

— Why don't you two go together? I said.

Kate looked at me, shocked.

— What?

— I can't go because of Chen. But I wouldn't want you to miss it on account of me.

— Are you sure you can't get out of teaching that night? asked Wu solemnly.

— I'm sure.

It occurred to me to let them go together, partly as an act of defiance, and partly to vex the demon in me that saw more to their friendship. I wanted to leave them ample space to create their own version of things. That way, Kate's choice would be unfettered.

— Harry, we'll tell you about it when we come back, said Wu.

13

I was wrong about the Ouroboros. I finally found a book on it and realized that the article I'd read in the *Tribune* was inaccurate, or I had remembered it incorrectly. I found the book in an obscure technical bookshop on Ho Ping Lu. It was written by the inventor of the Ouroboros, a man named W. D. Ellis, of Brainlike Devices, a company founded to build his computers (so far, only twelve had been made) and sell them to scientists who had almost impossible problems to figure out. He had invented the machine while a student at a northeastern university, similar to the one I had attended. The book was in English, and the shop had only one copy for an astronomical fee that I paid immediately, thinking my future was in the balance. Even though Kate's jests danced in my head, I was thrilled to have an entire book about the marvelous machine, this thing which had so entranced me.

But when I began to read the book, my spirits plunged. This was a highly complex object, this Ouroboros Series 1, far more complex than anything I had encountered before. It was labyrinthine. It was intricate and complex all the way down from its general structure to its tiny "processing nodes."

But though I was boggled by the array of formulas in the book, I was inflamed, intellectually I guess, by the picture of the machine on the cover. It was a huge black cube made up of smaller black cubes, and shining through its misty black surface along the top were hundreds of blue lights. It looked like an ideal of sorts, a beautiful magic box constructed by alchemists, or a geometric black pearl pulled from a giant oyster. When I looked at it I felt viscerally inspired, and I almost shook at the thought of its power.

But, as I said, the book proved the subject to be tremendously complicated. There was much to digest. Actually, most of what the *Tribune* had highlighted was not what the computer itself was all about. After plowing through the first chapter I had to throw out many of my suppositions. But, using a highly amateurish approach, I was able to develop for myself a working description of the machine, which I now deliver as I understood it.

The Ouroboros Series 1 is a black cube, as I've already explained. It stands about seven feet high, and is approximately the same in width. It is divided into eight subcubes, each containing forty-five boards that slide into the machine vertically, like tall, thin black books. On each board is an array of 6,630 objects called, by Ellis, "memory/will cells." All told, the computer is made up of 298,350 of these cells. Each of them is too small to do anything important on its own, but when all the cells are connected in a huge network, the machine can "think" very effectively, just as ant colonies can "think" through problems that the single ant doesn't even know exist.

This structure is fundamentally different from the ordinary computers that crowd around our daily lives. As explained by Ellis, common computers are built within the parameters designed in the 1940s by John von Neumann and his colleagues. Von Neumann built the earliest computers with a divided structure. On one side there was memory (which at that time was made up of vacuum tubes, as in the old television sets), and on the other side was the will of the computer, or what is ordinarily called the processor (made up of basic switching components). Splitting these two at the time made perfect sense, because they were composed of different mechanisms. This structure has been called, appropriately, the "von Neumann architecture," and it was the standard for all digital computers until quite recently.

When a problem is entered into a von Neumann computer (that is, almost every computer encountered today), the will of the computer (that is, the processor) must work to remain in constant contact with the memory, since no problem can be solved without the interdependence of the two. But, being in different locations, the will and the memory must at every moment communicate across a gap. This was nothing to be concerned about long ago when a computer was a simple apparatus and had a relatively small memory. But as time went on, and computers became more complex, and their memories became bigger and bigger, the distance between memory and will became an obstacle. The reason can be explained with this completely fabricated analogy.

Imagine that there are two brothers. One has a vast memory, with an acute sense of the past in great detail, but he is extremely passive, doesn't relate to the present, and thinks so much that he doesn't even use his body anymore. He sits around day after day in a haze of contemplation. The other brother has the opposite problem. He can't remember back more than one or two seconds. He is without a sense of self, doesn't even know his name, and cannot identify his own hand when it is held in front of his face. But he is strong and powerful, and has an insatiable desire to do things.

These two brothers grow up together, but early in their lives each realizes he cannot go on without the other's help. In order to survive, they build separate shacks next to each other (because each wants to have his own place) and connect the private houses with a passageway. That way, whenever the strong brother wants to act sensibly, with a knowledge of the past, he crosses the passageway, and the thoughtful brother thinks things out for him. When the thoughtful brother needs something done, even the most simple task, he yells (he's immobile and sits forever in his chair), and the strong one immediately comes over to help.

With time, the two brothers grow rich, and each, still owning his individual plot, builds a huge skyscraper on the spot where the shack once stood. Of course, they keep the passageway intact, being unable to exist without direct contact at every moment.

Eventually, over many, many years, two separate cities evolve, like towering columns, still connected by the one, ancient passageway on the ground. Even hundreds of years after the brothers have grown old and died, the people of the two cities, now numbering in the millions, struggle to carry on as always, still using the one archaic passageway. On one side, there are millions of people who can only remember, and on the other side, millions of people who can only do. As the cities get larger and more powerful, they are also pushing themselves to extinction, because most of the energy of the population is expended in getting through the grimy old corridor, just to find out what must be done next.

This, as I understood it from a much more mathematical analogy provided by W. D. Ellis, is the problem with traditional computers. The larger and more complex a computer gets, the more energy is required to move data between will and memory. In other words, no matter how forceful the will gets, or how vast and experienced the memory becomes, if there is a gap between them, it will always dominate the relationship.

This constraint has been dubbed the "von Neumann bottleneck." The larger a computer gets, the less useful it becomes. This is what Ellis set out to solve.

The solution to the problem, states Ellis, is "correlation" or, to be more precise, a homogeneous computing machine in which memory and will are one. Each of these memory/will cells communicates with the others by uniform connections. The passageway becomes obsolete. It's as if, in the analogy of the two cities, each person in the memory city has a child with a person in the will city, combining the talents in one offspring. The new generation destroys the passageway, and all live together in one huge city, remembering and doing all at one time. That is the Ouroboros.

It's a very democratic thing, and this is part of what drew me in even further, the way it seemed to have ideal principles secretly woven into its foundation. So that after reading the second chapter of the book about the Ouroboros Series 1, even though all the preliminary, basic language had disappeared long ago, and I found myself almost up to my eyes in murky equations, I pressed on. I was totally hooked by it. Slightly obsessed. It was a gorgeous thing, inside and out, in the mind and as an object.

It was getting to be the hot time of year in Taipei and I was settling into my tutoring position, and uneasily settling into the role of a perplexed and somewhat unfortunate lover, but the Ouroboros gleamed in my mind with all the brightness of a golden cup, like the Holy Grail. It was something miraculous and beautiful, and represented life's more admirable virtues, and yet . . . and this was the twist . . . it was a *machine*. I was infatuated with a *machine*.

Kate was getting ready to go with Wu to their English class dinner. I had been asked, but I didn't feel like going, because I'd been to one or two and found that invariably everyone talked at lightning speed in Chinese. My Chinese was getting better, but it wasn't great. I would smile and nod, sitting next to Kate, and she would translate, but eventually I'd drop through the cracks of the conversation.

Wu and Kate and I had gone out a few times together for tea and a couple of odd three-way walks, and I'd satisfied myself for the time being that Kate had no deep-down attraction to him. She definitely liked him, of course, but I decided her side of things wasn't particularly dangerous. It was *his* enthusiasm that worried me.

Kate was getting ready in the bathroom. She was taking an awfully long time and so, feeling more sure of myself (by way of my recent adventures in studying the Ouroboros) than I had for a long time, I put my mind to talking with Wu P'ei-fu. There was an awkward silence between us, and he rocked back and forth on his feet, making his shoes squeak. I'd just come back from downtown and had passed a statue of General Chiang. His stolid figure, with its benevolent eyes, loomed over the traffic, and as my bus skirted the monument's base I had the illusion that the big man was aloft, like a float in the Thanksgiving Day parade.

— What do you think of the veneration of Chiang Kai-shek?

He's all over the place. I find it amazing, I said, just off the top of my head.

Wu stopped rocking for a second.

— He is a hero. The most important hero, probably, of democratic China.

— I just wondered, I said. I see the pictures and the statues everywhere. Mister Chen has several likenesses of Chiang in his house.

Wu chuckled.

— Chen has pictures of Chiang?

— Yes. And a statue. A small one.

An ironic look passed over Wu's face, but it disappeared quickly when Kate, with the boom of the door hitting the wall as it opened, swept out of the bathroom. She looked beautiful but a bit too madeup, I thought. Too much lipstick. Her lips were iridescent. But, besides that, and the excess rouge, she was very attractive.

— You sure you don't want to come, Harry?

— Nope.

She gave me a serious look, her hand on her hip. She looked like a harlequin.

— Please come.

— Leave him alone. He's been to too many English class dinners, said Wu, nodding to me as if we were both in on a droll joke about boring dinners.

— Okay, said Kate.

She's not pleading with me, I thought, suddenly panicking. Bad sign. But then I looked at Wu. He was performing a crisp, manly lean against the wall.

There were many moments, like this, when I'd see him affect a stance so blatantly theatrical, so self-conscious, that I wanted to wave my hands and distract him to see if he'd fall down. He was always trying to balance perfectly in the moment. There was something in his face that was reminiscent of Rudolph Valentino posing in a catatonic, silent-film rigor mortis. He glowed with that awkward and overly potent sense of self that I had gladly smothered when I turned eighteen. And even though I considered him a rival of sorts, I was always a little afraid that he'd embarrass himself by doing something foolish. Something small, like dropping food from his mouth while he talked, or sliding off the wall, like right now, during a dramatic lean. Exaggerated self-awareness lends itself to sudden humiliation. And in those few moments when I was able to detach myself from my resentment, I found him endearing.

— All right, Wu, I said in a gravelly, fatherly voice. Have fun.

He smiled nervously.

— Thank you, Harry, he said.

Then they went out the door, saying goodbye, with Kate like a blond clown, swinging her pocketbook like a bag of rocks.

The next morning, tiptoeing so as not to wake Kate, I came out of our bedroom around dawn, naked, looking for a handkerchief to blow my nose in because my head was like lead and I was sure I had a cold.

That's when I saw someone coming out of Frederick's bedroom, tiptoeing, like me. For a moment I had one of those early morning disjunctions of perception, and I thought it was just an image of me looking for a handkerchief that was looming so large in my groggy mind that I had projected it outward into the room. But I realized one wouldn't see oneself that way, and as I was realizing this, the person heard me and turned around. Then I spied a green mark on the person's face and was jolted into recognition.

— Null, I said, completely surprised.

The Ouroboros

He flushed, staring at me while I grabbed a towel from the bathroom door.

— Harr-ee, why, hello, he said. I was just leafing.

We stood there for a moment, not knowing what to say, and then he resumed his tiptoeing, waving to me vaguely, and slipped out the door, closing it quietly behind him.

The first thought that came to me in a flash of fear was that he had sneaked in at night and murdered Frederick. I ran to Frederick's doorway and looked in. He was snoring, asleep in his bed, his mustache flat against his face. Blankets were on the floor beside the bed. My eyes focused on the blankets, and on the impression of a body that had been there, and, not quite comprehending, I turned around and went back into my bedroom and lay down next to Kate. I mean, if he'd been in Frederick's bed, it might have made some sense. But he hadn't.

There was too much to think about at that hour, and I couldn't concentrate. I began to think of the handkerchief that I'd gone in search of but had forgotten. Thinking about that, I gradually gave in to sleep again, but not before I turned toward Kate and gazed at her sleeping beside me. I smiled to myself. She'd come home late and hadn't done a good job of removing her lipstick, and there was a red wobbly stripe across her pillow.

14

During the drive to Chen's house I'd made it a habit to carry around the book on the Ouroboros and lazily glide my eyes over the incomprehensible sections. I knew that it was beholden upon me to begin to learn the meaning, for instance, of this equation:

$$P(\text{tail} \geq k) = 1 - (\sum_{x=0}^{k-1} \binom{n}{x} p^x (1-p)^{n-x})^N \approx 1 - e(-N \sum_{x=k}^{n} \binom{n}{x} p^x (1-p)^{n=x})$$

I looked at this thing on the page and was awed by its meticulous beauty. It reminded me of inscriptions on ancient temples; like them, it could be admired completely apart from its original intent. But that's about as far as I got during the ride to Chen's: admiring the physical beauty of equations.

On the day I admired the above equation we went up the driveway, as usual, past the guards, and reached the slate walk, only to see Chen and his assistant (the man with the lifeless tie) hurrying toward the car. This was a little out of the ordinary. Chen was wearing what could only be called a sport jacket, or what used to be called a sport jacket in the old Bing Crosby movies. It had a yellow madras pattern with stripes of black and greenish beige.

Chen leaned down to talk to me through the car window.

— Would you like to go to the moo-zee-um? I have arranged a trip for us to go to Gugong Buo-yu Yuan . . . to the Palace Moo-zee-um. Many anti-kwee-tees. Old, old. We can have our lesson there.

— All right, I said, realizing I had no choice in the matter anyway.

At the other end of the slate walk, near the house, I saw two men in suits standing near the guards. They were watching us. They talked quietly, and one lit a cigarette. They looked official, on boring but necessary business.

We got into another car, a larger one with darker windows, the three of us: Chen, myself, and the assistant, whose name, I learned, was Su, and who was grinning at me the whole time like the Cheshire Cat. We were all squashed together, even though the back seat was huge, because Chen sat in the middle and caused the seat to slant toward him, and Su and I found ourselves practically hugging him. Finally Su elected to get up front, and then we went down the driveway, under the blank stares of the guards, and out into the smooth streets of the suburban neighborhood.

— Su, I'm going to close the window now, said Chen, and he reached forward and shut the partition that divided us from the driver's seat.

Su's grinning face vanished behind the dark-tinted glass, except for a moment, when I could see his white-toothed smile shining through for a few seconds, disembodied. Then Chen busied himself with unfolding the little table that came out of the seat in front of us.

— One moment, one moment, he said, and reached into his pocket.

This was the first time, in all the months I'd known him, that I sensed something about Chen that made me positive he wasn't quite the same as other people. There had always been something on the edge of my mind, but I could never name it. When his yellow madras jacket stretched across his broad shoulders as he strained against its seams to reach into his pocket, and I heard his strange nasal breathing and observed his quiet, gentle, but labored preoccupation with what he was doing (and I knew exactly what he was reaching for), I saw in him a touch of something screwy, something a little off mentally, and it unsettled me that I hadn't recognized it before.

— There, he said, and placed the dragon on the small fold-out table.

He had concealed it with great difficulty in the tight pocket of his sport jacket. His face relaxed, and he looked infinitely relieved, watching it with a smile, even though it chattered up and down on the wood owing to the jostling of the car.

— You see, he said. It is now feeding. Yes? It breathes it in. And he inhaled and exhaled deeply.

— I have something to tell you. That's why we are going to the moo-zee-um. Sometimes they listen at home, he said, waving his hand over his shoulder.

He scratched his head.

— Moo-zee-um? Is that correct?

— Museum, I said. Say "Mew."

— Moo.

— Almost.

He waved this aside, not wanting to discuss it any further.

— I want to warn you, he said.

— Warn me?

— Yes. No one is going to warn you, so I will warn you. There are sara-ton officials in my government, officials I know well, who do not smile upon your association with a sara-ton person.

— Who?

— Your friend Mister Wu P'ei-fu, he said abruptly, and with great emphasis on *fu*. He is a friend?

I remembered my answer to Mai Kai-lin in Chen's house, and was embarrassed.

— No, not really. I mean . . . I know him. But I certainly couldn't call him a friend. But, Mister Chen, I assure you, it was after . . . I mean, honestly . . . I met him only after the talk with the woman from the Education Ministry.

— But they have seen you with him, on Ho Ping Bei Lu. They said that your wife and you spay-end time with him. That just two days ago you were seen on Ho Ping Bei Lu with him.

— My wife?

— She teaches him?

— But . . . he is a corporal in the army.

Chen smiled.

— Yes. But his gray-ett-grandfather was a chün-fa. A famous chün-fa. He was the most smart.

— What is a chün-fa?

— A warlord. During the communist insurrection, there were many warlords. Some fought with the communists, some fought with the Nah-sha-nalists, some fought only for themselves. Wu P'ei-fu, the gray-ett-grandfather, was an indah-pendent chün-fa. He fought against the communists, but also against the Kuomintang and Chiang Kai-shek.

When he uttered Chiang's name he bowed his head, and I thought he was praying. In fact, he was solemnly uttering some incantation. Suddenly he scratched his nose and, seized with what seemed like a fit of itches, began to scratch his entire face with tiny finger movements. He scratched his nose and forehead, his ears, and finally all along his upper lip, where he stopped.

— But that was almost seventy years ago.

— Still, he was a chün-fa. China is still at war. Although you do not see soldiers marching, there is a war, he said, waving his hand to indicate the peaceful neighborhood that rolled by outside.

— Taiwan is always threatened. Sara-ton officials do not like Wu P'ei-fu's gray-ett-grandson. He is not a good Nah-sha-nal-ist. He is known to have ideas. They do not like you meeting with the gray-ett-grandson of a chün-fa. Pah-teek-arly that gray-ett-grandson.

He reached out and touched the dragon, gingerly, at the end of his sentence, as if he were in a dark hallway and was reaching out to touch the wall.

— I see, I said.

After a few minutes of silence we arrived at the museum. It was a huge reconstructed Chinese palace with high yellow walls, blue-tiled roofs, and a series of different levels of steps leading up to the door. We got out and climbed the stairs. The driver of our car came with us and consulted seriously for a few minutes with the museum guards in a hushed tone.

Then the three of us, Chen, Su and I, went into the museum, Chen leading the way, and obviously on a path that he knew well. We were followed, at a respectful distance, by a guard in a blue uniform and a hat that was too big for him. His ears were the only things that prevented the hat, with its shiny medallion, from slipping down over his face. Hair would have helped. He had a severe crew cut. He watched us dispassionately, standing still every time we stood still, walking quickly whenever we did.

There were very few people there, and the long hallways were cool and vacant, and it was humorous to look back and see him attempting to look inconspicuous, a little man trying to blend in with high white walls.

I wondered about Chen's real position in the government. There was the sense that he was being baby-sat rather than protected. It was hard to justify the presence of so many guards at his house, or the goofy guard who followed us now.

We went down a corridor lined with illuminated cases. Brilliant Chinese robes were spread out, like butterflies, in each one. Chen glanced at them but hurried on.

— Fang-zian zai nali? Chen asked Su, who was trying to keep up with him while still appearing composed.

— Yu zhuan, said Su.

Chen took a right down another corridor and we bustled along, unable to look at anything, and unable to carry on one of our inane English lessons. Chen was intent on getting to a specific part of the museum. Half walking, half skipping to keep up with us, the guard in the big hat stayed about fifteen feet back.

— Yizhi zou, said Su breathlessly, pointing with jabs of his hand.

— Bu hao! said Chen.

He was asking directions from Su, and then staunchly ignoring them. Su took this all in stride gracefully.

We turned a corner and Chen halted abruptly. Su almost collided with Chen's bearish back, but stopped just in time and teetered for a second, staring at the jacket's stripes, before regaining his balance.

On the wall, in a secluded alcove, was an immense scroll covered with sweeping dark swirls of ink. But it was only when I looked closer that I could see scaly faces in the dim paint, peeking out here and there from behind rounded, boiling clouds.

Then, in various places, I could see angry claws, some clench-ing white balls. In other places, all over the scroll, were bared, pointed teeth and dark red tongues. All told there were nine dragons, twisted around one another, writhing, sawing the clouds with their mouths, their tails swooping in vast arcs.

— Hao, hao, said Su softly, admitting his defeat in finding the scroll.

Su smiled at me again, shrugged, and stood by Chen, who stared at the scroll with a shining expression on his face.

— Yes, said Chen. Here are the loong jiu . . . the nine drah-gones. Here they are . . .

— Hao, hao, mumbled Su, nodding to no one in particular while glancing without interest at the nine jagged faces on the wall.

— You see, these are like the chün-fa, said Chen, wagging his finger at the scroll and looking at me brightly. Chiang, you know, was also a chün-fa. But everyone called him chün-*fei* fa. A *good* warlord. Even so, he was a warlord. They were all like cree-tchurrs too big for their time, and so, because they were too strong for this woord, could only fight each other because that is the only fight that was large enough for them.

Chen looked back at the scroll, and I watched his baby-ish mouth, which became exaggeratedly puckered and self-satisfied with what it had just said.

— If they were the dragons, too big for their time and all that, what is everyone else? Are we the right size? What are we? I blurted out, staring with him up at the wall.

— *We?* We are not drah-gones. He laughed, making a sour face. *We?* Maybe we are leetle bee-tales crawling through the grass.

He walked up to the wall and pointed carefully, with his fat finger, at an infinitesimal spot at the bottom of the scroll.

— This . . . is you, he said, wrinkling his nose.

I looked at the tiny spot and said nothing, feeling somewhat bruised.

— *You*. Do you see you? *Here*, he said, pointing again.

— Okay, okay, I get it. I'm a beetle.

But then he searched around at the bottom of the scroll and finally pointed to another spot, equally small, a few inches away.

— This is me, he said, wrinkling his nose and squinting once again, as if he were really pointing out a tiny, tiny creature that disgusted him.

Ah, so we were equal, I thought.

— And here, said Chen, pointing to another black dot. This is Su.

Su, understanding only hazily, laughed and nodded.

— Su . . . jegga Su, he said, shaking his head with amusement.

— And this, said Chen, is our guard.

He pointed to another minuscule black spot. He was getting a little carried away with his simile. I was thinking, great, Chen, pretty soon we can start an ant farm.

— *We* are not drah-gones, said Chen. We are ink.

— Come on, Chen, I said as offhandedly as possible . . .

The whole demonstration was getting pretty silly.

— Why can't we be dragons? I mean, you'd think in a democratic society everybody would get a chance. You can be what you want.

— No. We are too small. People are too small now. You know how the drah-gone in my pocket? — he patted his jacket — how it feeds? You know. I told you. Noh-ting does that anymore. There is noh-ting you can find that *eats* — and he thrashed out his hand violently in my direction, clenched like a claw — that *eats* the ee-vall in the woord. The great drah-gones

were both the creators and the eaters of ee-vall. Without them
we are nothing. The woord . . .

— The world?

— Yes, the woord is no longer protected. There are no more
large people . . . no more drah-gones. They are dead. Without
them we are a woord of bee-tales.

— Fine, fine, I understand. But what is good in the world?
Look around you, what is good? What is *not* evil? I said half
smiling and having, at the same time, a lurking sense of déjà
vu.

— Taiwan, said Chen. Taiwan is good. All here, wrapped in
the hands of the people, the memory of Chiang and his teach-
ings, is also good. Your country is good . . . *was* good . . . but it
has lost its drah-gones, and is now attracted to the ee-vall. Tries
now to be friends with the Soviet. Tries now to be nice, to be
blind and forgiving of the sickness on China's mainland.

So that sums it up, I thought. There was much compelling
sentiment in what he was saying about the dragons, but then he
went off on all the communism stuff. I wasn't sure whether to
be sarcastic.

— I'm not sure that I understand. What do you think is
good?

— Su . . . for instance . . . Su is not ee-vall, said Chen. Su is
part of the *good* in the woord.

I didn't even know Su, but it was easy, in a general, harmless
way, to assert that he was good.

— Yes . . . I said, looking at Su.

— The guard, also, is good, said Chen. He is another good
pear-son in the woord.

I didn't answer him this time. I was beginning to catch on.
People who weren't threatening were good. Su was like that. He
looked up at everybody deferentially. And the guard was good,
because he was pitiable, with his big hat and his Dumbo ears,

and he was a harmless sort. So he was good, in Chen's eyes, because he threatened no one.

— You, however, *you* . . . Harry . . . are not good at all, said Chen, as if he were saying something kind to me, smiling, and with the same mild certainty with which he'd passed judgment on the rest.

— I'm not good?

— No, he said, as if the matter were settled.

— And why not? You mean they get to be good and I don't? Why? I was trying to treat it all as sort of a joke.

Chen began to stroll back down the hallway absently, and we followed behind, like a bunch of schoolchildren. We walked past a row of terra cotta statues from the twelfth century, their hands out in rigid positions, clasping spears that were no longer there, so that their hands formed perfect circles around nothing.

— It is because you lie, said Chen. And, although you are a nice pear-son, you have ee-vall in you. It is simple. And it is too bad.

Su looked at me and smiled, nodding as he had before.

— Hao, hao . . . jegga lies . . . jegga lies . . .

15

The next morning, Kate still asleep, Frederick at sword practice, I sat down and took up my book on the Ouroboros Series 1. When I turned to the page where I'd left off, and started to examine the incomprehensible equations I'd been battling with, I suddenly found myself very upset about the things Chen had said to me in the museum.

First, he'd given me that vague warning about Wu. I debated with myself about the best way to tell Kate. Then I wondered, Should I tell her at all? I wasn't sure. Wouldn't it be an effective way to have her stop seeing him? But Kate wasn't going to stop being Wu's friend just because Chen had said a few cautionary, gossipy things. In fact, she might take it as a sign that Wu was heroic, and that would only enhance his appeal in her eyes. If he was an enemy of the government — and we all knew, or were supposed to think, that it was a vile government — Kate would stand by his side more firmly. Although it made me feel a little guilty, I decided I wouldn't tell her about my conversation with Chen. At least not yet. I'd wait.

Then, after fudging the solution to that worry, I found myself worrying about the other thing Chen had said. How could he have so glibly asserted that I was an evil person? All that hogwash about lying. Was he talking about the California story? No. Impossible. That was hardly evil. And his little dragon and the eating of all the "ee-vall" . . . in some ways the man was infuriatingly hokey. What the hell was a good person in his eyes anyway? Somebody like Su. A man who at times reminded me of a friendly idiot.

From that I fell into a safe haven: thoughts about the Ouroboros, which at that point was the only satisfying, painless thing in my life. I looked at the book and turned to the photograph. Maybe I could escape into the computer, I said to myself. I imagined getting into the computer, going into the depths of its innards to live a safe life apart from my troubles. But when I was honest about it, I realized that most likely what I really wanted, my secret desire, that is, was to be the Ouroboros itself, or, if that wasn't possible, to have it grafted, in some way, onto my brain. But because I could not become the computer, or attach it to myself in any way, I felt bereft of knowing it well.

This made me drowsy. Everything of worth felt out of reach. Ultimately, being the Ouroboros was the only path to salvation, I thought. Then Wu came into my thoughts, lurking through the thousands of Memory/Will cells in the Ouroboros Series 1 like a ghost.

— Shoo, I said, sleepily.

That's when I fell asleep with my head on the page and had a fantasy about a celebration for the computer. It was a dream in which many venerable scientists were gathered around, toasting the Ouroboros. The computer stood in the middle of the room. Confetti lay on the floor and streamers were attached to the ceiling. The party, however, began to loosen and dissolve as everyone drank, and around the perfect black cube the once orderly, restrained scientists began to throw off their clothes. A bacchanalia was taking place, with the brooding computer at the center. Male scientists chased female scientists, and vice versa, and chaos descended on the once subdued gathering. Eventually everyone, having ripped off one another's clothes, all naked now, some with the remnants of their white lab coats dragging behind them, joined hands and danced around the cube, singing to it drunkenly. A few people fell from the dance and dozed off at the side, and the others continued, until only two of the scientists were left. But they barely looked like scientists anymore. They had become wild, angry Neanderthal men. They'd lost their power of reasoning, and the two of them stared at each other with wide eyes. Then they stopped. At the same instant, with the scattered sleeping bodies and the carnage of the party around them, they both realized the value of the silent, impassive computer, blinking softly, its thoughts intact inside. And both of them looked at it with awe and a nostalgia for their own lost intelligence, although they had only a dim memory of what it was.

Suddenly, it dawned on them, as feeding time might dawn on hyenas in the veldt, that they were now competitors. The computer was the only thinking thing left. They clenched their hands, and their nostrils dilated.

That's when I awoke with a jerk, frightened that I was going to be caught in the fight, and groggily lifted my head off the page. Looking around the apartment, I realized something had stuck in my thoughts from the dream, like the imprint of the book on my chin. I had an idea. It was, I admitted, a pretty superficial way to interpret the dream. But, regardless, I had a real idea.

I'd throw a party for all of our friends. Just as in the dream. Everyone would come. And I'd invite Wu. I was convinced, deep inside, that a party would secure a resolution to my problems. Something would happen. The gathering of people, of me, Kate, and Wu, and all the rest, would work, in a cabalistic fashion. I was certain of it.

With a sense of giddy relief, a kind of musical feeling, I felt I had to get started right away, set it up, as it were. I had to make the necessary moves immediately. A dream had given me an epiphany.

I headed outside, and almost skipped down Wei Chi Street, past the tired old palm trees, past the man who sold steamed bread on the corner, around the corner and past the Kungyuan market, past Tai Da, and onward in the direction of the Military Academy, feeling pushed and urged on by a new impetus, to the barracks house where I happened to know Wu spent most of his time.

When I got there I climbed the steps and entered the austere building. The main hallway was filled with uniformed men, and there were posters on the walls with a variety of slogans I couldn't read. Many of the soldiers stared at me. This was not a place I should be, I thought. But I was moved by the moment, still in a great mood. Then I was stopped at a second doorway, where a guard at a table loudly asked me to halt. Several military women nearby looked at me disapprovingly.

— I'm looking for Wu P'ei-fu. Wu P'ei-fu?

A few people turned their heads when they heard the name.

The guard pointed me down a corridor. But as I was walking down the corridor, looking into the offices, I felt a sudden, severe tap on my shoulder. I turned around.

It was Wu himself. He looked at me contemptuously, as if I were a water rat he'd discovered scampering along the hall.

— Harry, what are you doing here?

— I'm sorry, Wu. I came because I wanted to ask you in person.

— Ask me what?

— To a party.

— A party?

— Yes. Kate and I are giving a party. On Friday. We just decided today. Around eight o'clock. Will you come?

He surveyed my face. The disdain in his eyes was almost toxic.

— This is Kate's party, too?

— Yes.

Military personnel brushed by us on both sides, with sharp-brimmed cadet hats, stripes, stars, arm bands, and the sound of shoes clacking on the polished floors. A few people turned around to look at us, and then continued. I caught a glance of a passive, watchful face like Su's, Chen's assistant, but it quickly disappeared into the crowd.

— All right, said Wu slowly. Yes. Thank you. I'll come.

— Good.

We stood there, wordless for a moment.

— Should I show you to the exit? he said.

— No. I know my way.

For an instant a fog of suspicion washed across his eyes, but then his mouth curled into his usual supercilious smirk, and he nodded to me, just the faintest of nods.

Well, I'd started it. As I walked out and down the academy
steps I began to whistle. I whistled "When Johnny Comes
Marching Home." I suppose it was all the soldiers. But I was
ecstatic. I had done something concrete. I had acted. I had followed an instinct. There was no going back now. A party had to
be arranged.

I went back to Wei Chi Street and gathered up as much
money as I could afford and went directly (whispering to myself the whole way about what I would get) to the market, and
began buying things in a heat. I'd tell Kate about it later.

I had a vision, finally, of how I might influence events, and it
seemed to hinge on my exhilaration. *Buy,* I said. Buy things that
will set the stage. I needed a stage. And so, with the kind of
frenzy you arrive at by breaking a law, or something equally
forbidden, I surged in fitful bouts of walking and running
under the dim market tent looking for things for the party. I
had a feeling — as if I were a sculptor — for a form of something.

I bought a dozen peacock feathers. (What the hell, I thought.
It's all because of a fucking dream.) I bought several bottles of
plum wine, and foul-smelling incense. I bought sausage and
cabbage, and I liked the colors of the mangoes, so I bought
about twelve of them, even though a couple were almost rotten.
I also bought black candles, sugared beans, and freeze-dried
coffee.

Finally I went to buy the things I'd secretly been thinking
about since I'd lifted my head off the table with the imprint of
the book on my chin. Even though it seemed ridiculous and
fairly disgusting when it first occurred to me, I had a hankering
to get them. They were to form the centerpiece of the whole
deal. I admit, it was peculiar. But there was no questioning allowed, I decided. If you are going to follow the guidelines of

phantasms in your head, you have to go the way the images lead you.

I'd come out of the dream thinking of the Neanderthal scientists. And in that groggy state I thought of the monkey at the opera, and his mad dash through the audience, and how he had terrorized us all. So I went to the back of the market to a place Frederick had pointed out to me one day, a medicine booth, and I bargained with the man. I bought three of them: a trio of severed monkey heads, mummified, their eyes squashed closed into wrinkled areas of calm.

Home I went. The three monkey heads bumped against each other in the bag with a faint *knock, knock,* and I felt like a milkman. Bringing all those things home I also thought of my father, for some reason, back in Baltimore, bringing home a new car in the spring. This was a distinct image from home. Buying things was always curative. We went out and left our money with someone else so that we could smell new plastic and look at the trees reflected in the doors. And the engine sounded even and throaty. There was something strong and forceful about the act of buying. My monkey heads, strange as it may seem, gave me a feeling of a new horizon, a sense of the future, because they were now mine and they were going to, somehow, contribute to the party. Granted, they were taken from several poor beings who sat in trees. But they were possessions now, objects, and I wanted them to preside over the party, like a jury. They would replace the great, black, brooding Ouroboros, which could not be present.

I came to our doorstep and was happy to be home. It occurred to me that Kate and I had come very far from our roots, from where we belonged. I thought of her parents in their modern house overlooking the valley, and I thought of my parents on their small street in Baltimore, and a shiver went up my spine thinking about how different our lives were. And here we were, in our apartment in China. I mean, we weren't even close anymore, even geographically.

I looked into the bag and saw the three of them, with their close-lidded meditations, all darkly clustered together, almost sleeping, disconnected from the rest of themselves. And I walked in, like the father figure in a good, solid sitcom.

— Honey, I'm home.

16

There's always been a part of me that has wanted to believe that if you can figure out the proper order of things, set yourself in accordance with them, and then wait: the world will change on your behalf. This is the way I saw the party. There was the feeling of correctness about it. After I'd invited everyone I became convinced that I was on the verge of being freed forever of the menacing corporal. I mean, I'd accept the results as they fell, no matter what. But I was *moved* to buy the severed monkey heads, just like that, the way certain low-level biblical figures are moved to follow this or that cantankerous prophet in a dirty robe.

On a less substantial whim, on the night of the party I placed the three monkey heads on the bamboo table, and got a dark blue scarf of Kate's and draped it over them so that they glistened like a three-humped camel sleeping under a silk blanket.

Then I put on a jazz tape of Frederick's and I put out the plum wine on the table, spread the mangoes around, lit some candles, and brought out all of our glasses and mugs and plastic cups and arranged them on the table and felt very satisfied with myself.

Kate came home first with shopping bags full of food, and dumped them, and kissed me, and ran into the shower, flinging her clothes into the bedroom.

— Harry, could you put that stuff in a bowl?

— Yup, I said, and dutifully dumped the food into bowls and arranged them around the room.

— What is that under my scarf? she called from inside the shower.

— A surprise.

I could hear her scrubbing her head.

— Great. What kind of surprise?

There was a knock at the door.

— You'll see, I said, and shut the bathroom door, and then went to open the front door.

It was Null, who I'd forgotten might come, smelling of some rank cologne and holding flowers wrapped in paper. He was in good spirits.

— These are for Katey, he said, handing me the flowers.

— Thanks, Null.

He walked in, self-assured and odiferous. There were no circles under his eyes. He was content, and in a rosy frame of mind.

— Is Free-derick here?

— Not yet.

— He's coming?

— Of course, Null, he lives here. He went out.

— And Katey is in the shower?

— Yeah. Want a drink?

He swung around the room inspecting things, his little tattoo like a green S on his face. He took a glass of plum wine, and swayed it in front of his eyes.

— Hello, Null, said Kate, splattering across the floor in her towel.

— Hello, Katey. There are flowers here. For you.

He turned to me and nodded and winked.

— She likes them, he said.

— Yes, she will, I said, a bit unnerved by him.

Ulla, finding the door unlocked, strolled in and embraced me and with a whining voice sang out a few lines from the song that she was listening to on her earphones. She pulled them out of her ears.

— This is so great, you guys, that you guys, you and Kate, have a party . . . Hello, Null.

They began to talk, and Ulla took the liberty of swallowing a large, aggressive gulp of Null's wine.

— What's that Harry? she said, pointing at the scarf and its three round lumps.

— Don't touch it.

— Oh, said Ulla. So it's that kind of a party. What do you think, Null?

Then she giggled and meandered into the kitchen to fetch herself some wine. More people arrived. Klaus and Sally came with Roger Theef, who was wearing a white suit and a light blue shirt and sneakers. Sally took off her shoes. And Frederick arrived, frightened, it seemed, by Null's presence, and even more so by Null's fabulous mood, his strong, luxurious smell, and his strange attention to all of the women. In fact, Frederick skulked around the edges of the room, sipping demurely a small beer that he'd found at the back of the refrigerator.

But Wu hadn't arrived yet, and I watched the door in anticipation of his coming in, even looking forward to it, almost missing him, strangely. I even fantasized about what he'd do when he arrived, how he'd go right to Kate (I knew that) and would ignore everyone else. I was even looking forward to his smart uniform, his smart face, his smart mind thinking things about me, making up titles for me in his head: Harry the Interloper, Harry the Westerner Ignorant of the West, Harry the Laughable Husband-type.

I was relishing his downfall, though I had no idea how I was going to bring it about. I looked over to the three mounds covered with silk.

Then, like a cold wind, he arrived. He walked right through the door, said a curt hello to the few unknowns lingering there, and, just as I'd predicted, went right over to Kate as if she were a magnet, and, like a storybook Victorian gentleman, gallant and resplendent in his uniform, he kissed her hand. I couldn't believe it. She gave it to him softly, with a trace of embarrassment. And his face hovered down there after the kiss, as if he were staring minutely at her hand.

Everyone was impressed and turned around to look. There was a general quietening of talk, even though Theef could be heard over the low music and the momentary silence.

— No, no, that was in Hong Kong. Yes, it *was* a lot of money. It was *quite* a lot of money . . .

Wu spoke to Kate in a low voice, and Kate laughed, and the party flared up again and everyone started talking, although I'm positive a few people looked at me.

— So, the general over there likes Kate . . . No? said Null, loudly sipping wine, strolling over to where Frederick and I stood with Ulla, who was dancing in place. She licked her lips.

— He's a corporal, not a general, I said.

— He came only to see Kate, said Ulla, smiling at me and bumping her hip against me.

— Free-derick, can I speak to you for a sek-oond, said Null quietly.

— Well, yes, Null. I suppose.

Nervously, Frederick walked over with Null to the window, close to the drapèd heads, and I watched them carefully to make sure they didn't touch the scarf. I had a notion about a kind of macabre unveiling later, after everyone had gotten drunk.

— Harry, why is it that you always seem to be worrying? said Ulla.

— Because no one else is, I said angrily, not really paying attention to her.

The party continued for a while, wandering through quiet periods and periods of loud, rapid talk. But I always watched the corporal, and he was always near Kate. Every so often she'd move away and talk to someone else, but he'd follow. I slowly began to despair of any resolution arising from my contrived gathering. What made me do this? What was I waiting for?

As time passed, over the room descended a shadowy atmosphere, as if it were about to rain right there in the apartment, and there was the rustling of conversation and the clinking of glasses. But when I looked out the big window, I realized that it really was about to rain. And I was sad, and felt that a torrent of emotion was about to pour down upon my heart. I was bound up, and I wanted desperately for the world to rip open and reveal how I should act.

I would like to say that God spoke to me at that moment, and that staring into the gray sky and the tops of the bedraggled palm trees along Wei Chi Street, I was called by some voice other than my own. And indeed, I could make a case for it. But I was unprepared for whatever it was, and when it came to me (the godless American), I wanted desperately to call it God because it was so deep inside me that it would have been disappointing to sully it with my own image. I heard a rumbling far down in my innards that churned like a bass drum and wobbled all the organs in my belly, or in that hollow cavity which I imagine to be right below my heart. I felt tremendously moved, but was slightly ashamed, because it was the kind of whir and rush of emotion I remembered feeling when I was fourteen, when a girl I had a crush on walked by, or when I was in a field all by myself and the grandiose and absurd idea of the future made me want to burst. I sensed Ulla next to me, her attention gone back to the party, tapping her foot, drawing on a cigarette, and I felt close to her, accepting of her, grateful for all sorts of Ulla-like things she did. And then the rumbling in me focused into a voice, clear and low and firmly chiseled in my head, and it said something that sounded like "Now, Harry. This is it. Go ahead. Turn around and look."

And so I turned around slowly, afraid of shattering the spell, and when I had turned completely, I looked up to see Wu. But there, where Wu P'ei-fu had stood, was a horrible, reptilian creature.

I swear that is exactly what I saw — no vapors, or squinting to make things blurry. In real life, standing three-dimensionally, there was a beast with scales, clothed in a military uniform, upright like an odiously dressed iguana, its slithery tongue flipping back and forth, red and shiny. Wu was gone. Poof. He wasn't there. In his place was this thing. This scaly thing. I could see its eyes, cold and small, like black marbles set in a green rug.

And I understood, finally. The voice said, "You understand?" And I nodded to this booming question inside me and walked across the room, absolutely resolute now, as if propelled through high clouds. People glided by me like seraphim, or those forward-leaning statues of saints that hang solemnly in cathedrals.

The thing, the reptile, was speaking to Kate, and I could see very clearly how deeply she had been fooled, how subtly this undulating beast had insinuated itself into her life, into her daily routine, into her friendship, and how it wanted desperately to insinuate itself inside her, how it desperately wanted to enter her. And he had planned it so well. But now I could see. I was armed with sight.

— Wu, I said.

He turned around, and his yellow, knife-shaped pupils met mine. His shriveled snout, his rank breath, his scales rippling down his neck and disappearing into his collar, repulsed me. He, or it, was a terrifying sight. I could see the tips of his fangs peeking out from beneath his green lip, and his gnarled hand gripping the glass. And for a moment he so repelled me that I could barely keep my eyes on him, barely speak. I wanted to run. He and I were not made of the same substance. Now, finally, I was sure of that.

Thinking himself unseen, he smiled. And Kate also turned her attention to me.

I reached out quickly with both hands, afraid but also compelled by the force that was emerging, and I grabbed the huge lizard by his collar and shook him with all my might, furiously, so that he wagged back and forth, and back and forth jerkily, again and again, his eyes spinning around and his little glass of wine toppling out of his hand and spilling on the floor.

— You dirty, evil son of a bitch! What are you? What horrible thing are you? I shouted.

Everyone rushed toward us, arms flailing.

— Harry! yelled Kate and, along with the others, she jumped forward to pull me off the lizard.

— Stop! yelled the lizard.

— Stop! No, no, pleeez! yelled Null and Frederick together.

— What are you? I yelled, and I heard my voice break and tremble with fear at what was happening.

He was so caught off guard that he at first did nothing. But then he grabbed my arms and tried to right himself. His scaly legs had become all tangled. I drew him up, and with all my strength I flung him right past Kate and against the wall, where he glanced off and fell sideways against a chair. He got up quickly and met me as I came at him again, and this time he managed to grab my shoulders. But I spun him around and once again flung him, in another direction. That's when he fell back and, reaching out to break his fall, grabbed the silk scarf on the table. And when he hit the floor, it whipped away with a swish.

In a flash the three scowling faces were revealed as if on a dais, like a bunch of sleeping, disapproving old men, gazing down at the lizard man.

Everyone fell silent and stared. The only sound was of Wu trying to unravel himself from the scarf on the floor.

— What is tha-tha-that? said Null, covering his mouth.

— Yuck, said Sally.

— Have you gone mad? said Frederick, glaring at me. Is this a joke? Is this a joke . . . about me?

— Harry, are you *crazy*? said Kate, spitting with anger, and going over with a few others to help Wu get up.

Wu got to his feet.

— You . . . he said, pointing his finger menacingly at me. You *fuck* . . . boy! You . . . fuck!

While everyone stared at me, I watched the scales, one by one, vanishing from his neck, and watched his reptilian eyes transforming from knife-shaped pupils back into ordinary human eyes. And when he opened his mouth, the forked tongue was already flattening and filling out the split.

— Keep your fucking hands off Kate, you snake, you . . . I said, appalled that I didn't have the visual proof anymore.

— Harry! shouted Kate.

— For why are the gorilla heads? said Ulla quietly, making a nauseated face.

I turned toward Ulla. Then I turned toward Kate, and was about to speak calmly to her, when a firm knock came at the front door.

Everyone stood still, not knowing what to do.

— One second, I said apologetically, and gingerly stepped over the fallen chair and went to open the door.

Everyone gaped at me, speechless.

Standing in the doorway, flanked by two burly men in uniform was the mild Mr. Chen, looking massive and paternal. He was turning the little jade dragon around and around in his hand, a faint smile on his smooth face.

—– Ex-kuse me, Harry, he said. Hello, hello, he said politely to the group behind me, waving his hand vaguely. Ex-kuse me, but, sorry to disturb you, but, you see, this man, the Mister Wu P'ei-fu here, must be coming with us.

Everyone stood stark still.

— He has been summoned to be kwesh-toned. I am very sorry.

Wu was stunned. He straightened himself up and smoothed his uniform. We all stared at Chen.

— It is nothing seri-ooz, but rules of cone-duck have been broken. As you see, it is not attrah-ca-teeve to have our corporals fighting with forah-nahs. I am very sorry.

The two burly men shuffled into the apartment toward Wu, but Frederick, who was taller than either of them, raised his hand and stepped in front of them.

— No, no, said Frederick, shaking his head. We will not let you take Wu P'ei-fu to be interro . . . interrogated. We may be foreigners, but we cannot look the other way. No, I am sorry. Now us foreigners in Taiwan must say no.

— He is a friend of yours, Frederick? said Ulla under her breath, glancing briefly at me nervously.

— He is . . . in a way . . . and Harree, well, I am sorry, but we cannot, even in these circumstances, let your Mister Chen come in and take Wu.

I looked at Kate, and saw that she was burning with silent fury at me.

— Harry, are you going to let Chen walk into our apartment . . . just saunter in here . . . and take Wu off for some fabricated reason?

Chen's smile flickered back and forth into a disappointed frown.

— Kate, I said, but I found myself looking into Wu's desperate eyes. Kate . . .

— *Coward!* someone said loudly at the back of the room.

I thought it was Wilcox, the British malcontent.

— Now wait a second, wait a second, I said, looking around at everyone. Wu . . . I mean . . . listen, Wu, I said, turning back to him, and squinting to make sure he was now in human form. You haven't done anything wrong, have you? If you haven't done anything wrong, then tell these guys, or rather, *we'll* tell them, I said, turning to face Chen.

And then the anger and the memory of what I had seen began to stir inside me.

— But I *saw* something just now . . .

— Harry, Harry, Harry, said Roger Theef, coming toward me and setting his drink down on the way over. He put his arm around me.

— Listen, Harry, calm down, he said quietly. This man is obviously a troublemaker. The whole thing is better off just dropped.

— Oh, *fuck* you! Kate yelled in Theef's face.

Chen jumped back a step.

— Katey, shhhh, said Null.

— Fuck you, Roger. And Harry, *fuck you!*

She almost spat in my face, and I suddenly felt hit with pain, because I realized that Kate had quickly lowered me to the rank of Theef. I was as lowly to her as that shallow optimist.

A huge division loomed up inside me. On one side I saw one Harry, who was as weak and cowardly as I could imagine. He was wretched, and in my mind I saw his blunt face and it reminded me of the scrawny thug who'd hit me back at the bottomless lake, with his close-set eyes and sad, drooping socks. This person was now in the spotlight, and fused onto him unhappily, like a hostage soul, was the other part of me, the strong core of me, the real me. Yet they both had a common purpose. They both desperately wanted to see clearly, to act clearly, to win back the love of Kate. And they'd both seen Wu looking like a strange reptile.

— Ex-kuse me, said Chen over the din of argument, raising his hand to interrupt. Mister Wu, would you pleez to come with us?

— No, said Wu. I am at a party with friends.

The room fell silent. Chen looked around.

— These are your friends? he asked, gesturing directly toward me. I think that your "friends," as you call them, have been thrat-eening at you. There has been fighting? Yes? Fighting between a Nah-shaa-nalist officer and a forah-nah? This is why, sadly, there must be an investigation. We must prow-teck you from dishonoring yourself. Fighting, as you know, is forbidden.

— I was not fighting, sir, said Wu.

Chen looked around the room, smiling slightly, as if he was now gaining control and was just dallying for a moment. Then his gaze fell on the three monkey heads, and a look of mild shock passed over his face. Then it brightened, and he puckered his big baby lips and pointed to them.

— You are a friend, Corporal Wu. And these are their friends as well? You see, Corporal Wu . . . you see what they do to their friends?

Everyone looked at the sorrowful heads.

— An unhappy thing. Maybe it is unfortunate to lose face. But to lose head! This is *worse,* much worse, said Chen with a dark chuckle.

Wu looked over at the hairy row of heads and cracked a smile. Chen, his cheeks pink, opened up his mouth and laughed with complete freedom, leaning back so far that we could all see his round potbelly filling out his starched white shirt.

Chen was obviously no minor legislator; he was somebody of completely different rank. And it struck me that it was possible that Chen had always known of Kate's attachment to Wu, that he had always known of my attachment to Kate, and that possibly, no, probably, I had been hired as a tutor for reasons completely separate from my command of the English language.

I swung around and looked for Theef, the man who'd gotten me the job in the first place, but he'd managed to slip out the door.

I was flabbergasted. But I couldn't be sure. I wasn't sure. Chen was sharing his amusing moment with his quarry, the hated Corporal Wu, and Wu was even chuckling along with him, and in a weird way, looking at them again, I felt embarrassed for him.

Everyone became hollow-looking. Frederick, however, was still angry, and the blood had risen in his forehead.

— Go ahead, laugh with him, he lashed out at Wu. Go ahead, laugh. He is the one who will put you in the jail after we have all gone. Go ahead. You will not be laughing in your dark, your loan-ly jail. For what? Going to a party? Ha! And then you are sharing jokes with him . . .

Chen glared at Frederick.

— Ah, yes, said Chen, now truly impatient to get on with it. It is a Gerr-mon, no? The Gerr-mon is lecturing us? They wanted to roo the woord. In Woord War Two, they try to roo the woord. But now you tell us that *we* are no good? How do you dare? This . . . the man from Gerr-money — telling *us!*

Frederick shrank back, his lip curling. His height diminished, and he retreated into the room a few steps.

But Wu stepped forward.

— Please stop, he said, now glum and pale.

He dusted off his pants, went over and picked up his hat, and planted it securely on his head. But first, as was his habit, he smoothed his shiny hair with a long, precise movement of his hand. Then he went directly to Kate and bowed to her. They looked each other in the eyes for what seemed many minutes, and my insides twisted. He then came over to me and clicked his heels in a mock salute, but his face was steely and impenetrable, and his eyes were cold. He hated me. It was different from the way I hated him; it was a hate completely free of doubt. His lack of doubt was one of the things I detested most in him, his lack of conscience, or the semblance of a possibility of regret. If there had been one flicker of uncertainty in his eyes about blatantly wooing my woman, I would have backed down. But there was none. He wanted me to disappear, and if I didn't, he would curse and humiliate me by acting as if I already had.

Then, with a military bearing, he walked out the doorway and was led away by Chen's guards on either side of him.

Chen nodded to us all, as a group, and caught my eye as he closed the door, but I could see not one iota of apology or regret in his face, only a straightforward gaze under his wide brow that told me immediately our association was over forever. It had served its purpose, and he would now remember me as the American boy who, in order to impress him, had invented a couple of ridiculous stories about California.

The door shut, and the first thing I felt was a hard slap on the back of my head delivered by the hand of Kate.

A little stunned, not even turning around to acknowledge the insult, I pushed through the crowd, trying to get to the window. As I passed Frederick, who glowered at me, his mustache twitching, he said in a hoarse voice, pointing at the severed heads:

— Those are a joke on me? Those are your joke on me . . . hey, Harree? The dead moan-keys? Hey, Harree? The dead moan-keys? Very funny.

I didn't respond. I went directly to the windows and yanked them open and stepped out onto the balcony, throwing an old mop aside. It had started to rain, and puddles were already forming on the street. Down below, Wu was being helped into Chen's car, and Chen was getting in at the other side, while at the same time talking to Wu, his voice eerily soothing, almost kind. Wu nodded, listening to him. Then the doors shut, and the car pulled away. For a moment I felt like crying. Strangely, I felt a sudden surge of remorse and concern for the man who moments before had possibly been revealed to me as an evil creature, a demon in disguise.

17

Did you have to slap me on the head? I said to Kate in a broken voice after everyone had left (except for Frederick, who sullenly mumbled around in his room).

— Yes, because you're a total fool. I always knew that. But I never knew you were a *violent* fool. Frankly, Harry . . . I mean, look at you, attacking Wu. Can't you just ask me, quietly, aside, to me, can't you just ask . . . Kate, are you in love with that guy? As ridiculous as it sounds. And it *is* ridiculous. Even so, you could just ask. Or a less *violent* approach might be to say, I'm jealous. Stop seeing him. Couldn't you say that? But instead you attack him!

— I saw something, Kate, I said in a low voice. What I did may have looked weird to you, but sometimes one has to act on what one sees.

She looked at me and shook her head.

— You don't know what you're talking about.

— It doesn't matter. He wants you.

— How do you know?

— It's obvious! You're blind if you don't notice it. At least I know my own gender. I know that much. But he . . . he's something else . . .

— Chinese?

— No. Evil. Something like that.

— You're a xenophobe. Maybe a bigot.

— I don't give a damn that he's Chinese.

Frederick slammed his door loudly.

— He could have been anything, anybody, it's irrelevant . . . I saw . . . for a moment I think I finally understood . . .

But at that moment Chen's face came into my mind. First I thought of him twirling the little dragon in his hand. Then I remembered his house, and Su popping in and out, and the electronic *I Ching,* and I was suddenly furious. Particularly after his moral lecture to me in the museum.

— I can't believe Chen came after Wu. I can't believe it.

— Did you tell him Wu was coming to the party?

— Of course not. Why would I? I had no idea he had it in for Wu.

— I don't know . . . it all works out conveniently for you, doesn't it? I mean, come on, Harry. You suddenly, out of the blue, decide to have a party. *You,* of all people. That didn't make sense to me. Not only that, but you invited Wu. In fact, you go all the way to the Military Academy to invite him, this man whom you supposedly despise. That was pretty odd. Then *(and this is the strangest part),* of all people, your student, an official in the government, shows up and takes Wu away on the grounds that he was fighting with a foreigner. And who was the fucking "foreigner" who started a fight with him? I mean, come on. Seriously, Harry, I mean *seriously,* you can't tell me it was a coincidence.

— Kate, listen to me. I know it's hard to believe, but . . .

I began to wonder about myself. Had I known it was going to happen? I became confused. Had I planned it that way? It was unbelievably brilliant if I had. Had I known all along? Was there some secret message in my dream about the Ouroboros? No. Impossible. It was a total coincidence.

— Kate, I'm very confused.

She gave me a scornful look.

— Well, that's not good enough. In fact, I think you and I should reassess this whole relationship, she said acidly.

— Okay, I said, rubbing my face. Maybe we should separate for a while.

At that moment Frederick walked into the living room and looked at us, completely ignoring what was going on.

— Harree, he said gesturing toward the monkey heads. Harree, these dead any-malls . . .

— Frederick, I said imploringly, I didn't bring these out because of your monkey bite at the opera. It wasn't a joke. That had nothing to do with it. It's hard to explain.

— It don't matter to me why, he said morosely. They are dead, maybe unhealthy, and because of your pushing Mister Wu, like you want to kill him . . . I don't know. I had hopes for you. I thought you would study sword dancing. I thought you came to here for a *reason.* Maybe to get knowledge. But then you are pushing.

He shrugged, and he threw up his hands as if he didn't care anymore.

— Go ahead. I am sorry. You can argue now.

He shuffled into his room and closed the door.

— Maybe we should separate for a while? Is that what you said? she asked, uneasily.

— Yes. I can't stay in Taipei.

— Why? she said, softer than before.

— I'm a pariah here now. And I suppose I don't blame them. All the people we know here think I'm a crackpot. I mean . . . even Frederick . . .

— Don't be ridiculous. Frederick is upset. He still likes you.

— Anyway, I want to leave this damned country. I seem to have done enough damage . . . although still, I'm positive he's in love with you. And Kate, you never put up much resistance. I mean, you could have stopped being so damned nice to him.

She frowned.

— You only encouraged him. It was irresponsible. You like his attention and you do nothing to stop it.

She folded her arms and said nothing, but her lip got hawk-like.

— I think you should at least take partial responsibility for what just happened here, I said angrily.

— Shut up, Harry, she said sharply.

We glared at each other for a few seconds.

— Listen. Maybe I should go away for a while, I said, trying to be conciliatory. I've got a little money now, from teaching Chen.

She scowled.

— Okay, I know, but still, it's money. I could go away, do a little traveling. You could join me later. Maybe it would be good.

I wanted very much to have her agree with me about something, anything that sounded like an optimistic plan to fix what I had evidently done. I had accidentally stumbled directly into the very sort of clumsy act I had always tried to avoid.

— What do you think? I'll go away for a month and give you some breathing room.

She seemed interested. And even though I was annoyed by

the hasty babble of desperation in my voice, what I was saying sounded plausible to me.

— Just to cool things off between us. Maybe I'll go to the mainland. I haven't seen the mainland. Or how about Hong Kong? It's only an hour or so on the plane to Hong Kong. I know a guy there I could stay with. Then you could come over and join me and we'll travel together. Remember that guy from college? Swan Fisk? He now works for a big American bank in Hong Kong. Do you remember Swan?

— No, she said curtly.

— You remember him, you just don't remember him now.

— I don't remember him. Christ, Harry, if I say I don't remember him, that means I don't remember him!

— Okay, okay.

— You want to split up for a while? she asked in whisper.

— Do you?

— I could see it would have benefits, she said sadly.

I was getting tremendously upset, and my nose began to run. Then she started to cry, just on the edge of her eyes.

— All right, she said, getting hold of herself. Why don't we split up for a month? It wouldn't be bad for us. You go to Hong Kong, and I'll come over in a month. But listen, if this bullshit continues after we get back together . . . if you keep doing lunatic things, then that's it. Do you understand? I can't take it. I mean, also, I've got to stay and see if I can find a way to help out Wu. We can't just abandon him in this situation.

— Maybe I should stay. I'm the reason he's in trouble. Maybe they'll listen to me.

— No. It would get worse. Something would happen. I just know it. You go. I'll see what I can do, and I'll come and join you in Hong Kong. It will be good for us.

— Okay, I said.

But it sounded to me as if I were fleeing, as if I were a conspirator or a dishonorable lout. I can't leave, I thought.

— Kate, I *can't* just go. I'll stay and help work this all out. I'll help you get Wu out of this jam.

— No, she said emphatically. Please, Harry. Do it for me, will you? Please, just do it. Okay? We'll be together in a month. We'll travel together for a while, and we'll be alone.

She stared at me for a moment, and as her tears dried I could see a series of moods pass behind her eyes, some of which I couldn't identify. She was observing me, thinking about me, and comparing me to some hidden object in her head. And for that moment I felt scared, as if I were all alone in the room.

— All right, I said. I'll go.

18

Swan Fisk charged down the hallway. His tie was flung over his shoulder, and he bellowed . . .

— What are all these Americans doing in Asia?

I had been in Hong Kong for a little over a week, staying in a dilapidated hotel called the Chung King Mansion, because I hadn't gotten up the courage to call Swan yet, and I had a deep need to spend some time alone. Then I called, and his voice was so familiar and strong over the phone, and he was so happy to hear from me, that I decided to go right over to see him, even though we hadn't been very close in college.

Swan worked in a huge skyscraper. In the elevator I was forced to look at myself in the mirrored walls. There was the pervasive aura of disheveled exhaustion in my bearing. I noticed, with a sigh, how shabby my clothes looked, and I realized that the effect was exaggerated by the atmosphere of the modern building. Everything I was wearing looked wrinkled. Then there was a *ding*, and the doors opened on a gleaming white office where people rushed to and fro.

— Harry, Harry, Harry. So how are you? said Swan, coming down the long corridor toward me.

His colleagues, all neatly buttoned down in suits, turned their heads and looked over their desks to observe me standing there, waiting for Fisk. His stride was strong and somewhat scary in its forward-moving force; he was like a bull charging down a field in a blue silk suit.

He grabbed my hand and shook it earnestly. For a second I had the impression that we were vying to see whose grip was more severe. Then he let go and threw his arm around me to steer me into his office, but first we swept past several secretaries, their hands poised above their keyboards.

— Harry, he whispered. I'm finally in *love*.

He had intimated something about this on the phone, and I'd been a little taken aback by his desire to talk about it immediately with a distant friend arriving out of the blue. He was breathless and perky, with a shade of anxiety at the back of his voice. And I'd wondered about it, because I didn't remember Fisk as being the jittery, romantic sort.

— Yes, you mentioned it on the phone. That's great, Swan.

— She's wonderful. I want you to meet her. It's great to have an old friend here to tell it to . . . I've got no *normal* friends here at all. But I'm happy — he laughed — I really am. Finally. Don't you remember how depressed I was at college?

— No, I thought you were fairly happy.

— Really? Me? That's amazing. That's truly amazing, Harry. Most miserable years of my life.

We veered into his office, which was dominated by a very large poster of a Mondrian painting.

There was an awkward shuffling as we both sat down, Swan behind an ornate red wood desk, and me in an overly comfortable chair that leaned back so far, my head almost touched the floor.

— I thought you were living with some woman in Taiwan.

— I was.

— It's over?

— No. Not really.

— That's good. As for me, Harry, this time I'm really in love.

— Yeah?

I stared at his tie, which was dark blue with little silver diamonds. In each diamond there was a round black spot. It was a jarring tie because the design looked faintly like a small field of eyes. I stared at it, disconcerted for a few seconds, my head still way down in the chair.

— Her name is Rachel. I met her two weeks ago. We slept together for the first time three nights ago. I swear to God I'm unglued. Harry, she's got black hair and green eyes and she's beautiful. But that's not it . . . it's really not that she's beautiful, which she is. It's also that she and I have this thing . . . this remarkable feeling between us.

— That's wonderful, I said. What does she do?

— Do? he said incredulously. Harry, you're so American. We're both so fucking American. Do? She's a woman.

— I know that, Swan.

— All right. All right . . . She's an investment banker.

It was late in the afternoon and Swan suggested we get something to eat. We took the streetcar to a crowded neighborhood and ended up eating in a local restaurant that was shabby but had become popular because of its good food. Amidst its Hong Kong dinginess, seated at every table in their dark suits, were young business men and women, many of them European and American, wolfing down their meals and talking loudly.

— Sure. Kate. I remember her, said Swan. The brainy one with the nice ass.

— Great, Swan. That's a wonderful description of someone who's probably the love of my life.

— She's not the love of your life, Harry. That's obvious.

— How?

— This wouldn't be happening. This P'ei-fu guy. He wouldn't be buzzing around.

I hadn't told Swan the whole story, but I ended up telling him half of it. I told him about Wu's attraction to Kate, and how it had infuriated me. But I didn't touch on the rest. It would be hard to describe all of it without incriminating myself; it sounded so preposterous. But, besides that, I was becoming, moment by moment, aware of Fisk as a man who'd somehow found the success that had evaded me. And I didn't want to widen the gap between us. Dressed in expensive clothes, handling himself with poignant self-assurance, crossing with ease from his business to his new love, he was like a storybook prince for whom money and love were perpetually matched, part of the same goal. My life, in comparison, was a dark swirl of erratic emotions, peculiar theories, and a thousand misunderstandings.

— Soup? said Swan.

— Yes, I said, watching him closely.

— You may have been temporarily separated from your girlfriend, Harry. But let's not be depressed. Not now. It's an amazing day. We've got great food, and I, me, Swan, your old friend, am finally, truly, completely in love.

As he said this, even though it was a bit pompous, I had a strong, respectful intuition that Fisk was better at living than I was, even though he was nothing like what I wanted to be. He managed daily life well. He was a forceful daylight person. An impressive man. Not the manners stuff, just the style and the poise with which he arrived at it all, as if he had been born in a seamless suit of armor. And on top of that he was in love, or thought he was. His having convinced himself of that was enough to make me regard him with respect.

— I want to go to the harbor, he said. Harry, I'll take you on the company boat. I've got the use of it. Would you like that? Why not? Out into the harbor?

We went along the winding streets to the harbor. There we came to a private dock with a little boathouse, newly painted white. The bank that Swan worked for was named AmeriBank, and the logo had an urgent tilt to it, as if it were rushing right-ward. It was omnipresent, and could be seen all over the dock pasted to life preservers, crates, paddles, and almost everything else that offered enough blank space to display the name. A young Chinese man was reading inside the boathouse, but when he saw us through the porthole window, he put his book down and came out to talk to Fisk.

The company boat was tied to the side of the dock by a fat white rope. It was a large, glittering motor cruiser of about seventy feet, rocking in the low waves and nudging the blue dock bumpers with a persistent, muffled *bump, bump*. On its stern was painted its name in overly elegant script: *The Profit Motive*.

Swan went into the boathouse and made a phone call. He waved to me through the window, as if I were far away. Then he made another phone call and while he talked his face got businesslike. He scratched his receding hairline. I watched him. He looked in the square frame of the window like one of those portraits, very detailed, of pale medieval men, earrings in their ears, slightly feminine, holding a watch or a leaf in their soft hands. In this case, Swan twirled the phone cord around his thumb. He was nonchalantly royal, and still looked boyish, almost untouched.

— Right, said Swan to the young man as he came out of the boathouse.

The young man was dressed as if he had gone to prep school in the United States. He wore white tennis shoes, pressed khaki pants, a green sport shirt, frayed at the collar, with the small crocodile patch peeling off slightly on the breast.

— And there's some beer in the refrigerator, said the young man, without a trace of an accent.

— Right, thanks, Marty, said Fisk. There's a bunch coming down from the bank. Apparently, we're going to have a last-minute meeting. Oh, yes. You remember Rachel? She'll be here soon. Just show her up.

Marty nodded.

We climbed up the little ladder. Swan insisted I put sneakers on. They had a locker full of white-soled deck shoes of all sizes, but incredibly my size wasn't available. I felt ducklike in a large pair Swan picked out for me.

— I want to get your opinion, he said, striding across the deck while I walked behind with the *smack, smack* of my big shoes.

— Of what?

— Of Rachel. She's coming. But I'm sorry, Harry, there's going to have to be a meeting with some bank people. It's un-expected. My partners are on their way down so we can discuss business on the way to the island. Maybe you could keep Rachel company while I'm busy.

— The island?

— Yeah. AmeriBank has a private island out there, he said, waving his hand out toward the bay. There's a gym, a swimming pool. It's a spa.

We sat down on a bench. I was feeling sad, and something in me wanted to confide in Swan. In college, he'd been part of the fraternity crowd, but I had tried to remain independent from groups. I always felt watered down in groups, so I'd avoided them. Sometimes, in very large gatherings, I felt as if I'd disappeared altogether.

Fisk had been very popular. Being adored in school provides you with confidence about your opinions, your actions, so that in later life you retain something of that glow of certainty. I expected Swan to be able to steer me in the right direction, if only because he'd never considered that he'd gone in any other way. This was the right kind of person, I decided, to spend time with before I saw Kate again. And yet, regardless of this, I found a pervasive melancholy in everything since arriving in Hong Kong.

Just then some men wearing business suits began to climb the ladder. They were all carrying briefcases, which each managed to force awkwardly through the railing or swing over onto the deck.

— Hey, Swaneeee.

— Hey, Fisk, did you get that third-quarter report from Carmichael?

— Yup, said Swan, not particularly pleased to see them.

— Can you get me a copy? said a rotund, bald man who was having difficulty getting his briefcase through the railing.

Fisk did not see fit to introduce me to these men, even though, as they landed one by one on the deck, they looked at me apprehensively, as if they were supposed to know who I was but couldn't remember. They all trooped to the stern of the boat, where there was a stretch of deck covered with a blue-and-white awning, the official colors of AmeriBank. Here they flopped down in canvas chairs, bitching and moaning, dropping large bundles of papers and folders on the small cocktail tables beside them.

— I'll be with you guys in a second, said Swan, nervously

looking over the side toward the dock and the street beyond.

He smiled at me and patted me on the back. Then, as if seized by a sudden fright, he swung around.

— Oh, hey! Guys! This is Harry! Harry, these are the guys. Cronenberg, Mitchell, Wang, and Mister Phillips . . . the rogue Australian . . . and our brilliant man from Japan, Hanashi, and of course everyone's favorite sweet face, Mister Weiss.

He pointed at each. They all nodded hello while they flipped through their papers.

— So, Swaneee. Tell the captain that we're ready to go. Let's get out of here.

— Can't, Weiss. I'm waiting for Rachel.

— Rachel?

— Ooooo, they all chimed in.

— The babe, said Cronenberg, who had an unusually high forehead but small, dim-witted eyes.

— Well, she'd better hurry up, said Weiss. We've got to be back with this preliminary report by five-thirty. Five-thirty the latest.

— She'll be here any second, said Swan, watching the street nervously.

It was only a few minutes later, after Swan and I had paced the deck together once or twice, that a black cab drove up.

— She's here, he whispered to me.

Swan ran up the stairs to the cabin, where a crew was waiting, employed by AmeriBank for the sole purpose of conveying its brokers around Hong Kong harbor. White water burbled around the sides of the boat. Marty, the prep school dock tender, untied the ropes. And the elegant legs of Rachel came over the side.

— Hello, she said to me.

I was the first one she encountered on boarding. I stood there like a duck man in my big sneakers, trying to observe her without appearing to stare. She was extraordinarily beautiful.

— Hello, I said. I'm Harry.

We shook hands. Her hand was long and cool.

— I'm a friend of Swan's from college. He was a year ahead of me.

— Oh, really? she said, taking off her sunglasses and revealing green eyes.

For some reason I recalled the woman whose boyfriend hit me. I smelled the dead leaves and saw the view through them and the grass from the vantage point of the ground, looking out toward the bottomless lake.

— Rachel, called Swan from the top of the ladder.

There was a plaintive tone in his voice. We both looked up to see him coming down the ladder, his legs moving quickly and his cuffed pants fluttering around his legs. He hopped onto the deck and they embraced. The wind blew. Her hair flipped up and over her head and onto his. She had lush black hair, and she drew her head back, her hair pulling slowly off his head.

— This is Harry, said Swan, pulling some of her hair from his face.

— We've met.

— Harry's another American lost in Asia.

— I don't think you're so lost, I said to Swan.

— Listen, said Swan, ignoring my comment. I've got to get some work done with these guys. Why don't you two walk around the deck, or get something to eat inside? I'm going to be done in a little while. Oh, yeah, Rachel, you'll get to meet Trialson. He's coming out too, on his boat.

Then he jabbered a few apologies and shuffled down the deck to join the others.

— Great, said Rachel with a touch of sarcasm. Trialson. He's the Great Black Hope. Swan's boss. Swan worships him.

— Oh?

— Yeah. He's supposed to be a genius or something.

She glanced briefly at my feet, and then looked at me and smiled warmly. No doubt she thought the large sneakers were endearing.

— I hope we get back soon. I should get back to work in the evening, she said.

— You're an investment banker?

— Yup. But I hate it. I went to business school only because my father's a lawyer and he was desperate to keep me out of law. He says it's only for people who want to make unhappiness into a career. Little did he know.

A big laugh came from the other side of the deck, where the meeting was going on.

— Sounds like they're getting a lot done, huh? she said with a grin.

There was a taste of cynicism that lingered after everything she said. I had the impression that for her Swan was a last-ditch attempt at believing in the conventional. She had the jaded quality that certain attractive, smart women from well-off families get when they've tried almost every conceivable way to make themselves happy but still find themselves perpetually aware of an absence. Women of this sort are possibly a variety of American archetype: well-educated and seamlessly poised and pretty women for whom everything seems guaranteed, everything assured, but through whose fingers each opportunity for happiness slips like a slippery sea creature.

As we headed into the harbor the waves plunked and splashed against *The Profit Motive*. Hong Kong stood behind us like a high, jagged set of false teeth coming out of the water. Here and there green could be seen beneath the buildings, and a gray haze hung behind the city.

— Where are you from? I asked.

— California, she said, looking down at the water.

I thought of Chen listening to me in his study, turning the jade dragon around in his hand.

— Where in California?

— L.A. She turned to look at me through her sunglasses. Santa Monica. Do you know L.A. at all?

— No. Never been there, I said.

My eyes drifted surreptitiously to her shirt, to her legs, and then back to her sunglasses, where, disconcertingly, I saw myself staring back, a ball-like, shadowy midget, with a nose like the rear end of a Volkswagen bug.

Another bellow of laughter came from down the deck, and a shiver went through me. This was Swan's girlfriend. I straightened myself up and shook the image of Rachel from my mind, though it lingered for a second, fuzzy and sour. And then, like an arriving wind, Kate descended into my thoughts, correct and well known, her body cool, logical, and blond, her thighs a milky color, her feet landing upon the deck with the light, hollow thump of clean toes touching wood.

— You want a drink? I asked, motioning toward the cabin.

— No, thanks, said Rachel.

I teetered away from her to the cabin, Kate pressing down on my thoughts.

It occurred to me, as I fumbled with a bottle of ginger ale, that I hadn't properly disposed of the monkey heads before I left. I'd put them into a brown paper bag and thrown it into a trash can, but I'd forgotten that the woman superintendent poked through the trash looking for salvageable items. No doubt she'd wonder. She'd complain to Kate about animal heads in the trash. She thought we were married. That was the only way to explain our living together in the same room. Frederick was amused by this, and from time to time he called me Mr. Kate. But the superintendent was always convinced that Kate and I were putting something over on her. She watched us carefully. Monkey heads would cause suspicion. Kate would have a hard time explaining. She'd tell me all about what had happened when she arrived in Hong Kong. She'd give me the details.

When I went back onto the deck, the boat was nearing a rocky spit of barren land. Several previously unseen crewmen in white sailor suits busied themselves with docking procedures.

— Oh, boy, said Cronenberg, coming suddenly around to our side, striding by with a computer printout trailing from his arm and a cup of coffee in his hand. Trialson is already here. He's the president of our division. We're going to have him breathing down our fucking necks . . .

He strode down the deck and I heard him speak through a porthole, his coffee spilling as he leaned in.

Then the dock swung into view and Rachel took off her sunglasses to observe the gleaming hull of a wide, well-trimmed boat that sat in its slip, already moored, bristling with its own network of radar and antennae. The name painted on the stern in black letters read *Bucephalus*.

Cronenberg loped by again, spilling more of his coffee in abrupt little cascades on the deck.

— Damn, there's his boat, he muttered to us. And then, louder: Weiss! He's here already!

And off he went around the corner, the long tail of computer paper fluttering behind him in the breeze.

19

With his arm around Rachel, Swan conveyed us through various checkpoints until we came to the side of a long pool. There, beside it, a large black man, mostly bald but with closely cropped white hair on the back of his head, sat under a blue umbrella looking through a bunch of business charts. On the table next to him were two or three neat piles of paper. He wore a bathing suit, sandals, and a button-down shirt, untucked, under which was a blue, overwashed T-shirt with the faded logo of AmeriBank on his chest.

Even after all of us had assembled around him he still stared violently at the charts in his hand with a furrowed brow.

— Excuse me, Mister Trialson, said Cronenberg.

— Yes? he said in a gravelly voice, not looking up.

— Are you going to join us for the meeting on the Singapore deal? We're going to go over the details right now.

— Yes. Fine, Bob, so I heard, he said, looking up at Cronenberg and at the same time smiling, completely breaking off his concentration from the charts, but now focusing it, with a look of mild joy, on the rather joyless face of Cronenberg.

— There was the suggestion that you wanted to keep tabs on the report.

— Absolutely. Why don't you guys go through it here at the pool?

All of them dropped their briefcases and began quickly searching for chairs. Swan was on the edge of introducing Rachel and me to Trialson, but he hesitated a moment, interrupted by Trialson's shouting out to Weiss that he should make sure he had the so-and-so data or the whole damned thing would be a waste of time. Fisk then lost his courage, and turned to Rachel and me and suggested we wander about the place until they were finished with the meeting.

Rachel, tall and languorous, walked with me down a cinder path away from the pool, toward a manicured little bluff.

— So, Swan . . . is that your girlfriend? Trialson could be heard saying as Rachel and I walked away.

— Yes, sir, said Swan.

We walked out of earshot, through a gate, and onto the bluff. We sat on a white bench. The jagged grayness of Hong Kong glittered vaguely across the water. Huge boats wandered back and forth.

— Isn't that a destroyer? I said, pointing to where a slate-colored mass of a ship moved heavily on the bay.

— I don't know, said Rachel.

We watched the ship. It was British. The Union Jack flapped on a wire. It was menacing as it lurked through the harbor, like a large, angry wall of stone. A stone wall in the ocean. Inexplicably, I was reminded of the stone wall at Chen's house, and recalled the man with the headband who had climbed over it and gotten caught. And then I wondered about Chen. He'd given me his sanctimonious speech about who was good and who was not, and he'd managed, on the basis of a few of my own puny falsehoods, to make me doubt my integrity. However, it was his integrity that was finally in doubt. I had been blind to him.

And thinking on this, I realized there was a wall inside me that obscured a full view of things, much as the destroyer was able to obscure the spiky skyline of Hong Kong that rose out of the ocean. This wall in me sometimes shifted, and sometimes I could see around it, like the boat, but it was always there. What worried me, though, was a heavy feeling that I was responsible for this at some level. I had constructed my own blindness. It was something wrought by me, or by the way I allowed myself to think. And at this realization I felt sad and disappointed with myself.

— I'm sure that's a destroyer, I said, concentrating on the boat again to draw myself away from my thoughts.

— What's a destroyer?

— A warship. They made them in World War Two. See the big guns? They can hit the shore from several miles away. The shells themselves are as long as this bench.

— No.

— Yup. Look at how big it is. It's amazing that something that large and made of steel can float on the water.

But as I said this I remembered watching Kate asleep one night in bed in Taipei, and seeing her like a large cloud, like a huge, weighty object floating in the sky, and a gust of hope swept into me. Wasn't it Kate I was missing after all? Wasn't that, finally, the limitation I was feeling in myself?

I looked over at Rachel, who was shielding her eyes to gaze out at the ship passing, her hand raised elegantly, softly touching her eyebrows.

Suddenly Swan appeared, with an air of urgency in his walk and a rosy color in his cheeks. He strode with an aggressive *crunch, crunch, crunch* down the cinder path.

— Hey . . . there you are. We're taking a break. Trialson's having the report sent over from the bank. It's being faxed over now. He said it's okay if you two want to swim.

— I don't think so, said Rachel. I'd feel uncomfortable with all your friends watching.

— Harry? said Swan, eagerly.

— No, thanks. Anyway, I don't have a bathing suit.

— There are plenty in the changing room.

— Thanks anyway, I'd rather not.

He stood there shifting his weight, his shoes squeaking.

— What are you afraid of? It's a great pool, he said, putting his hands on his hips, and allowing his good mood to be only slightly tarnished by my obstinance.

— Swan, said Rachel. Harry doesn't want to swim.

Swan shrugged.

— I was just trying to be a good host. I feel guilty that you guys have to sit around waiting.

— That's all right, I said, irritated.

I was beginning to wonder why I had come to Hong Kong at all. Everything that was happening seemed artificial and wrong: this petty argument with Swan, for instance, and these detached, airy conversations with Rachel. In the back of my mind Kate lay on the bamboo mat in our room in Taipei. I saw her lips, and her eyes, and her breast rising and falling, and I heard her say something kind to me, soft but to the point. I missed that.

— Well, then, why don't you two come sit by the pool? I'm sure Trialson won't mind. You can order a drink if you want. Okay, honey? he said to Rachel.

It finally occurred to me that Swan wanted Trialson and the others to see Rachel. He wanted them to admire her. Rachel must have realized this too.

— Okay, she said. Come on, Harry, let's go sit by the pool.

We walked down the cinder path and seated ourselves down on the other side of the pool from the brokers. Swan took his place with them, nodding to us as he took up his papers.

Trialson had put his glasses on and was inspecting a document that had been spit out of the fax machine. His glasses were perched on the end of his nose and he scowled, his face tilted slightly upward. He held up the piece of paper so that the sunlight could catch it. The others fiddled with their reports.

— All right, he said finally in his resonant, velvet voice. All right, I think I've got it. I've got it.

They all became silent. The light blue water of the pool rippled gently. Swan looked across at us and smiled, and Rachel waved a concealed flap of her fingers at him.

— Hello, babe, she said, barely above a whisper.

She was hoping he could read her lips. Weiss, though, also received this message, since he happened to be gazing at Rachel at the same moment. He seemed shocked that she should be whispering something to him, and immediately flushed, but then craned his neck around and saw Fisk behind him, and relaxed.

— All right, said Trialson once again. It starts at three hundred and sixty-five million in nineteen seventy-six, and then we get a marginal rise through the mid-eighties, ending with, at the time of the merger, a measly four hundred and ten million . . .

— Yeah, but Ben, you've got to remember, said Cronenberg,

blinking his tiny eyes, to take into consideration their holdings in gallium, the value of which no one could have predicted back then.

Trialson slapped the paper down on the table and got up suddenly. The others jumped in their seats. He put his glasses up on his forehead, and, with his arms behind his back, began to pace around the pool, still looking in the air at an angle, as if he were balancing something on his nose. They all turned in their seats to watch him. He took big strides, and his long black legs swung under him gracefully. Making his way to the shallow end, he looked into the clear water.

— Who here knows anything about gallium?

— It's used in thermometers, said Wang, tapping his lip with a pencil. That in itself is a steady, medium-size market.

— What else?

— Well, there's gallium arsenide, said Hanashi. It's used in high-speed computer chips. Everyone knows that. Mix gallium with arsenic and it gets a higher speed chip. Frankly, this is a takeover target and we feel it's going to be Mitsaki Industries, or one of the other large Japanese chip manufacturers . . .

The Ouroboros Series 1 used gallium arsenide chips. Gallium was a bluish-white metal. Combined with arsenic it becomes a perfect low-temperature compound for conducting high-speed computer signals and storing information. I smiled. I was pleased to encounter the Ouroboros here, where I was feeling out of place. The great black cube hovered in my thoughts like the possibility of a solution to all messy, unhappy things. In my head was the image of the original Ouroboros: the snake curved in a circle, devouring its tail. All these snakes in my life, I thought. Bad snakes and good snakes. But there probably were not many good snakes. Snakes have always represented what's evil in us. It occurred to me, in a joking fashion, that when a snake was itself, it was like a penis, but when it curved in a circle, it became a vagina. Why was a penis supposed to be evil? The Ouroboros, I supposed, was actually a dark thing to the alchemists, an evil that became divine through inverting itself. Male into female. A straight line into a perfect, unending ring. Lead into gold. Kate was gold. She had golden hair.

And then my thoughts flicked back to the computer, the Ouroboros Series 1, in which, as in alchemy, strange substances had been combined to create something fantastical. Gallium and arsenic, white metal and poison. The bones of a magic, all-seeing machine.

Trialson continued around the pool, toward where Rachel and I were sitting, still looking airily upward. He had a slight paunch. With a big smile he stopped at our chairs and looked down at Rachel. Then he held out his hand.

— Why, hello. You're Swan's girlfriend.

Rachel took his hand, and instantly, across the pool, Swan leaped up from his seat.

— Sorry, Ben, I meant to introduce you. This is Rachel . . . Rachel, Ben Trialson. And that's Harry, a friend from home.

Trialson glowered at me in mid-handshake with Rachel. He got how she fit in, but not me.

— Hello, Harry.

— Hi.

— So, Swan. Who's next, your parents? Are we to be graced by your brothers and sisters? These meetings are becoming pretty folksy. Last week Porter brought his cat. Something about feline diabetes.

— Sorry, Ben, I didn't know we were having a meeting. I was just going to take them out in the boat.

— No, no. Just giving you a hard time. But in the future . . .

— Of course. Sorry, Ben, said Swan weakly.

Trialson grinned down at us and continued around the pool.

Across the water, Swan sat back down in an exasperated heap. But then Trialson turned around quickly, as if inspired.

— Want to go for a swim? he said expansively, with an open hand toward the water.

— No, thanks, I said quickly.

— Rachel?

— Um, she said, hesitating.

— It's a great pool. Warm water.

The others all watched from the other side of the pool, some tapping their fingers and rustling papers. Swan appeared to be in great pain. His mouth got a wrinkled, screwed-up look, as if he'd eaten a lemon.

— Go ahead, Rachel, if you want, he barked, unable to conceal the urgency in his voice.

— You bring a suit? asked Trialson.

— Well, yes, but . . .

— Right over there, he added calmly. There's a changing room.

— Okay, thanks, said Rachel.

She got up and, taking her bag, disappeared into a little building at the far end of the pool. I kept my place rigidly, afraid that I would be forced, out of fear for Swan's mental health and reputation, to go swimming as well. But Trialson turned on his heel and once again made his way silently around the edge of the pool, pondering, with his face tilted slightly upward.

— Arsenic! he bellowed. Arsenic and gallium. Okay, Hanashi, this is interesting. But our clients haven't been able to leverage their gallium holdings into anything substantial. Look, gentlemen, in the third quarter . . .

After a few minutes, Rachel emerged from the changing room. We all looked. But I immediately looked away, because I didn't want to be caught gaping. She was magnificent. Lithe and covered in an iridescent one-piece green suit, her body was almost unreal. And for a moment I caught a glimpse of Swan across the pool, his face once again turning red, but this time because he hadn't realized she would have to parade like this. He felt bad for her, because he knew she was being stared at and was feeling self-conscious; but also, he was ashamed of her physical magnificence, the way certain people are ashamed of their wealth when their immense salaries are disclosed.

She walked gingerly up to the water, dipped her toe in, and smiled at everybody. Having touched the water, she seemed to relax. They all smiled back at her with one big show of teeth, as if all connected to the same switch. She ignored this demurely. And then she dove in, with barely a ripple.

Trialson glanced at her and stopped talking. He continued around the pool. There was a dense stillness that came from the table of young brokers.

Rachel began swimming laps, intensely, knifing along with rhythmic plunks of her hands and feet. Her mouth kept coming up every few seconds for air and her hair streamed behind her like wet black silk.

Trialson strolled back to where the others were, but he kept going, right past them, watching the water in the general vicinity of Rachel's body, but never quite landing his eyes on her. He seemed to be looking just to the side, at the ripples she was making. And we all sat there for a long time in silence, a little ill at ease, while Rachel swam.

— She's a good swimmer, Fisk, Trialson said finally, his arms behind his back, his forehead gleaming in the sun. A very capable swimmer.

— Yes, I know.

— I think she's got the right idea there. Yes, I do. It's a hot day. What do you all say to the idea of us going in for a swim? he asked, turning to the table of pale men.

— Now? said Mitchell, who had remained completely quiet up to this point.

He looked precious, with a smoothly coiffed head and sharp chin.

The others chuckled.

— Yes, Stan. Now.

— What about the meeting?

— We'll conduct the meeting in the pool. Anything wrong with that?

— No, but I don't see the purpose of it.

— Maybe that's why you should do it. Come on, said Trialson, clapping his hands. You guys get into the changing room. There's lots of suits in there emblazoned with AmeriBank's name. You know where they are. Come on, let's go . . .

They all sat there for a moment, staring. Then Weiss got up and started toward the changing room, dutiful and plump, his shirt untucked in back.

— Come on, guys! said Trialson. Just think of this as a new management technique.

They all got up. Cronenberg was last. He just nodded skeptically, but eventually got to his feet and followed the others. He had a loping gait with a big head and hunched shoulders. You could tell he'd played basketball at one time, but no doubt he'd given it up.

Rachel surged through the water, her heels bobbing up, round and pretty. Finally Trialson looked over at me, surprised to see me still there.

— You're welcome to join us.

— No, thanks.

He nodded and then followed the others.

The sun was becoming dimmed by clouds, and the pool had that dusky, cool look pools get when they're too cold to swim in. On top of that, I had no desire to bob around in the water during an aquatic bank meeting. I could hear, from behind the wall, the muffled chatter of all the men changing, and the sound of shoes hitting the floor.

Rachel stopped in the water and looked up. She smoothed back her long hair and cleared the water from her eyes.

— Where is everybody?

— They've gone to change, I said. They're all coming in for a swim. They're going to continue the meeting in the pool.

— Oh, she said, perplexed.

Slightly embarrassed, she put her head back down into the water and started swimming again. I watched and felt calmed by the sight of this one graceful woman swimming in this one pool with no one around, and the mesmerizing splash of her hands and feet.

When I closed my eyes, I heard what sounded like a river or a stream, and then I thought of Kate on the rock in the middle of that stream near Taipei a month ago, sitting upright and proud, her face partly in shade, partly in sun, her eyelashes spiked with light. And, with my eyes closed, Rachel's swimming sounded like the persistent splashing of my own feet in the water that day, circling Kate, round and round, round and round, like a bird of prey, a hawk, or the piercing eye of the Ouroboros examining the factual world, watching her, hoping to see her completely, to be, in regard to Kate, all-seeing and all-knowing.

And when I opened my eyes I felt quite alone, even though Rachel was nearby, submerged.

As the evening settled down on Hong Kong, the splashing wake of *The Profit Motive* appeared bone white against the waves. On the deck, a few feet away, Rachel spoke quietly and soothingly to Swan. Swan had decided that Trialson hated him, and wondered out loud whether he should continue at the bank.

I felt a drop or two of rain on my face. Wind was blowing across the boat, and, watching the two of them, I wondered briefly about the rainy season, and whether we were entering colder months now. As the sun went down, everything on the deck became dark, edged with blue, so that a large lifeboat hanging from winches evolved into an oblong, menacing thing above us. Their voices mingled, hers soft, his sharp and abrupt, up and down, and then, when I looked over, their mouths met, and the little crack of light between their faces disappeared. They were in shadow. Then a tower of dark clouds materialized above and behind them over the sea.

A brisk wind hit me in the face. It was several degrees colder than the air around me. And the sky opened, releasing a torrent of rain upon us.

We were drenched immediately, and the three of us ran for cover, fighting with our hands through the falling water, until we made it under an arch of a doorway. I looked up, and the first thing I saw as we shook ourselves off were Rachel's breasts revealed like ghostly orbs through the veil of her wet shirt. She covered herself when she got the water out of her eyes.

Swan was soaked.

— Shit! My suit! he yelled.

But his voice was drowned out by the sound of the rain hitting the deck. My big shoes had filled with rain quickly. Swan led the way and we made it into a cabin.

— Look, said Rachel, pointing at me. See! They forced you to take a swim after all.

We laughed, but Swan glared. He trooped to the back of the cabin and took off his suit. Somewhere we found some dry AmeriBank shirts to put on, and we dried our pants next to a heater and sat in towels in the cabin while the boat churned through the rain with a humming whir of engines. Swan sat silently for the most part, his hair combed back like a movie idol's, looking troubled and handsome.

It was dark when we docked, and the rain was a foggy drizzle. We were going to go out for a beer, but first Swan wanted to call his answering machine. When he came out of the boathouse he said there was a garbled message for me from someone with a foreign accent.

— Whoever it is, he's got my address and said he'd go straight there from the airport. He says he has something for you, Harry. Sounds important.

— Did he leave his name?

— No, said Swan. He spoke as if you'd recognize his voice.

We arrived at Swan Fisk's tall apartment building, high on a hill overlooking Hong Kong, and the taxi swerved around the circle outside. My impression of the expanse of Hong Kong below, and the general atmosphere of Swan's wealth, was quickly forgotten when I saw a familiar figure standing in the doorway next to a much shorter, nervous doorman, who was surveying the visitor with a look of distaste.

It was Frederick. He was sopping wet, having also been caught in the rain, and his mustache was uncurled and sagging down both sides of his face.

— Harree! he called and waved as I got out of the car.

— What are you doing here? I said, laughing.

I was very happy to see him. His face reminded me of home. Swan and Rachel hovered behind me.

— I'm going to the mainland, Harree. I've left Taiwan. It's all a mess back there. Everyone we know is leaving. The group is splitting up and moving on. I had to come to Hong Kong to get my visa. But that's not the point. Kate . . . you see . . . Kate asked me to find you before I left. She sent you a letter. She was afraid it wouldn't get to you. So I promised I'd deliver it myself.

Swan looked at Frederick's drenched clothes.

— Would you like to come up and change? he asked.

— A letter from Kate? Couldn't she send it?

— Well, yes. But Harree, it's no good . . . you see. I was coming through, and she felt you should get it soon.

There was a tone in his voice, and a worried expression in his eyes, that made my heart flicker.

— Why? I said nervously.

Frederick paused and looked at me. Then he opened up his leather carrying case and began searching through it.

— Come on, let's go up, said Swan jovially, herding us into the building.

Frederick came in, grudgingly. I introduced everyone quickly and we all crammed into the elevator.

— What's up? I asked. Is everything all right?

Frederick nodded and handed me a crumpled letter with Kate's rounded little scrawl across the front in green ink. What's the worst? I thought. She's coming later. She's still angry and wants more time.

I opened the letter and began to read, my hand trembling slightly. Rachel's perfume, ignited by the rain, filled the elevator.

Dear Harry,

I'm sorry it's come to this, but I'm sure you're not surprised. I'm not coming to Hong Kong, I've decided, finally. The reason is, Harry, that I've fallen in love with someone else.

The air in my lungs disappeared. I looked up from the letter. Frederick watched me uneasily, clutching his leather bag against his chest, his wet head almost touching the ceiling of the elevator. I read on.

You know that things were ending for us. It was just a matter of time. Frankly, when I saw the way you acted that night, you no longer were the person I had fallen in love with. You've gone overboard, Harry. You've got to realize that. And I don't think our staying together will help. In fact, I think your being with me makes you more peculiar, more screwy, than you would be otherwise.

I've fallen in love, as I said, with a guy I think you'd like, actually, maybe. But I'm leaving Taiwan with him. And I'm sorry if this hurts you, but it's the truth. I had to tell you the truth. I didn't want to lie to you.

The whole incident at the party, and all the rest, I've put behind me and I completely forgive you for all of it. I'll be glad to leave this island, and all the things that happened here.

Good luck with the computers. Take care of yourself, and please, Harry, go back home soon.

Love,
Kate

20

We fell. And while falling there was a sensation of nausea and a long, airy, swirling view of the river far below. And there were bits of rock. And I saw my shoes over my head, and a guttural yelp came up from my belly but got caught somewhere in my throat.

When I hit the first ledge I reached out with my hands but slid fast beyond, and I saw the other guy blow by me in a blaze of dust. We went over and down again and I was aware of the approach of death. It stood there, silent and windy, offering only a clear, lonely, jewel-like view of the cold peaks of the Himalayas.

Down. I slammed against another ledge. Rocks dislodged and constellated in the air around my head for a moment, and then the fall continued. An outcropping appeared. Again I threw my arm out, but it caught me in the armpit and ripped through my shirt. This time I went head first. The other guy hit the outcropping seconds after me, and there was an explosion of sand and rock and a shout of pain.

Then my face hit sand. It burned. I did seven or eight somersaults, whacking my feet with a *whump* each time. And then, in a cloud of dust, I came to an abrupt stop. I continued to hear falling sounds, but it wasn't me.

There was silence. My chest throbbed. My cheek was burning, and my chin was bleeding. Groans issued from a few feet away.

I looked up. We were in a dry riverbed. We'd tried to take a shortcut. Fuck it. Why did we try to take a shortcut? I thought some of my bones were broken. I tried to move. I could move. I gradually hoisted myself to a sitting position, and sand came down off my head. I looked at the pile of clothes and equipment several feet away, where the groans were coming from.

— You okay?

— I don't know.

Two weeks before, while we were sitting at Ben Trialson's dinner table in Hong Kong, a couple of days after the visit to AmeriBank's island, Trialson's son had asked, very politely, with great intensity while leaning over the table, whether he could, whether it would be possible if, didn't I need a hiking partner when I went to Nepal?

Reticent and stolidly unhappy, I was like a ghoulish presence at the dinner table because of a remark that Swan had made. I had announced at the beginning of dinner that I was planning a trip to the Himalayas. The reasons were left murky. I'd made my decision that morning on the spur of the moment. Ben Trialson, at the head of the table, after cherry pie had been placed in front of us by the cook, asked me why I wanted to go to Nepal. "That unfortunate place," he called it.

Swan raised his eyebrows but said nothing.

— For the hell of it, I said.

— Everyone goes there now, said Trialson in his soft-growling voice. And I promise you, it's not the way you imagine it. There's tourists. Lots. They're climbing everywhere. I've been there, he said, slicing his pie with a fork.

His son, William, listened carefully. He was wearing a big white shirt that read BLACK TO THE FUTURE. He was listening carefully to everything that was said. They're an upper-class family, I thought; an upper-class American black family in a foreign country, and consequently William had a very refined quality about him. He had a tough look in his eye, but he was obviously from wealth. There was a solid confidence, without any concealed uncertainty, in his bearing.

— Dad, there can't be *crowds* of people in those mountains.

Trialson replied that there weren't crowds per se, but a lot of people, and that it took away from the adventure of the mountains. You always saw yourself as an adventurer in the Himalayas, he said, but the facts of the place in the late twentieth-century kept you from experiencing yourself that way. People were everywhere, and they had cameras. It wasn't an adventure anymore.

— Adventures are dead, Will, unless you go into space.

Along with some of the others who had been at the pool meeting, we'd been invited over to Trialson's for dinner. Swan was unhappy because he felt Trialson had been harder on him since the meeting. But Rachel had assured him that Trialson, or Ben, actually liked Swan, and was hard on him solely because he had affection for him and wanted him to be the best at AmeriBank.

— You should see the Nepalese when they see a black man, said Trialson. They *stare* at you. Particularly if you're wearing nice clothes. Some will follow you down the street to see what you'll do, and when you do normal things, like *buy* something or *eat* something, they'll stare at you as if you've revealed something remarkable, even scary, about buying and eating.

It was a relaxed dinner, except for the tension that existed among the young white brokers. All (though some more than others) seemed to want to demonstrate how happy they were that a man of African heritage was their boss. They did this by trying to talk about racial schisms (such as the one just mentioned by Trialson) in a familiar and mirthful tone of voice. Trialson saw all this for what it was, but for reasons that remained elusive to me it didn't bother him, even their overeagerness to concur and nod with commiseration at his descriptions of a black man's uneasiness in Nepal.

Since the topic of Nepal had come up, Trialson had turned his attention toward me. He talked as if I were yet another example of middle-class folly. He seemed to have devised an intricate anthropology concerning young, white, American aspirations, and, with a certain sarcasm, he showed interest in getting me to air my reasons.

— Why the hell are you going there anyway? he asked.

I turned around the ceramic coffee cup in my hand and looked at the blue and white stripes on it. I noticed how beautiful all the furniture in Trialson's apartment was, all burnished wood, and delicate Chinese lamps with rice paper shades.

When I got out of the elevator on the day that I read Kate's note, I immediately pushed Frederick up against the wall, tall as he was, and looked up at his unshaven face, past his soggy mustache, into his bleary, blue eyes, and I shouted.

— Who is it?! Who is she supposedly in love with?

— Harree . . . please . . . don't get upset. There's nothing to do, said Frederick.

— Damn it! Tell me!

My mouth felt wrinkled and contorted, and my eyes were reddening, so that I had to blink repeatedly.

— Together, said Frederick firmly, as if that were an explanation. They went on a trip together, Harree. And I told her it was cruel to you but she don't listen.

His English was loosening. I knew I could get the answer from him in this guilty state.

— Harry, said Swan. I'm sure that Fred here had nothing to do with it . . .

— Who was it, Frederick?

Frederick looked at me fearfully. There was something recognizable in his eye, like something I should know, and when I saw it, the hair stood up on the back of my neck.

— It can't be. Not him.

— Harree, please, said Frederick. I knew you would be saying this.

— It's the snake? The corporal? Wu P'ei-fu?

— *Yes,* Harree, he bellowed down at me, shoving me away. So now are you happy? Now that you are seeing . . . you see that you're right . . . *what difference does it make? You didn't do anything about it anyway!*

Everything got very quiet. My blood went cold. I felt aching and empty, but calm.

— How did he get out of jail? Was he ever in jail?

— He was being held. But Kate helped him, said Frederick. She got some papers and got him out.

Rachel quickly disappeared into Fisk's apartment, and Swan, glaring at me over his shoulder, followed her.

I slumped against the wall.

— I can't believe it.

— Well, it's true, said Frederick acidly. Kate got him released. About a week after you left. She got some papers . . .

It was several hours later, when I lay on a bed in a guest room in Swan's huge apartment and stared at the ceiling, sweating, with the other three murmuring out in the farther room, that I began to see the horror of it all. I saw Kate and Wu together, finally alone, making love, as if on a dense vapor platform, deep, deep in the middle of an impassable country, far away from any roads or lights or telephones frantically ringing, their bodies different shades of white and olive, moving together. And the shape of Wu's body scared me because he looked virile and yet crooked, like an iguana, and his arm looked like a green mossy branch laid across Kate's thigh . . .

— Sounds as if you've been planning this trip for a long time, said Trialson.

— What do you mean? I said, suddenly jolted from looking at a white stripe around my cup.

— You seem to take the question awfully seriously. I just wondered why you wanted to go to Nepal.

— I've always wanted to go. Doesn't everyone want to go and see the highest mountains in the world?

Swan snorted. Rachel looked at me with her head tilted, as if to say, "Is this really the way to go about it?" She was the figure of reason now. Umpteen times since I read that letter in the elevator she'd said measured things to me about considering my actions, lying low, getting in touch with myself.

— What's so funny, Swan? said Trialson.

— Nothing. It's just that Harry's totally irrational. If you only knew the whole story. He's moved by his gut. I don't think he's thought this trip through, he added, giving me a meaningful stare.

— Give him a break, said Cronenberg. He wants to go to the Himalayas. What's wrong with that?

— I still don't think you should go, said Swan to me across the table, ignoring Cronenberg. You're being impetuous. That's not the way to solve something like that. You won't find them.

— Find who? asked Cronenberg.

— Find *them,* said Swan.

— I'm going to look for some friends of mine who are in Nepal, I said tersely, trying to pre-empt the discussion.

— Friends? said Swan, his voice cracking. That's beautiful. Harry, you're perfect, he said, shaking his head.

— What? Is that just a way of saying you're going there to find God or something? said Trialson with a smile. You're not going there to become a Buddhist, are you? Well, he said, chuckling, you're not the first.

— I'm going for personal reasons, I said. Nothing religious. Some friends of mine are over there, and I hear the mountains are beautiful.

— Well, then, said Trialson, looking up from his pie. Well, then, at least that sounds level-headed. I say go. Go, and don't listen to all these doubters. See the mountains and have a hell of a time.

And Trialson reached over and gave me an abrupt, affectionate whack on the back.

The lump of clothing moved in the dust and then sat up, with puffs of smoke coming off it, and resolved itself, after a few familiar movements, into a tall man sitting in the dirt, a mustache, like a foolish, antiquated remark, curling below his nose.

Frederick dusted himself off.

"It's on the way to China," he'd said in explanation when he sat down next to me in the plane just before takeoff. But I knew that he was really thinking, Harry's doing something crazy. I was the one who told him. I'm responsible for what happens. Damn it! I'll have to go with him. A small detour . . .

And here we were, Frederick and I, sitting in some nameless, waterless river, as if we were bathing together in the imaginary water, in the middle of a country on the other side of the globe.

I saw that all of it, the whole progression from the moment I first saw Kate dancing in the barn at the party at college, was to this end: to have my love tested by Wu P'ei-fu, to have his presence make me doubt myself completely, and then to seek him out and somehow win over him, thereby proclaiming my final awakening to my love for Kate.

I'd lost the first round. Now was the time to finish this dispute. I had been able to see, briefly, what was truly important, and now it would not escape.

Frederick stood in the dusty streambed and patted his pants so that all around him, as the dust billowed, there floated the pervasive reds and browns and beiges that color everything in a dusty country. We had flown to Kathmandu and had found out by asking at the permit office that Kate and Wu had gotten a permit for the mountain trails. I stared at Kate's signature on the green card and winced, rubbing my thumb on it. It was her handwriting. There was no doubt about it. The sight of it shot fear through my chest. She was here. So was he. A Chinese signature in flashy lines was beside her name.

Frederick worried that he shouldn't go, that I shouldn't go, that we should stop and he should talk some sense into me and send me packing back to Baltimore, where, he seemed to think, a big protective family would nurse me back to normality in a tree-shaded house with Buicks parked outside.

— Harree, this is a journey doomed, he said darkly, as we picked through a heap of army surplus gear (about a week before our plunge down the cliff) at a store on a small street in the middle of Kathmandu.

It was a dirty city with people and oxen in the streets, and dogs roving from sewer puddle to sewer puddle, and thin boys rolling hoops down alleys with sticks.

— Frederick, I'm going into the mountains. Remember, I didn't ask you to come. You should leave.

— I can't leave you. You'll get hurt. Something will happen and I'll be responsible.

— You're not responsible for me, I said, picking up an old backpack and inspecting the seams.

— Maybe no. But I cannot just leave, and hear later that you never came back. And I carried the letter! he said again, smacking his forehead. Why did I ever bring that letter?

I spent the evening buying maps. The permit indicated that Kate and Wu had gone up the eastern trail that circles Annapurna.

— You are going blindly. You are going for what end? This is jelly-owsy . . . rah-venge . . . and it will come to no good. Harree, listen to me, anger leads to no good if you act it out.

My decision had been made, though. I was going into the mountains to find them. I'd keep going until my money ran out. I'd come down through the various levels of disappointment, through the stages of companionship, sexual joy, common friendship, then disillusion, doubt, naïve hope, lack of understanding, apparent blindness. I'd even come through the twisted triumph of having discovered her unfaithfulness, as if at last getting it right. Then I'd orchestrated the party, and managed to humiliate everyone at once, particularly myself. All of it, the entire pilgrimage toward Kate, farcical as it was, would have been in vain if I let them both just slip away into the mountains. It all would have been for nothing. I had to find them.

Otherwise I'd be as low and purposeless in my own memory as I most certainly was in Wu's. I had to show Kate, finally, that I really loved her now.

Frederick and I were walking through a square in which there was an ancient building with detailed wood carvings around its eaves and fine, thin screens that had been carved, each one, out of a single piece of wood. In the screens there were tiny pictures of men and women erotically intertwined. Men eased themselves acrobatically into the open thighs of smiling women, their arms twisted around their lovers' necks, legs encircling, hands open in divine gestures. Beyond them were the dark recesses of the interior, and above, along the underside of the eaves, was a series of large, soft, eroding sculptures that held up the roof. They were lifesize couples, their legs gripping each other, their faces still, their eyes open yet blank.

— These are very old, said Frederick matter-of-factly, noticing my fascination with the sculptures. It's all from the Kama Sutra, he added.

Above the bodies of the lovers, the roof sloped up, covered with brown shingles, until all sides met in a single, shining gold point.

— You seem to be attracted to religion, said Frederick thoughtfully.

— What do you mean? I'm admiring the luck of those people.

I found myself trying to see between the thighs of one of the female figures. But I turned away, feeling unhappy and unsettled. The issue of Wu and Kate hung like a poisonous fog, or an assemblage of collected evils, over the beauty of the statues. I felt polluted.

— Even so, Harree, you must meditate, ask for some guidance. You're not on a good path . . . Bah! he said, interrupting himself suddenly. What am I preaching to you about? You look up there and all you see is sex, he said, disgusted. Harree, look into those faces. You will see detachment, an attitude toward love that you will never have.

— No one will ever have it, Frederick. That's why the statues are so beautiful.

Frederick laughed quietly.

The wind blew across the square, and the dust blew directly in my teeth.

It was a week later, Frederick still following me like a priest attempting to get a condemned man to convert, that we took the shortcut and ended up falling down the cliff, many miles northwest of Kathmandu.

It was all because I felt that if I hurried I had a chance of catching up to Wu and Kate. Even in the bus depot in Kathmandu, while boys threw luggage on the roof of the battered bus and people yelled and the sun beat down, Frederick, chopping his hand up and down for emphasis, argued that it was wrong to chase them into the mountains. He even asked me, out of desperation, as the bus revved up its engine and I listened to him with my head sticking out one of the bus windows, to accompany him to China instead.

Then the old bus let out a burst of exhaust and began to pull away. And Frederick suddenly jumped on, in midsentence. He lumbered back to my seat through the hot, crowded aisle with a terrible look on his face. For several miles he cursed me. Then, after gloomily staring out the window at the ravines and the passing fields, he said,

— Just this bus ride, Harree. Then I'm out of here. I can't be-leaf I came with you.

We took the bus to Dumray, a windy, desolate town about three hours west of Kathmandu. A dusty highway went through the middle of it, and on either side was a single row of decrepit shacks. Emaciated dogs traipsed about with their tongues hanging out, sniffing the ground with dry, dirty noses.

Frederick followed me through the shops of Dumray as I stocked up on cans of food for my trek into the mountains.

— There's no way, Harree . . . there's no way that I am going to follow you into those Himall-yahs.

For a long time he'd been planning to go to China to see the great sword dancers, and possibly to study with them. I remembered how he had talked about them in Taiwan.

— You'd be much happier in China. Think of what you'll learn, think of the sword dancers there. They're worth your time. It's very good of you to be so concerned. But there's nothing in it for you. You should go.

He watched me, his drawn face and his eyes showing his age. He was nearing forty, but the weariness in him seemed much older. It was finally occurring to him that I was serious, that I was really going after Wu and Kate, and nothing he could say would stop me. His face deflated, like a mustachioed balloon, and he sat there in silence, staring at me as we sat in one of Dumray's fly-infested cafés. The Kathmandu bus idled nearby. Beyond the dead, shadowy shacks across the dust-blown road the jagged peaks and subpeaks of snowy Annapurna stood high in the sky, jutting up into the blue.

— You are going?

— Yup.

— What do you intend to do? That is, if you are so lucky to find them?

At that point a little boy came up and began to tug at Frederick's sleeve. He said, over and over again, "Rupee, sir, rupee, sir, rupee, rupee . . ."

— Maybe I'll kill him, I said over the boy's voice.

— Ha! Frederick laughed. You don't know the first thing about killing. Harree, you really are an old-fashioned naïve type . . . a naïve romantic. That's not the way things work. Wu would get you first.

— I'll challenge him to a duel, I said.

And as I said, it, although my words sounded almost childishly operatic, it caused a glimmer of hope in me that I had a specific goal.

— I want Kate to understand how much I love her. I want to restore my honor.

Frederick rolled his eyes.

The boy's pleading got louder, and I tried to wave him away as politely as possible. But instead, he shut up and continued to stand next to the table, staring at us.

— Anyway, I know I'll win. I've seen what Wu's all about. He's not good. He's wicked. I can win.

— You sound so positive.

— I am.

— How?

— Because, Frederick, I said, leaning toward him for emphasis, in this situation, at least, I'm not the underhanded one. That's on my side.

— What is? I don't get it.

— Whatever it is that showed me his true self. I have a feeling that something allowed me to see him in a very simple form. In reality, I believe, he has only one attribute. I can't name that attribute, because words can't describe all the nuances of what I saw. I mean, it's more of an instinctive thing. It has nothing to do with Kate, really. She's part of it, obviously. And the issue of Kate and the issue of Wu have gotten mixed. There's losing her. And then there's him. They're jumbled together. But distinct from her, distinct from my doubts about her and me, there is something very clear that I now see, and that I saw at that party. You could describe it as a vision. I believe that every so often one is allowed to see something clearly in his life, something point-blank and true. I saw, or I was allowed to see, Wu P'ei-fu as he really is, absolutely, in some realm of reality. He was monstrous and loathsome. He was a reptile — a dragon or a snake. But that was just a picture. When it comes right down to it, only one word comes close to all of the many impressions. Evil.

— Oh, said Frederick. Now, you see, you're talking about religion, but you don't admit it. You be-leaf God is on your side. To be-leaf that you have to bel-leaf in God.

— It's not a religious issue, Frederick. It's not like that. It's an issue of good and not-good.

Frederick nodded and smiled. But he really didn't understand at all. Although I was very serious, he was convinced I was unknowingly opening myself to him.

The boy took the pause in our conversation as encouragement, and once again he held out his hand and began to murmur, "Rupee . . . rupee . . . rupee."

— I'll tell you what. I will go with you as far as the Moan-key Temple, said Frederick. Remember, in my room in Taipei I had a photograph of it from a may-gazine? I've always wanted to see it, and now, so close, it would be sad not to go.

He patted me on the shoulder and grinned, as if everything were settled.

— It's a very holy place. It's in the direction you are going. I will go with you as far as there, and then I'll turn back. Maybe you will turn back with me, he said, and winked slyly.

The little boy continued his singsong whining. I looked at him. For some reason that I'd failed to comprehend, he'd been bothering only Frederick, and stood beside him, thin as a post, his hands out and his mouth open like the bottom of a small bell, chanting and stepping agitatedly from one foot to the other as if he were cold.

— Here, said Frederick. Go away.

Frederick reached out and pushed a ten-rupee note into the boy's hand. The boy looked at what had been given him and became immediately silent. He clutched the money and gaped at it. That's when, also looking at the money Frederick had given him, I saw that his little hand was deformed and that his fingernails looked like ruffled pieces of shell.

He ran out of the café, and Frederick looked up again.

— Did you see his fingernails? I said.

— No, said Frederick.

— They were all twisted.

— Really? he said without interest, and he drank his tea in one gulp.

— The Moan-key Temple, Harree, he continued. I've only seen pick-toors of it. But I found it on the map today. It's north of Talapna. Nice name, eh? Talapna. You know, it's funny, but if I hadn't been fool enough to follow you, I would never have seen the Moan-key Temple. I guess I could always see it in pick-toors. But the real thing, you know, to see the real thing is *always* better.

21

From where we stood in the dusty riverbed I could see the part of the path, far above, that had given way when Frederick and I fell. I felt a burn on my chin, which turned out to be a slight cut, and I discovered that my right arm was twisted.

— My back . . . it hit against the rock up there. Oof. It's lucky that we came down to sand, said Frederick, wincing.

His backpack had rolled away from him and sat a few feet off, roughed up and slightly mangled.

I pulled out my map, dusted it, and traced my finger along the winding dark blue line of the Marysandi River, which we'd been following into the mountains. I'd figured that they could be only four days ahead at the most. That's why I'd tried to work out some shortcuts in order to gain ground on them. One of the shortcuts had taken us directly across a lowland forest with no path, at which point I jogged to make up time. Frederick snarled at me from behind, intermittently jogging, walking, and cursing in German. The second shortcut took us over the part of the path that gave way and tossed us into the ravine.

By now, Frederick was on the verge of giving up his congenial trek with me to the Monkey Temple. But after bandaging our cuts, I looked at the map and found we were near a small town named Updu, and I suggested to Frederick that we find our way there, albeit limping, and recover from our fall.

He agreed, but his anger and impatience were now completely evident.

— You'll never find them, he said peevishly, dusting himself off with hard whacks of his hand. And now we are falling and almost becoming kilt, he blurted out. Face it, Harree! They are probably long ago around the northern path and going down the western side. It's all over and this is just a waste. She doesn't love you anymore!

— It doesn't matter, Frederick, I said as calmly as possible. That's not the point.

— What? What's the point now? I seem to have for-goatten it, he bellowed.

In the silence after his yell he looked at me wearily, as if I were an infant. He had a saggy expression on his face, which made him look much older and gray around the mouth. It occurred to me, looking at him looking at me, that he must have gone through a great deal of pain when he left his wife. I had never thought about it before. All the time I lived with him and he stood by as Kate and I frolicked together, giggling late at night. Now I could see in his face a whole range of remorse that I'd never noticed before. He never told me what had happened. I'd thought it slightly amusing when he wrote to his son with his sword beside him like a steel security blanket. But there was evidence in his face of someone who'd lost a great deal. It was odd to see it now, when he was shouting at me. There was something compassionate in him, underneath the superficial curl of the mustache. He looked at me pityingly. And the slap-stick image of him jumping away from the dog in Taipei came into my mind and was transformed. He wasn't foolish, I thought. He was grandly farcical, in a tragic vein. Below the surface there was a man of supreme, almost ridiculous vulner-ability.

— This is just a man! he shouted at me. A Chinese man, Har-ree. He is not "The Enemy."

I didn't have anything to say at that moment. So I started walking again. And he started to walk, too, with a vague limp.

We trekked along in silence for several miles until we came, dejectedly, into the tiny town of Updu, composed of several stone lean-tos with a few mangy ponies chewing monotonously outside, a small stream, and a filthy rooster bobbing his head in the grass like a mechanical toy.

A man came out of one of the shacks.

— Hello, hello, he said, beckoning us to enter his house. There is food . . . tea . . . food . . .

Famished and exhausted, we followed him into the dark low doorway.

It was smoky inside and there was a fire in the middle of the room, but the bulk of the smoke went up through a round hole in the ceiling. The ceiling was low and covered with soot so that, looking up, all one could see was the opaque, bituminous color of ash. There were three other occupants of the shack besides the man, Frederick, and myself. One was an ancient woman who looked blind. She sat in the shadows under a low rafter at the far end, staring out, one eye completely white, the eyeball turned up into her head, the other gazing obliquely off to her left. Her white hair was bundled behind her head in a ball, but a few wild strands curled in the air and caught the light of the fire, making it appear as if a cobweb had formed behind her head.

There was also a teenage boy who had dusty black hair that hung over his eyes. He was kneeling at the fire stirring ashes beneath a kettle. He gave us a disinterested look and went back to tending the fire. A different figure sat on a stump by the fire, dressed in bright clothes, and she jumped up as soon as we entered.

She was a woman of about seventy, but her quick movements gave evidence of an athletic energy. She came forward and took our hands and shook them with great enthusiasm.

— Hello! she said. I just got here myself. Half an hour ago. Came down from Manang. Thought I'd have tea. Awfully pretty day.

She had a large face with dark eyes close together, glasses, and white curly hair coiffed with a certain hiking practicality in mind. She wore big khaki shorts and suede hiking boots with white socks poking out. She was drinking tea from a collapsible camping cup. We all sat down on stools around the fire, and she immediately told us, in a jovial but aggressive manner, about herself.

She was Canadian, from Toronto, and had decided to see the Himalayas before she "kicked the bucket." She'd taken all her savings (which I got the feeling were quite a lot) and come to Nepal.

— And where are you from? asked the boy, who'd been listening to the conversation, and obviously had a working knowledge of English. He directed his question to me.

— The United States. My friend is from West Germany.

The father asked the boy what had been said and the boy replied in Nepalese. Nodding slowly, he surveyed us while he listened to his son. Then the father called back to the blind woman in the shadows. She took this in, staring blankly at the ceiling, and then answered in a shrill, grainy voice, speaking to the boy.

— My grandmother wants to know if you want supplies for your trip into the mountains. We have many supplies.

— No, thank you, said Frederick. We are only on a short trek.

— Around Annapurna? asked the Canadian woman.

— No, I said.

— That doesn't sound especially adventurous, she murmured with a chuckle.

— He may go, said Frederick. I'm going to the Monkey Temple near Talapna.

— Yes, I've heard of that, she said. But you . . . she said, chiding me. You're just going to wander around?

— Not really.

She looked annoyed. She had a fierce desire to gab. She waited to see if I was going to talk, and then continued on her own.

— Ah. But it's beautiful up there. The pine woods and then the glacial terrain, then the snow . . .

She stopped herself and peered at me. Then she leaned forward and studied my face at close range. In the dim light she was like a snowy-headed grandmother from a dream.

— You don't look well. Are you sick?

— No. I'm not sick, I said.

— You've got a gash there on your chin and you look pale.

— He *is* sick, said Frederick. He's been a little off. Are you a doctor?

— No, I'm not. But he says he's not sick.

— I'm not, I said, giving Frederick a stern look. Where did you get the idea that I was sick?

— He is, said Frederick firmly, turning slightly away from me.

— You drank the water down at the hot spring?

— It's more of a sigh-cow-logical thing, said Frederick, tapping his head.

— Oh, said the Canadian woman. It's his disposition? She narrowed her gaze on me.

— He's no longer in control of himself, said Frederick. He's got a day-mon in him.

At this remark the young boy got very uneasy and began to stare at me. His father called out to him to translate, which the boy did, and afterward the old blind woman began to mumble to herself as if she were singing a little song.

— A demon? said the Canadian woman. He just looks queasy.

The boy came over to me, up close, and looked furtively into my left eye, as if he were peeking into a keyhole, trying to look into my head. He nodded.

— Yes. He has one. Inside him.

— How can you tell? I said with a sigh.

— Your eye, he said ambiguously, and then sat back down at the fire.

— Oh, bosh, said the woman. You have no demons in you. You just drank the water in the hot spring. Perhaps you've got parasites.

— What do you do for day-mons? asked Frederick, taking this new turn in the conversation with great earnestness.

— You have to kill another one, said the boy, poking the fire. They see through your eyes, so when you kill another . . . the demon inside you sees it and he gets . . . he gets . . .

— Frightened?

— Yes. Then goes away. Flies out, he said, flitting his hand up. You know.

— Now wait, said the Canadian woman impatiently. You believe in them?

— Yes, said the boy, simply.

— You think the American man has demons inside him right now? At this moment?

The boy shrugged. The woman was speaking in an annoying tone, and he was not unaware of it. He had the look in his face of someone much older. He couldn't have been more than fifteen, but he had that dullness in his face of the deeply cynical. There was an ashy, listless color to his face, and a flat quality in his eye that stayed constant and unflickering while he talked.

— He has demons . . . maybe, he said.

— Maybe? Ah, but for me maybe isn't enough, she said somewhat smugly.

— What's unusual about day-mons? Frederick said, angrily.

— Everyone likes to believe in such things these days, she said. Do you? Reincarnation, spirits, that sort of thing?

— Maybe, said Frederick, shrugging slightly. I don't *not* believe in them, he said.

The boy glared at Frederick suspiciously.

— But tell me, honestly now, how does this fit into our world, all these maybe's? asked the Canadian, shifting her large bottom on the stool.

— There's only one maybe now that you know of, said Frederick testily. And that's the day-mons.

— But still, it's just a myth. What good does it do anyone? It's not connected to anything. It's just an imaginary thing out there that fills up a hole so it doesn't look as if there's a hole there. My gosh, she said, looking at me again, as if I were the only sane witness. It seems all anybody wants these days is nice stories. Myths. Now everybody back home is fascinated by these tales.

The boy translated as best he could for his father, but his father remained silent, pretending not to listen. He went about preparing tea and a large pan of wet rice. The room was becoming very smoky.

— I did not say I be-leafed in day-mons, said Frederick. But I won't rule anything out, you see. Things are not easy to explain.

— Well, said the woman, scratching her head, I'm not sure how fancy myths and stories help that. I mean, it's everywhere, isn't it? Vague religions and so on. Pray to this one, pray to that one. Karma this, karma that. It's just a lot of shifting sand. Nothing substantial.

Frederick smiled.

— We had shifting sand today, he said jovially. We just, two hours ago, fell off a path south of here, when the sand goes out from under us.

— Went, said the woman.

— What?

— Went out from under us. It's correct to say "the sand went out from under us."

— Thank you, said Frederick under his breath.

— Well, well, I suppose it works. It's an attitude that plugs up a few holes, she continued, muttering to herself. I suppose it makes no difference. But it bothers me. There are no guiding principles. It's just a lot of sticky, gooey special effects that pass for convictions.

— Excuse me? said Frederick, not hearing her clearly, thinking she was saying something derogatory about him.

— Why are you going to the Monkey Temple? she asked suddenly. Are you a Buddhist?

— No. I've heard many things about it. It's supposed to be a very spiritual place. What's wrong with that?

— Nothing. Nothing at all, she said, but she was obviously disgusted.

The man came over and gave each of us a steaming plate of rice covered with yellow curry sauce. We began to eat, though Frederick and the Canadian woman remained poised to continue their conversation. Frederick was searching his mind for something to say to her to defend an eclectic view of the world. He strongly believed in fairness. He didn't want myths and vague spiritual beliefs condemned just because they were imprecise. He seemed to feel that it was a benevolent act to allow imprecise beliefs, and that open-mindedness and refraining from judgment created the feeling that the world was indeed a good place. Any interpretation of God or the rest of it should be equal to any other. It was only fair. In some ways, I think he saw it as his right, as a spiritual man, to believe in as many things as possible. To Frederick, belief itself was the important commodity.

— And what do you think? she said to me, her mouth full of rice. You're the one with the supposed demons. Are you sick or possessed?

— What bothers you so much about the idea that there may, or may not be, spirits? It's just a conjecture, I replied glibly. I don't see what difference it makes.

— Because, frankly, I don't like it one bit, the way we all pick up and worship pieces of other cultures. It's unhealthy. None of it means anything. Yes, sure, it provides an attractive means of getting through the bleakness of the day. You become a Buddhist, or you become a Unitarian, or you meditate, or on your bookshelf, along with *The Hobbit* and *The Joy of Sex,* you put the Torah, the Koran, the Upanishads, and some book on tai chi. It's an attitude. An ignorant attitude, she said, glowering at Frederick, who ate his rice self-consciously. We ultimately don't "believe" in anything, do we? We're just "moved" by the sentiments. What's actually going on is that we're desperate. With no faith of our own, we play with pretty ideas that have fallen off other people's faith. That's all that reincarnation is, you know. It's an idea that's fallen off a religion, like a nose off a statue.

The boy laughed. With his shoulders hunched down, sitting

close to the fire, he laughed a few dry *yuck, yucks,* his eye lit by the fire for a moment.

— She is *good,* he said to Frederick and me. Yes? I don't understand much, but she is *good.*

He spoke as if it were incredible to him that a woman would speak this way, particularly an old woman, and he addressed himself to us as if she were a gag we had concocted.

— Why are you so angry? said Frederick to her softly. We were only talking calmly of being . . . in der dämonische Gewalt, ah, how do you say? In the power . . . in the power of something. Which he definitely is. I did not mean, lee-terally, that he has creatures in him with the horns and the wings. If you knew him, you'd know he is acting not like himself. Now, I do not be-leaf in day-mons as they are in drawings, or as gaagoy-aahls. But I also, I *also,* do not be-leaf that everything makes sense. Some things do not make sense. I came to Asia, thinking maybe I need a spiritual discipline. This is why I came. Now . . . I think it is fair to say I am a very good sword dancer. Through the dancing my inner self has become calm. Once I was, like Harree, very angry and very full of questions. Now I am not. In some ways I have been cured of my ego . . . my ego-filled . . .

The Canadian woman snorted.

— My ego . . . how do you say? It doesn't matter, said Frederick. You mock the people from home, from the West, who come here for answers. You say it is bad, or fake. But maybe this is what must be done anyway. Maybe it makes the world look young again . . . for us from Europe and Amer-eeca, where everywhere you look — and Frederick imitated looking about — it looks like mankind is in fast decline.

— Maybe, said the Canadian woman. Maybe you will be buried beneath all of your maybe's. There's not much to hold on to there.

— And you? What do you believe in? asked Frederick, inclining his head to the side, trying, as he felt was right, to be patient.

— I believe in science, said the woman. I've taught school, and studied and catalogued animals for many years. But believe me, I know what you're talking about. I've seen it first-hand. My parents were missionaries.

At that moment, abruptly, the old blind woman stood up and shuffled toward us, and as she came close she became more visible. She was wearing an old musty black shawl under which was a shirt that had once been white but now was an uneven yellow. Her skirt was dusty, and she wore frayed sandals. Her feet were large and callused, and they appeared strangely out of scale, moving stiffly under her hem, gnarled from walking over rough land with heavy burdens. She was ugly and had whiskers. But the eye that stared off, sideways, into the distance, retained a certain color and youth, and you could tell, just by the youth in that one eye, that she had been, many decades ago, an attractive woman. She came close to the fire and reached her hand out to the boy, who guided her to him with his voice, until her hand rested on his shoulder.

She spoke with a grainy voice.

— She says she wants to sit close to all of you. She says she likes the sound of the foreign voices, said the boy.

She gradually lowered herself onto the bench next to him and took his hand in hers to steady herself. In her presence all of us fell silent. But after a few minutes the Canadian woman spoke quietly to Frederick, under her breath, as if she were embarrassed in the presence of the old woman.

— I'm sorry if I seem inflamed by this topic, she said. It's close to the bone for me. My father fancied himself an expert on all this and . . . well. I don't even know your name. I'm Dorothy. Dorothy Krasnick.

— Frederick.

— Harry, I said, putting out my hand.

But at the sound of our talk the old blind woman began, strangely, to giggle wheezily. She put her wrinkled hand over her mouth. The boy nudged her with his knee. We all looked at her. She giggled for a few moments, and then stopped.

— It will take a day or two to reach the Monkey Temple, said Dorothy, trying to ignore the uneasiness the old woman's giggling had aroused.

The old woman began tittering again. She rocked herself back and forth. The father grumbled at her, and she stopped, once again putting her hand over her mouth. But she continued to listen, waiting for the sound of our voices.

— It's an unusual time to head into the mountains, said the Canadian, trying to ignore the laughing. But although I didn't go to the Monkey Temple, I did go by the crossroads leading to the path up to it. A beautiful spot. A real view. You can look right across the mountains eastward. There was a lovely couple that I met there. You meet a lot of nice people when you're trekking. The young woman was an American. Her husband, or boyfriend, was a charming Oriental man. We all thought the view was marvelous.

My heart froze. It missed several beats, and then, furiously, started thumping again.

Frederick looked at me, his eyes wide.

— What did she look like? I asked hoarsely.

— The American girl? Very pretty. Interesting features. Blond. Sweet. Traveling together. Very romantic. You know . . . in the mountains together. I remember wanting to do things like that, but it took me until I was sixty-eight and single to get around to it.

My blood shot through my veins. I felt my heartbeat right in my temples, and all the energy that had drained out of me listening to the conversation came steaming back. I wanted to leap up and charge out. She was near. She was near to me. They were near. Suddenly I missed her desperately.

But then a sense of shame and humiliation pervaded everything around me. The fire, being poked by the boy with a stick, became dull and lowly because of its proximity to me. The food I was eating looked paltry and poor. And those around me, Frederick, the young boy, the blind hag, the father, and the sanctimonious Canadian woman glowering through the smoke, all became unfortunate, pitiful beings solely because they sat near me. My chest became airless and concave, and the saliva in my mouth tasted stale and sour.

The old blind woman began to giggle inexplicably once again, and I began to hate myself. How was it that I had let this happen? How was it that I meant so little to Kate? No doubt there had been something detestable about me recently, and my following them into the Himalayas was even more detestable. Yet, in the growing nausea I felt in my own presence, at the sound of my own whining heart, I once again, moment by moment, became certain that I had done the right thing. I looked up again and made an effort to breathe deeply.

— Because these mountains, this part of the world, should be experienced when you're in love. Then the peaks, the tall, tall peaks, make such a soaring feeling in you.

— Let's go, I said abruptly.

— But, Harree. Now? said Frederick nervously.

— Yes. Now.

— You haven't finished your rice, said the Canadian woman. My goodness. Relax. We're not in New York, you know. No need to rush.

— Unfortunately I've got to go now. There's no time, I said, shivering at the realization that my own voice had once again begun to sound reedy and repulsive to me.

They were out there somewhere, together. She was talking to him intimately. Touching him. She was leaving behind all the intimate things we had done together, erasing them. I had to move quickly before they convinced themselves that they were living out the *real* romance.

I got up quickly and grabbed my backpack.

— Harree, please, not yet. Let me finish my rice, said Frederick anxiously.

Now that he knew we were on the same path as the other two, his apprehension and anxiety had tripled.

— You can finish your rice. I've got to start up the trail.

The blind Nepalese woman laughed, now uproariously, slapping her thighs, her creased face stretching into a long, lined howl.

— *Hush!* said the boy.

I put my backpack on, left a few rupees on the bench for what I'd eaten, and made my way through the dark, smoky interior to the door and finally out into the airy daylight.

— Don't drink the water from the hot springs! shouted Dorothy.

— Harree! Wait! said Frederick.

I heard him grabbing his pack and hurriedly saying goodbye. He politely offered a quick word of thanks to each person there in turn, even thanking the old blind woman, whose muffled giggling I could still hear as I headed past the other shacks, past the dirty rooster jerking his head back and forth in the grass, past a few children playing in a dusty courtyard, and out toward the path that led northward into the mountains.

22

The steps of the Monkey Temple of Kyparuna ascend, embedded into the dry cliffs just east of the town of Talapna, until they stop, far above the valley, on a plateau on which the great, crumbling temple sits overlooking windy foothills. Annapurna stares down on it like a large, diamond-headed cat, brooding beneath a mantle of snow. From the valley we could just make out the tattered orange prayer flags flapping in the wind way up there, beyond the ledge of the plateau. We were at twelve thousand feet above sea level, and by the looks of it the temple sat another five hundred feet above us, a long steep climb up a huge staircase of wide, cracked steps.

Frederick stared up at the temple with a kind of grim ecstasy, keeping his own counsel about the thrill of arriving. He'd lost faith in me as any sort of co-believer, even though what he had wanted me to believe was unclear. He was finding my stalking of the escaped couple increasingly distasteful. And it seemed that I was becoming more of an object lesson for him than a friend. Our long trek from Updu, in silence, him behind me most of the way, had only consolidated his growing unfavorable assessment of me. He was looking forward to being released from my company, and I think he longed for that time when he'd be spared the influence of my sophomoric, implacable notions of settling accounts. He didn't believe in settling accounts. He believed in absorbing them.

— Should we climb? he asked, staring at the steps hungrily, as if they were to a gourmet restaurant of the soul.

— Yup, I said, and started up the first steps, aware that this visiting of a holy place was all less complicated for me, because I had only one thing to do, and it was completely secular.

Frederick seemed anxious to approach in just the right way, in just the right frame of mind, so as not to disturb the karma of the moment. With a trace of sarcasm, I reviewed his little lecture of many months ago when I first arrived in Taipei: *"You've come to seek some sort of enlightenment. Hah! There isn't any!"* And I took note of how he climbed the steps, delicately, as if he were walking on one of his own fragile dreams, his eyes cast upward searchingly. He was like a man listening for a song that wasn't being sung. And he was like a buffoon to me then.

But I couldn't concentrate on his foibles too long because I became aware of a group of small children not far up from us on the staircase. They were milling about, as if they couldn't decide to go up or down, and sometimes grabbed one another, and frequently ran back and forth on the steps. They looked like poor village children scavenging for food, and the idea of coming face to face with them depressed me. Since seeing the boy in Dumray, I'd been depressed about the children, and I had no desire to see any more. I found I was always repulsed by them, but also, I felt repulsed by myself for being so healthy, and seeing the brightness of my new, well-made clothes next to their rags. There was the desire to help. But stronger was the desire to get away, as if I secretly feared I would catch poverty, like a disease. I was ashamed of this.

So when I saw them on the steps, I slowed my walking. They made strange, shifty gestures that seemed to indicate a malevolent, unhappy mood. They were like shadows crisscrossing.

— What are children doing here all alone? Who do you think they are?

— I don't know, said Frederick, looking up ahead.

But as we drew closer, step by step, the forms of the children gradually coalesced into hunched, hairy forms. We stopped in our tracks and peered closer.

They were monkeys.

Frederick's expression turned from one of intense fascination to a limp and fearful disgust. We could now see that at various points up the staircase there were little massings of these hairy beasts, and that hundreds, perhaps a thousand, of them sat, ran, chattered, and screamed on the steps between us and the high temple. They were the small scuttling kind of monkey, so that they appeared to be like a population of rats that had grown into human beings but had somehow gotten stuck halfway.

Group by group, with a shifting and turning of heads and a blinking of many eyes, they became aware of our presence.

— Moan-keys . . . moan-keys everywhere, said Frederick in a trembling whisper. But I am not going to miss this temple after coming so far, all this way, and falling down the cliff . . . also suffering through *you!* No! The apes, die Affen, will not get me this time.

He began a low humming to himself, something like an old marching song; and staring ahead, on the alert for any particularly angry monkey, he tugged my arm, and we continued cautiously up the steps. They were all looking at us, and many sat like fat men at the beach, with their legs splayed out on the steps, and observed our slow progress with their noses twitching.

Frederick slowly reached into his bag and withdrew a long pouch, which he undid with careful movements of his fingers, and gradually pulled out his long, shining Taiwanese sword. With the tassel on the handle he slung it through his belt, and lashed it so that it could be grabbed quickly. It bounced against his leg at each step and flashed in the sun, and when I looked at him, even though I could see his almost ninnyish fear, he seemed to me, high above the valley, with the white peaks behind and the gleaming weapon at his side, and his absurd mustache sticking out from his face, like a hero. A hero of ordinariness. He was like niceness itself, babyish and new and without even a thought, without prejudice or opinion, fallen into the world like a single flower petal dropped into a dirty lake. Kind, and fumbling for a way to believe in things, to believe in God or in divine powers, he was about the most banal form of good I would ever meet.

He drew his sword.

— Aha! he cried, and swung it in a great arc around his head.

I looked and saw several monkeys coming at us down the steps, their eyes agog and their hands and feet flashing over the steps.

Frederick swung. The sword nicked the step in front of us with a flinty *ping*, and the monkeys leaped backward, agitatedly running up the steps to safety a few feet away.

— Away, apes! shouted Frederick. Come on, Harry, he said, turning to me, quiet and firm, holding his sword in front of him in a professional stance and putting his foot on the next step. We will continue.

We climbed and Frederick kept his sword menacingly drawn to keep the monkeys at bay. As they watched us, their faces expressed all sorts of itching, angry impulses. The whole swarming, motley bunch of them were mangy and obviously starving, since they seemed to live off the remnants left by the few pilgrims to the temple. There was a pile of fly-covered meat on a step, dried and rotted by the sun, and a whole clutch of dull-coated, flea-bitten monkeys of all ages sat around it, guarding it, as if it were a precious heirloom. The babies huddled against their mothers as we passed, and the mothers loped off to the edge of the stairs with their children clutching their bellies. But all of them, the entire colony, scrutinized our every movement, and observed every foot of our progress jealously, as if bowls of colorful, newly picked fruit were concealed in our clothes.

A large old male with gray above his eyes defecated on a step directly in our path, and then he sat down beside it as if he'd created an intimate friend with whom he would now keep company. Frederick threatened him, poking the sword in his direction, and he watched us pass, one leg shivering with old age.

This is the way we moved up the long stairway, with Frederick's sword held out in warning, passing through the diseased horde of distant relations, poking at them when they went for us, or shouting and kicking when they approached from the back. Several times two or three lunged at us, but Frederick, like a spinning top, whirled and whooped, coming close to severing their heads from their bodies with one elegant motion. They'd stop in their tracks, and back off just in time. The blade blew by them with the *woof, woof* airy sound reminiscent of the big cloth sails of a windmill.

— They're pitiful, I said.

— Don't feel pity for them, they want to eat your flesh, said Frederick. They can't believe we have no food . . . or that we ourselves are not food . . .

— But they're pathetic. There's something grotesque about animals that hang around public places hoping to get fed. There's no dignity in them.

The image of the three monkey heads that I had obtained for the party came back to me, sitting in a row under blue silk.

— Dignity? Be-leaf me, Harree . . . all they want is to eat your arm or your leg.

We kept going. Behind us the stairs went in a steep slant back down to the valley. The monkeys that we had passed were hopping up the stairs, slowly following us, chattering, their hairy hands touching the steps lightly, their scampering feet making a pitter-patter of muffled footsteps. I suppose if we had faltered or fallen they would have covered us in a moment. But I doubted Frederick's assertion that they'd have eaten us. That was absurd. It was the hopping that got to me, though. It was unnerving. All the steps directly behind us were covered with black, furry beings with upturned, blinking eyes.

— Keep going! said Frederick.

Huffing and puffing, using our hands to reach the top steps, we made our way to the uppermost step and onto the plateau itself.

There were no more monkeys on the last steps. And there were none on the plateau itself. In their place, at this height, all around us, were the figures of tall, majestic men with shiny, bald heads walking to and fro, their papery orange robes flapping about their loins in a soft breeze. On high poles prayer flags ruffled and snapped. And in the midst of all this, through a maze of small white shrines, was the huge golden stupa of the temple, its bumblebee spire striking itself high into the blue. Two large and lustrous eyes were painted on its side, gazing at and beyond us like the two last remaining pieces of some lusty, voluptuous giant.

The stupa itself was a large breast-shaped mound, polished

and smooth. On top of the mound was a square block, where the eyes were painted, and on top of that was a rising pagoda tower consisting of about thirteen levels. On the very top, a crude stone lantern was almost lost in the clouds.

— Those are the steps toward Heaven, said Frederick, pointing. And below is the earth mountain. That's what they call it . . . it seem-bolizes the world. In between the earth mountain and Heaven are the eyes of the Buddha's con-shuss-nuss.

Staring at the temple, Frederick was lost in reverie. He breathed hard from the climb.

— You see, Harree . . . it is said that this temple was built many hundreds of years ago on the tomb of Chandaka. Chandaka was the Buddha's chariot driver.

— You mean his chauffeur?

— Yes, you might say that.

His awe made me uneasy. What did Frederick know about the Buddha's chauffeur anyway? Did the story impress him, the sense of history? Or was it something about being close to the life of the Buddha? In some ways I thought of Frederick as an appreciator of life, not one who was living it. And it angered me. He's like Chen, admiring the dragons of the past, I thought. But I looked at him and realized that the comparison was unfair. At least Frederick feels things deeply, I thought, even if he doesn't know precisely what they are. Still, he was annoying.

The monks walked back and forth with bowls of rice in their hands, and some carried palm fronds, some knelt, some laughed, and there was the smell of incense in the air. Frederick sighed and seemed to be on the verge of crying. He carefully put his sword back into its cover and tucked it gently back into his pack. The whole time he stared in silence and with a glow emanating from his face.

— Ah, he said. *Ah.*

Although I was seeing the same glorious sight that he saw, I found myself narrowing my eyes and picking my way through the crowd on the plateau, searching for strangers who looked out of place.

— Forget it, Harree, said Frederick. They are not here. Give in. You have arrived.

I was chagrined that Frederick had noticed my furtive glances about the plateau. But at that moment my heart was jerked by the sight of a person in the crowd, someone who definitely did not fit in. The walk was unusual; so were the clothes. As the monks parted to reveal this person, I became aware, even at a distance, that it was somebody I recognized. Yes. I knew him. His face came out of the crowd and began to rush toward us, until, as he came closer and closer, a speck, like a swipe of green calligraphy, could be seen on his cheek.

— Free-derick!

— My God, I said. It's Null Geschmack.

Frederick's eyes, first misted over but forward-gazing, now became wide and clear. He was at a loss for words; he gaped and his face began to sag, like someone robbed of his wits, as he focused on the approaching figure.

— No, it can't be him. It can't. It's *not* possible, he said in a hoarse, coughing voice.

Somewhere a bell sounded and the monks began to move in one direction, but through them, with his red hair in a ponytail and his feet slapping in a full run, came Null, happy as an idiot calf let out of a barn to play.

— You have come! You have come! Hooray! Free-derick . . . Free-derick! . . . und . . . und . . . Harr-ee. I knew you'd come here, Free-derick, he said breathlessly, stopping in front of us, panting, slapping his arms at his sides. And I am sorry, forgive me for surprising you . . . but I thought . . . well, I was inspy-erred by that pick-toor in your room, and . . . I heard . . . of course from Harr-ee's friend in Hong Kong you were coming to Nee-pall. So I knew you would get *here* eventually. I knew that you always wanted to come here, Free-derick. Remember? That pick-toor in your room? Of this place? So, not to miss you, I came the other way around the mountain. I paid some mare-chants to bring me by pony. And you came! And you came! I was right. I know you so *well*. So *well* . . .

The whole time he talked, ebullient and out of breath, the snake on his cheek pulsed against the red of his skin and the nimbus of his flame-red hair. He was flushed and looked quite healthy. And for the first time I had to concede that he was a man of forceful, almost handsome good looks. Ob-viously the mountains served him well. He wore a lot of new camping gear, including an army surplus flashlight that, for some reason, he'd hooked to his belt so that it dangled in front of him phallically.

— Yes, I see, said Frederick. You are here, Null. Very clever.

Null went to embrace Frederick, but Frederick caught his arms halfway and they clasped in an awkward, arm's-length grip.

— Willkommen in Kyparuna, said Null.

Then he swung around and with a large gesture presented us, as if on a game show, with the expanse of the temple and the plateau.

— Isn't it beautiful? It *is* beautiful, he said happily. And I know many things about this place bee-kaaz . . . bee-kaaz you, Free-derick, have often told me about the meanings of these things. Like that, for in-stahns . . . *that* . . . Harr-ee, is the eye of their god.

— Not really, said Frederick stiffly.

— Yes, Null, I've heard.

— Exciting? It is exciting. An ane-shinn relig-own and we are the bee-holders. But also, it is amazing that we have met. By chance! I am so glad to see you both. Oh, hold on now, what time is it? he said, hurriedly peeling back his sleeve to look at his watch. Oh, yes! Oh, yes! The sera-moany! It's still time . . . we've got to hurry, because I know Free-derick will want to see this. Pleez hurry, he said, yanking Frederick's arm and turning, beckoning me to follow.

Frederick was still in a daze. He stared down at Null tugging on his sleeve as if at an apparition.

The snowy peaks were isolated up in the sky like carefully painted vignettes, blue, white, and black, huge but far away. As Null tugged us along, I looked up at them and wondered where Kate and that reptile were. Were they in the snow yet?

— Come, hurry, said Null. I'm going to get my camera . . .

— No camera! said Frederick, grabbing his shoulder. We'll just go. Quietly, Null. Bitte benimm' dich. Please.

— All right, all right, Free-derick, if you want, said Null. I won't get the camera, but you will be sorry. When you want to see pick-toors and there are no pick-toors . . .

— Null, said Frederick firmly, interrupting him. Which way is the ceremony?

Null led the way, turning around every moment to give us a nod and a grin.

— You look well. You both look well, he said, peering over his shoulder at Frederick.

I looked at Frederick and noticed he was getting gray in the face. It seemed that Null's presence was making him grow older. He was growing sad very quickly.

On the other side of the stupa, where the view stretched un-impeded to the north, and where the long white wall of mountains in the distance marked the beginning of Tibet, a collection of monks, some with tall fringed hats, others bareheaded, walked solemnly in a processional circle, drums and gongs and smoke-trailing incense holders in their hands.

— Look, said Null. Look! I've seen this twice already. I've been here for two days waiting for you, and I've seen it twice.

Frederick scratched his forehead and watched the procession, trying not to hear Null. I watched too, momentarily distracted. But I felt strangely uninterested in the monks and their procession. It began to look like just another backdrop, with unusual props, for my private obsession, which began to bubble up in my thoughts like a once dormant acid as soon as I got over the shock of Null.

I pulled him aside.

— Null, have you seen Kate?

— Kate? he said, looking at me wide-eyed. No, Harr-ee. I haven't seen Kate since your party . . . with that poor man you pushed over. That was a strange party. How is Katey?

— Null. She's here, I said.

— Where?

— In Nepal. With *him*. Wu P'ei-fu.

— Woo who?

— *Null*, I almost yelled. She's come here with him. They've run off together. Kate left me.

Null gaped at me and then at Frederick.

— Is this true, Free-derick?

— Null! I said loudly, and several monks nearby looked over at us. I'm talking to you. Have you seen them? . . . God, this is ridiculous. Obviously you haven't!

I stamped my foot. Once again I was supremely aggravated by myself. Yelling had drawn attention to me. A few monks looked at me disapprovingly. I hated that I wasn't able to stay calm. But every time I remembered that Kate was close, very close now, somewhere out in those mountains, I couldn't find any patience, and I imagined her receding farther and farther into the distance.

— Harree. Don't be unkind to Null. Maybe he didn't know about you and Kate, said Frederick with barely veiled contempt for both of us.

I was steaming. And when I looked at Null, the idiocy of him almost burned my eyes out with fury.

— Harr-ee, be-leaf me. If I saw Katey here in the middle of the Himall-yaahs, I would have remembered, he said with a smile. Are you sure she came to Nee-pall?

— Yes. I'm sure.

— He's sure? said Null, turning to Frederick, as if I were not of sound judgment.

— Yes. This is the case. Unfortunately. I told him. It happened after Harree left. Then I saw him in Hong Kong. That is why he is here. He wants to find them. I told him I'd come as far as the Moan-key Temple.

— Yes, I knew it, said Null. I knew you'd be here, Free-der-ick, he said.

A gong sounded. Four old men in orange robes passed us and behind them came a double line of young monks, some with their hands clasped, some strewing the ground in front of them with flower petals. The wind blew and the petals tumbled along the plateau. Some were blown over the edge, and I watched as they blew away and down across the long staircase, where a few hairy black forms could be seen just over the edge, chasing the pink spots hither and thither.

The monks proceeded around the stupa, counterclockwise, and Frederick's face showed signs of being freed of agitation. Null watched the ceremony only partly, because he kept turning and observing Frederick. His adoration was amazing, I thought, and I found myself being impressed by his perseverance.

As the monks passed us, I tried to compare, in my mind, the

distances that were involved. There was the distance that I'd come to Asia to be with Kate, and then there was the distance she had now gone away from me. And along with this there was the distance between, for instance, us, the three Westerners, and these monks. There was a lot of space being negotiated, and those involved frequently forgot that space existed between themselves and that which they wanted. Take Null, for example. His adoration of Frederick was as indelible as the tattoo on his face, yet he was its victim. For him, the obvious structure of events and the composition of people's hearts were to be fought, to be overturned and proved wrong. Yet for all his insensitivity to the truth, it was evident that he knew the facts very well. I'm positive he feared there could be no good ending to his life. So he chased what he wanted with the dull genius of those who are doomed. And consequently, he had an innate feeling for the tragedy of himself. That in itself was something to be admired, or at least recognized. But it never was. That's what it was to be Null.

The chanting began, first in the wavering voice of the older monks, whose faces were set in a grimace, and then followed seconds later by the low, rhythmic chant of the others.

— Kaa . . . aa . . . deee, kaa . . . aa . . . deee . . . aaa, called the older monks.

— Kaa . . . aa . . . aa . . . deee, kaa . . . aa . . . aa . . . deee, answered the rest.

— Kaa . . . dee, kaa . . . dee, ka . . . dee, chanted the old monks again in a high, twirling tone.

The chant strung itself through the air, emanating from the phalanx of mouths. On and on they chanted until I found myself weaving dizzily on my feet. Off the dome of the stupa the chant reflected, and off the tiles on the ground, until the voices ebbed and flowed like a wave moving through our bodies.

It was intolerable.

— Wait a second, I said abruptly. What are they saying?

— Shhh, said Null.

— Are they saying what I think they're saying? Are they saying "Katey"?

I couldn't believe my ears.

— Get hold of yourself, said Frederick under his breath. They're saying "Kah-di," not "Katey." Harree, you're getting almost crazy. It means "How much?" It has to do with the cost of enlightenment.

— What does that mean? They're singing my girlfriend's name!

I felt feverish. This was getting absurd. These bald celibates were shouting out the name of my love, my escaped love. I hated it. It was as if insects were attacking me. I felt like scratching. I was itching all over with humiliation, and her name was everywhere, like some natural phenomenon, a wind, or the sound of animals in a field.

— This is preposterous. I can't take it!

Null turned around abruptly.

— *Shhh.* This is embarrassing. Listen to Free-derick. It has to do with Nirvana. *Not* Kate.

The chanting made the air viscous. I had to get away. I turned and walked quickly around to the other side of the stupa. There was no one on the other side, and the voices grew faint. Flower petals littered the ground, and there was a long high view of the mountains. I sat on the plateau wall.

From where I sat I could see down the jagged cliffs, and down the ravines to where the valley started, where Frederick and I had begun our climb. There was a wide view of the mountain range and of the successive peaks stepping up the side of Annapurna, and the tall peak itself, all white, soft-sided, yet sharp. And from the base of the staircase, which I could barely see off to the left just around the edge of the plateau, where a

few monkeys wandered about and picked fleas, I could make
out the light brown path that led away, in meandering curves,
up the valley and north into the foothills.

There was no vegetation at this height, just cold desert, boulders, and the flat faces of the hills. Here and there across the
valley large heaps of fallen moraine descended from the edge
of the ice sheets. It was a still, uncomplicated, and direct environment. No reminders of the confusing qualities of life
showed themselves. No squawking birds, no stinking swamps,
or armored insects buzzing at flowers, or cows waiting to be
slaughtered, or cars, or trash cans, or banking machines, or
even money, greasily fluttering loose in the air, flung from
somebody's wallet, or a sandwich, or the idea of a job and the
lurching, scrambling streets of cities where people stalked their
careers.

— Kaah-dee, kaah-dee, kaah-dee, chanted the warbling
throats behind the stupa.

My eye traced the progression into the mountains of the light
brown path, which was a couple of miles away, and at the same
time, feeling sorry for myself, I began to hum along, Katey,
Katey, Katey . . . How much? How much? Until part of me felt
there was tremendous vanity in revenge. And for no reason at
all I remembered walking through the hallway at college with
Kate and seeing the bust of Voltaire, and being somehow surprised at how similar the faces were.

— How much? How much? How much? they chanted, and I
could almost sense this enlightenment they were referring to,
this Buddha consciousness that the big sexy eyes on the stupa
were looking for out there in the mountains. It wasn't happiness. It wasn't an abstract television either, on which the entry
requirements to Paradise were pictured. It was simply a place
where deception never occurred. And, conceivably, this place
wasn't meant for the vague-headed individuals of my era, who

nevertheless put up an admirable, almost saintly struggle against an inability to believe in anything for very long.

I followed the big advertisementlike eyes outward into the foothills. And that's when I saw two figures making their way up the path, along a high ridge right near the snow line; two specks, a couple of miles away, walking together. There was something about them that was maddeningly familiar, even though they were barely large enough to be seen.

23

Turning away from the ceremony for just a moment, and angered finally by what he saw as my increasing mania, Frederick almost blew up.

— Harree, it's *very* unlikely!

— I saw them. I'm positive. Climbing the path a few miles north, from the other side of the stupa.

— Impossible.

— Harr-ee, said Null. I think you need rest. You look terr-eeble.

— I promise you. I saw them.

They both sighed. The chanting continued, but the monks were now on a different set of words, and the whole "Kahdee" thing seemed distant and sort of humorous. I waited for a response from the two of them, but they glanced at each other, and then at me, exasperated and at a loss for words.

— Well, it doesn't matter. I'm going.

I hoisted my pack on my shoulder and spun on my heel. I had no time for Frederick and his little drama with Null. I headed across the plateau toward the staircase.

— Harree! Scheisse! Don't be ridiculous! called Frederick, loud enough to be heard, though he was still mindful of not interrupting the monks.

I heard them talking furiously to each other in German, but that dwindled out when I reached the edge of the plateau and looked down the steep, monkey-infested flight of crumbling stairs. I decided that I just had to head through it fast. No doubt it would be easier going downhill.

I started down. But as I did, I heard the *flip-flopping* gait of Null behind me.

— Harr-ee, he said, standing at the top, calling after me. Harr-ee, Free-derick says wait and we'll both go with you! Wait . . . Just a few hours.

I turned around abruptly, scaring away a few monkeys on the uppermost steps. I wasn't angry. I just wanted to get on with it.

— Null! I shouted up the steps. I did not come to Nepal to hang around watching people sing about the half-price sale on enlightenment. I came to find Kate. It's as simple as that. I don't mind the mountains. I don't mind the scenery, but I've got to go after those two! Kate's only a few miles away!

Null nodded in disappointment.

— But Harr-ee, he called glumly. Even if you find them . . . what can you do? They are in love. You say, "It is as simple as that," and I agree. It is as simple as that. But they are in love. You will do better to come back. Come and listen to the singing. It's woon-der-full. I feel better already.

— Null! I shouted, barely able to control myself. Null! Why?

What's the point? What are *you* doing anyway? You're in love with Frederick and you don't even tell him . . . you just sit around mooning at him, following him around the world, hoping he'll pay attention to you one day, hoping he'll love you. But how is that a life? How can you stand it? At least . . . at least, Null, I'm going to *do* something!

And at that, stunned and flushed at the thought of having revealed Null so blatantly, I turned around, and, with his empty, vulnerable expression stuck in my mind, started down the steps like a bull, almost in a frenzy, frightening two mangy male monkeys who'd crept up behind me while I was talking and were fidgeting with my pack.

Monkeys scattered screeching as I came down the steps. I barked out to scare them, my legs pumping and the severe slant of the stairs dropping away from me like a cliff. It was then, occupied with not falling headlong down the stairs, aware only of the scattering animals and the great fall, that I heard Null shouting . . .

— *Harr-ee* . . . at least I *know!* At least I *know* I am not loved!

But I couldn't listen, because I could do nothing to keep myself from going faster and faster, and monkeys of all sizes were howling and jumping aside. I thought, I'm going to fall, I'm going to fall. I'd already fallen once that morning, down the cliff with Frederick, and I was sure that the second time I wouldn't be so lucky. So I moved my legs as fast as possible to meet the steps as they came.

They flashed by me, with dark, white-toothed panic. They reminded me of those people you feel sympathy for in televised disasters. They were afraid and threatened, but on an unapproachable level, far removed. So that, as their faces flew by, they became compelling only in the way a manual of physiognomy might be as a flashcard series. This one was mute, this one terrified, the upper lip pulled down low, round eyes blinking; this one is too surprised to panic, this one leaps sideways, eyebrows raised, yellow teeth almost smiling; this one's furious, furrows needling her hairy brow, her cheeks puffed out to show the indignity, clutching her child like a rag. As they went by I kicked a few by mistake, and as they dove to get away I stomped on their rotten meat.

After many minutes of pounding down the steps I came to the bottom and collapsed on my knees in the dust. With my big pack on my back, I rolled over like a turtle, breathing heavily, and looked up to see Null, still there, the prayer flags snapping behind him in the blue.

The monkeys were whimpering, but they'd already begun to limp back to their original positions.

Null waved. It was a silly gesture, like "Glad you got home all right." Then he moved away from the edge of the plateau and disappeared.

The best evidence I had that I'd changed irrevocably was that I discovered in myself, as I traipsed along the rocky path alone, only a scathing and sarcastic attitude toward the Ouroboros. There was a feeling that a preoccupation with blinking lights and synthetic intelligence was solely a method of masturbation, related now to Frederick's awe of "mysterious" spiritual notions. If you want to get things done, I said to myself, you can't allow yourself to be drawn into inactive dependencies, ideas or things that seem to offer to do the work of understanding, like religions or machines that think. The way out, I told myself, was to commit yourself to one simple, even inane, task and complete it. That was it. That was the axiom which floated to the surface whenever I thought of myself leafing through computer books in Taipei.

The computer no longer offered salvation. It's not *my* brain, I kept saying. The Ouroboros doesn't think *my* thoughts. It thinks the thoughts of a blank, pure, faceless, bloodless nobody. It thinks powerful, neutral thoughts. And the idea of thoughts without personality, without ethical or emotional goals, an idea that once grabbed my attention with force, now only made me recoil with revulsion. I decided that I wanted to speak in the form of unexpected, malarranged deeds, because the roads of thought had been completely steamrollered and made uniform by such faceless things as God and the Ouroboros.

So, like an angry child, I continued through the ravines — over the icy streams and across the rope bridges — with a pugnacious desire to remain dumb for as long as it took to find Kate and Wu. I want to be alone! I yelled at the enclosed part of my head. There is something I want to *do.*

I also arrived at another conclusion. I smelled. Not only did I smell, but I was beginning to believe that I had terribly bad breath. Or did I just imagine it? There was the growing feeling that I was repulsive to other people and that I was unaware of it.

I stopped at a rock and looked around. There was not a soul to be seen. I had the idea of taking out my shaving mirror and getting a good look at myself. The air was quiet, the atmosphere was thin, but the mountains stood sober and hard above me. I found the mirror and pointed it at my face. I did look bad. But not the way I expected. There was something sort of glued together about me, as if I'd found bits and pieces of a face and tried to make them match. My eyes looked as if they were different colors. My mouth sagged on one side, and on the other it got tight and thin. Just made of patches, I thought. "You look forlorn," Kate would have said.

I pushed on, and over the next ridge the path dipped down.

It was around the next bend that I came on a group of five men who turned out to be Nepalese policemen. They had tin badges and battered blue hats, and there were pistols on their belts in worn leather holsters. They had stopped on their way up the mountain. Their dusty ponies were tied up beside the path, and they sat in a circle around a small fire, eating out of dented metal dishes and gabbing loudly. As I approached, I noticed that there was a long box lashed to the back of one of the ponies. On its side was painted a red spot on a white rectangle, but on closer inspection I realized it was a small Japanese flag.

They offered me tea. Two or three of them spoke broken English, and the captain, a man with a graceful, bony face, spoke fluently, with a trace of a British accent. He'd been in the British Nepalese regiment after the war, he explained.

— What's the box for? I asked.

— It's a coffin. A Japanese man, a mountain climber, died up on the pass. Went up too late. After the sun rose. Sank in the snow. Climbers saw him on the pass. Reported him dead, and said the sun burned him like a cinder. Little atmosphere, you know, up there. Sun's very devilish. Probably had altitude sickness as well. The coffin was provided by the Japanese embassy.

I nodded. It sounded gruesome.

— Nice box, eh? said one of the other policemen, a bearded man with a gold tooth.

They all nodded and we turned around to look at it, sitting on top of the pony.

— The Japanese are good craftsmen, said the captain.

We nodded again. The pony shifted its weight under the coffin and swished its tail. It seemed to think the admiration was directed toward itself.

— Have you seen anyone else on this trail? Friends of mine, a Chinese man and a blond woman?

They shook their heads. They'd seen only some Nepalese traders carrying a load of Coca-Cola bottles down the mountain from one of the high towns. You can redeem them in Kathmandu.

— Only you, so far, said the captain.

I thanked them for the tea, left them around the fire, and headed once again northward up the path.

Heading into the mountains, I felt a peculiar freedom, but also an increasing loneliness. During the interminable hikes up thin, precarious paths, I found myself thinking about walking into Kate's room long before, studying the objects there, her bottle of skin lotion, her bowl full of bracelets. Once or twice, as a game, in order to humanize the cold, foreign environment of the Himalayas, I squinted at the dusk and imagined that the mountains surrounding me were those objects in her room, and that they had become gargantuan. The rounded peak of a tremendous bottle, the jutting lid of the highest cold cream jar in the world, their labels obscured by long shadows slanting across the snow. But after a moment the game seemed perverse, even though, when I thought about myself in her room long ago, the image I had was one of ascetic rapture and contemplation, like that of those monks at the temple; and it seemed to me that it was an attitude more in keeping with the Himalayas. Now there was something feral and fretful in me, something instinctively unhappy, like a desperate hunting animal, wild-eyed and mangy, as if I'd gone backward in human evolution. And sometimes my goal of finding Kate and Wu seemed to burn in my head, the only light in the top room of an abandoned building.

One night, after having pitched my tent on a hill above a river, I thought I heard someone outside and I took out my pocket penknife and waited for whoever it was to rip open my tent. Thieves reportedly lived in the mountains, and attacks on hikers were not uncommon. The penknife looked dull, and I felt foolish lying in my sleeping bag with just my underwear on waiting for an attack. Originally I would never have prayed, but

I did, because the cracking sound of sticks beneath boots outside the tent, in the absolute dark, paralyzed me with fear. The next morning, after waking up with my hand still clutching the knife, I felt dirty, as if I'd done something shameful the night before. I was slipping. I couldn't believe I was that weak-willed. In the morning light I decided, once and for all, that the world was a big, stupid place where you were forced to fend off short, hairy animals with sticky hands who were distantly related to you. It was possible to die, for instance, in a tent far away from home in your underwear, without anyone there to remark on the silliness of it.

For the curative feeling it gave me, at the next town, a dusty place called Baragachop, in a small dark shop that opened onto the passing main path, I bought from a wrinkled woman in black a large kukhri sword, like the swords used by the Gurkha regiments in which the police captain had served. It was shiny and had a menacing look, with an unusual hooked curve, like a surreal version of Frederick's sword.

I looked it over in the shop and wondered for a few moments about my intentions. But since they were unclear to me, I decided to view the purchase as a statement to myself more than anything else. It made me feel better, even though it was just a sword. I set off once again, my new purchase installed neatly in a long side pouch of my backpack, with renewed momentum and the desire, more than ever, to come face to face with Kate and Wu.

24

The moon at night in the Himalayas is boldly lit but somber, like a porthole shining down into the belly of a vast ship. I stood outside my tent, stalked, and spun, attempting from time to time to mimic from memory Frederick's body movements. The dim light gleamed on the blade. I envisioned lopping off Wu's head with one precise swipe, and then holding it up in my fist by the hair, like that statue of Perseus holding the head of the Medusa.

Then I cried a little, just a tear or two, because I fell to imagining the actual duel between myself and Wu. It continues for several minutes, while Kate gasps, sitting on a rock. She realizes she loves me. She gets tender. I die. Or Wu and I die at the same time.

But I stopped for a moment to consider some oddities that

had been plaguing me. How was it that Wu P'ei-fu got away from the wily Mr. Chen? It didn't make sense. It was evident at the party that Chen was out for blood. He had planned it all, at least it seemed that way, and I couldn't understand how he'd let Wu leave the country. It seemed a slip-up on Chen's part.

But enough dallying with the past, I said to myself . . . I'm no longer the memory. Now I'm the will.

Then, to test myself, I jumped into a position of attack once again and scurried about the little dirt clearing where my tent was pitched, fending, lunging, kicking up dirt, and once or twice getting my feet locked and stumbling. But all in all I felt I would be pretty good in a fight. I was sweating under the moon, and it made me feel great.

I ran across the clearing and leaped on a rock, pointing the sword at the sky, and bellowed out an optimistic yelp.

— Moon! I yelled, pointing my sword upward.

It was the first thing that came to my mind. The moon was glowing, and I was going to recite something, probably made up, about the moon and the coming day — something like that.

But I never got to it, because when I reached the top of the rock, in midyell, I looked down and saw a corpulent Nepalese man sitting on a pony with a pistol in his hand.

— Please to get down, he said.

He pointed the pistol at me, but not belligerently, just with a calm motion. It was one of the policemen I'd met before. His tin badge glinted in the moonlight, and he seemed to be chewing something, as if he were just finishing a meal. Jabbing the gun in the air, he spoke again, through his chewing.

— Come down, please. Please come down.

I could see food sticking to his beard. With the thumb of the hand that held the gun, he wiped his face. I came down the rock, hiding the sword behind my leg as much as possible. As I descended I became aware that all the policemen sat waiting on their ponies on the path several yards away. Two other figures stood beside them in the darkness.

Immediately I recognized them: Frederick and Null. When I got closer, I could see them standing like dejected, melancholy versions of the Good Citizen, with their white shirts and their white skin gleaming in the dark.

With a little difficulty the policeman got off his pony and, making a clicking noise through his teeth, gestured for me to give him the sword. I handed it over, wondering whether they'd witnessed my prancing around and yelling at the moon.

We made our way over to the others.

— I have him. He had this. He was shouting and jumping around with it, he said, handing it to the captain, who inspected it.

The policemen chuckled. Frederick and Null both looked at me gravely.

— Harree, I am sorry, but we couldn't let you go off like that all . . . well . . . all crazy. So I told the police you were up here somewhere . . . and we came to look for you. But Harree, I never thought that you would get a sword!

— I got the idea from you, Frederick.

— Oh, Harr-ee, this is sad. This is very sad, said Null, shaking his head and hugging himself against the evening chill.

The captain was not as amused as the others.

— So, we have found your friend, he said. Now you must take him back down to Kathmandu.

— No, that's all right. I'm perfectly all right. These two are just worried. I'm fine. Really, I am.

They all looked at me skeptically.

— All the same, said the officer. We can't have you running around the mountains threatening people with a sword.

— I haven't threatened anybody.

Frederick and the officer exchanged glances.

— All the same, you'll have to head down. I'm the authority up here. You'll camp with us tonight and first thing tomorrow all three of you will go back down. Is that understood?

— That is good with me, said Frederick.

— Yes, said Null.

— That's perfectly okay with me, I said. I was planning to head down tomorrow anyway.

Frederick looked at me with a sharply raised eyebrow.

— No, I'm serious, I added. I've basically come to the conclusion that what I'm doing is absurd. You were right, Frederick. But it was only after I bought the sword that I began to wonder what was going on. Frankly, if at all possible, I think we should head down tonight. I'd really like to get home.

— Impossible, said the captain. It's too dangerous on this path at night. Also, the trek back to Kathmandu will take several days. Better start tomorrow.

Frederick examined me, somewhat relieved, his face relaxing.

— Harree, stay tonight, he said in a kinder voice. We'll get a good sleep and head down in the morning.

He patted my shoulder.

— All right, I said.

The captain nodded approvingly, but looked me sternly in the eye for a moment. One of the policemen dismounted and led his pony, with the rest of us following, through a gap in some rocks and down a small path toward a clearing.

I had a plan. I'd made it up on the spot. No doubt it was total lunacy.

We all bedded down by the small river that ran down the mountain a hundred yards or so off the path. It was called the Kali Gandaki, and the sound of its tumbling water filled my head as the grumbling, chatting group of policemen set up two tents with old smoke-smelling tarps they'd unloaded from one of the pack ponies. And since it was already well into the night, it was decided that we should not pitch our tents, but sleep underneath the tarps so that we could leave early in the morning.

Frederick was eager to leave as early as possible, and he kept thanking the captain for his help, and apologized several times while everyone was setting up for having detained them from their mission. Null seemed to have been deputized by Frederick to stay by me at all times, which was ludicrous.

— Feeling okay, Harr-ee? asked Null, while Frederick was off in the distance.

— Yes, fine. Thanks, Null.

— I think it will be good to get back to Kathmandu. Do you have a return ticket back to the United States?

— Yup.

Null grinned.

When I first met him, standing over Frederick at the Chinese opera, Null had seemed like a lowlife. There had been that sniveling, obsequious quality about him which made me dislike him immediately. And I remembered looking into his hollow eyes, and observing his tattoo, and deciding he was thoroughly untrustworthy. Since then I'd become more tolerant of him, almost sympathetic, so I was surprised by how he took to the position of my volunteer guard. He seemed to be pleased that I was under his command, somewhat vindictively, but with an odd trace of motherliness. So that when he spoke to me he was kind, but with a slight tinge of resentment sparking his words.

— Harr-ee. Remember what you yelled at me at the temple?

— Yes, Null.

— I don't think that was nice, Harr-ee, he said, glancing over his shoulder to make sure we weren't overheard. I don't think you know about what you say.

— I'm sorry, Null. I wasn't thinking.

— No, he said, touching my arm. You don't think. You must assure me you deed not ever say what you said to Free-derick.

I was staring at the little picture on his face. It looked like a grownup worm, stuck there. His nostrils dilated as he glared at me, and his white skin was papery in the darkness.

— *Tell* me, he said whispering harshly. Pleez.

— No, Null. Of course I've never said anything to Frederick.

— What about Katey? Did Katey ever say any-ting?

— No, Null, I said, pulling back from him.

He had a fever in his face, and there was a petulant look in his eyes, as if he weren't sure whether or not he wanted to strike me. Wrenching my arm tighter, he leaned close to me, and I was forced to stare at the tattoo on his cheek at very close range. It was a good drawing. Its head was the shape of a smooth diamond and its eyes were red with black, knife-thin pupils. It swirled in an S and ended in a detailed yellow-green rattle. The skin was very smooth where the colors were.

— No, Null. Kate never talked to Frederick about you. Back at the temple I was just talking off the top of my head. I'm frustrated too, Null. I've got things I'm worrying about.

There was a silence between us, and Null kept moving from foot to foot. He was cold. I let the air leave my lungs and listened to the rushing water of the Kali Gandaki barely drowning out the voices of the policemen. Null released his grip on my arm.

— Well, you know, he said quietly, with a touch of sadness in his voice, I always liked you, Harr-ee. It's too bad . . . the way things worked out. And now you are going back. I felt we had many things in common. I think, no matter what they all say, that you are a good person.

— Thanks, Null.

He patted me on the back of the neck. Although I recoiled at

this gesture of tenderness on his part, and found myself jerking
away from his hand, I was on the verge of tears.

Null, I thought, Null of all people, saying these things to me.

That night, after waiting till everyone had fallen asleep, I crept
out from under the tarp and fumbled around in the darkness
until I found my pack. From it I took a scrap of paper, on
which, by the light of a match, I wrote the following note:

> Dear Frederick and Null,
>   I'm embarrassed about this mess, dragging you after me and
> all, and I'm upset that I've involved you both and caused so
> much trouble.
>   I couldn't wait for the morning. I want to get out of this
> damned country, and decided I'd be too ashamed to bother you
> anymore with escorting me down the mountain. I'm descending
> on my own. I feel foolish.
>   You were right, Frederick. This was all a big mistake.
>
> My fond regards,
Harry

I carefully pushed the note under Frederick's pillow, and
then, gathering up my things, tiptoed down to the river, making a detour past the policemen's lean-to, where my sword was
leaning against some equipment. I took it, careful not to let it
knock against anything, while they all snored sonorously under
the slanting tarp. Then I made my way down to the river in the
darkness, and, coming upon the ponies, felt my way among
them by touching their noses, until I came to the one on whose
back the coffin was lashed. The policemen were planning to
sleep only a few hours, so most of the packs and baggage had
been left on the ponies. Dawn was just a few hours away. The
animals rustled back and forth when I came, twitching their ears.

They were tied at a large cluster of rocks, which I climbed
onto and, from that elevation, managed to unhinge and quietly

slide the lid of the coffin open. There was another Japanese flag painted on the top of the lid, and although the red spot was inky and practically invisible in the darkness, the surrounding white rectangle was luminous.

I first put my pack in and shoved it with my foot to the bottom of the coffin. Then I cautiously got in, and lowered myself down. The pony's legs shifted about as I let go of the rock and put all my weight on its back. Then, feeling as if I were consigning myself to the grave, I slid the lid back over me. Inside, there was just enough room if I curved my legs around my pack.

Getting up the mountain was the important thing, I decided, no matter what I did to evade everyone who wanted to stop me. If I'd gone on foot, the policemen, riding the ponies on their own way up the mountain, would ultimately catch up to me. If I headed off the trail alone, I was certain to get lost. This was the only trail for many, many miles. The only way for me to continue was to be escorted by them without their knowing.

It was black and airless inside the coffin, and there was the smell of newly cut wood. The pony, perplexed, shook its mane and shuffled around a bit, but ultimately fell asleep. Then, after I had listened to the river for a long time, and fallen asleep and awakened several times, I saw the sun through the crack of the lid, and I heard voices outside and the sounds of the tarps being taken down, aired, and folded.

They were discussing my departure. The captain sounded disgusted. Frederick read him my note aloud, as if he were reading a liturgy, particularly when he had problems with the word "descending," and he read it over several times. The end of the letter was obscured by the sound of a pony pissing loudly on the ground below me. Frederick's voice disappeared and eventually I heard the policemen around me, speaking to one another in Nepalese. There was the smacking sound of mats and packs being thrown onto the backs of the ponies, and the bridles clattering into their mouths.

We set off, and the dark box swayed back and forth, as if I were at sea in an enclosed boat, and I was floating with no particular destination. I remembered how sailors were buried at sea, in watertight coffins, those long lozenges that go into the water like a shot, swallowed immediately with a splash. Maybe that's what I'm doing, I thought. Floating on some sea in a coffin without purpose, like a dead man. Or maybe I am always a dead man when I am not in Kate's presence. Purposeless, stiff, mute, and insubstantial. There was a certain force in that: floating upward into the mountains, a ghost, in the guise of death, until I am near her once again and am revived.

But it sat upon me, the darkness of the coffin and these impressions of death. I lifted the sword off the floor of the coffin and hefted it in my palm. Was this the kind of thing the dead thought about?

Then, placing the sword back on the coffin's floor, just before I was rocked to sleep by the swaying of the pony's haunches, I had to admit that what was bothering me was that my girlfriend had slept with another man. That was it. Period. She also claimed that she loved him. She said she no longer loved me. That was the extent of it.

Yet, after this thought, even though it belittled my mission, as I fell asleep I became certain that there was something fulfilling about the feeling of righteousness, even if it was over seemingly small emotional issues. Like a warrior in a Greek story who's protected by the gods, I felt cared for by higher powers, which hoped for my success, nurtured me, assured me that, as outlandish as it all was, there was something correct in what I was doing.

But, of course, I went to sleep feeling totally alone. I hugged myself, imitating the bigger feeling of being protected that, sadly, no longer seemed plausible, or honest, in those last few seconds before I drifted off to sleep.

25

I could smell her shirt, because my head was lying on her knee. I knew immediately the smell of her clean shirt and her sweat combined. I believed she was sitting next to me, and I had leaned over and fallen asleep. When I opened my eyes, the first thing I saw, in sunlight, was her tanned arm and the soft frill of bright blond hairs across its surface. She was stroking my head, and I heard her talking. And I awoke startled, thinking, How did this happen? How is she here?

— Which path is it? she asked.

— The Thorong path? asked a nearby voice.

— Yes.

— Over there . . . You walk that way . . .

We were on a veranda or a porch and were seated, I thought, across from the man with whom Kate was talking. But my eyes were half shut. I saw bright sunshine on her arm, but I didn't move my head for fear of disturbing the moment. So I opened my eyes wider, but even though I struggled, I still couldn't see clearly. I struggled again, but they wouldn't open. Finally, panicking, I pushed open my eyes with all my might and was immediately plunged into darkness.

I took several gasping breaths. It was pitch black. I was still in the coffin.

But her voice was there. I hadn't imagined it, although it faded for a moment. She was outside. She was talking. Then her voice became louder again.

— Oh, I get it, she said. Up around that bend.

— That's right.

I gathered my wits. She couldn't have been more than a few feet away. I had arrived. She was here. And as I had guessed I would, I felt the life pumping back into me, resuscitating me. I felt charged with energy and wide-awake. I had done it. I had found her. I put my hand on the lid of the coffin and was about to push up, but I stopped. My heart thudded.

— You see? Near the white rock. That's the path.

— Thank you, she said.

— Thank you, said another voice.

It was a painfully familiar, precise, accented, fastidious voice.

Something formed in my throat, a combination of a yell and a great sucking cough. And it vibrated halfway down my gullet like a fatal hiccup.

— Wu, Wu, Wu, Wu, I whispered to myself, the one syllable hovering, trying to get out.

Then it spilled into my mouth, and blew about there around my tongue, until it finally smashed up against the back of my teeth and formed into a tremendous yell.

— Wuuuuu!

I grabbed the sword and, with my shoulder pushing up, my knees unbuckling, I burst through the lid, and as it smacked open, I suddenly found myself standing in the coffin, wavering there, blinking at the bright light, swinging the sword over my head in a flashing arc.

It was apparent that the horses had been tied up and were alone with only one man tending them, the rest evidently having gone up the mountain to bring down the corpse. We were at the foot of the snowline. And in that one crystalline moment I saw the snow, the dirt, the line of terrified horses, the shocked Nepalese policeman, the wide-eyed, neatly dressed Corporal Wu, and Kate, glaringly colorful in a yellow sweater, gazing at me as if she were staring at the Devil himself, come to earth in the shape of her ex-boyfriend.

Her face was lovely, pale, and motionless.

— Harry? she murmured.

But the ponies had been scared by my rapid rise out of the coffin. And in a second, their ears way back, they reared, pulling on their ropes. When the policeman's pony took off at a gallop, the rest followed suit, including the one on which I was standing, who in one leap managed to slip out of the ropes that held the coffin on its back, and disappear from beneath me. I descended to the ground with a crash and tumbled out of the coffin.

Kate and Wu jumped back, and Wu tripped over a rock and fell on his ass. The ponies scattered in several directions.

As both Wu and I clambered to our feet, and hoofbeats rumbled down the path, I heard the familiar sweet voice of Kate saying,

— Harry? Harry? What the *hell* . . . ?

With as much composure as I could muster, I brushed away the dust that was plastered to my face.

— Hello, Kate. Hello, Wu.

Kate was shocked, but there was none of that veiled recognition you'd expect on encountering an old boyfriend.

— Harry . . . I mean *Harry* . . . what the . . . what the hell are you doing here?

— What do you think? I said. You think I travel in a coffin all the time?

There was silence as they both stared at me. Wu, wearing a blue shirt and army hiking boots, watched me keenly, as if he'd been insulted, but nothing more. There was the feeling that he didn't have time to be shocked. He struck me as one of those people who are always infuriatingly "ready" merely because they don't question the strangeness of life. Shallow. The guy's shallow, I asserted to myself. How else do you explain such an unruffled demeanor? He's red in the face. He's surprised. But he's not shocked.

Wu motioned to Kate to stand back, as if he were going to handle the situation. A few of the ponies strayed, ropes dangling, far down the path. We all glanced at them. They had the appearance of big dogs idling on a street with their leashes loose. Then they trotted amiably around the bend.

We were alone. The three of us.

— Harry, said Wu sternly. I am sorry things happened the way they did. Please, we both . . .

— Shut up, I said.

He did, promptly. I bent down and picked up the sword.

For a long moment I hefted it in my hand and considered what it was I wanted to do. It was all outlandish, what I had done. But it seemed important to continue the force of my original intention, regardless of how bizarre it sounded.

— I hereby challenge you, Wu P'ei-fu, to a duel.

Kate sputtered, half laughing.

— Harry, you're fucking crazy. What are you doing here? I

can't believe you followed us. In a damned coffin. I can't believe it!

— No, no. Shh, shh, said Wu to her quietly. Please, Katey. Don't get upset.

Katey? Null calls her that too, I thought angrily.

— Kate, I said, ignoring Wu and looking directly into her eyes. I don't understand why you gave me up for this man. I know you don't trust me anymore, and you think I've gone crazy . . . and you may have reason . . . but you have to admit, you *must* admit, that I have good intuition. You have to admit to me that regardless of how you feel about me now, I do have unquestionable instincts.

Wu looked over to Kate, waiting for her to respond.

— Yes, Harry, she said after a moment with a level voice. I'll give you that.

— All right. Good. Given that you admit my instincts, regardless of what kind of dope you may think I am, you must listen to me.

— Wait, Harry. This is not . . . said Wu, with a fluttering voice.

— Shut up, I said. This is between me and Kate.

Kate looked over at Wu.

— Let him speak, she said gently.

A silent assent passed between them, and my heart took a dip.

— Go on, she said.

— Kate, so help me, I know this man. I know him well. I've seen into him, into his soul. He's not what he pretends to be. Behind the face there's something deeply ugly that's gained your affection. He's evil, Kate. For some reason, I was allowed to see that. He may not be evil in the traditional sense, but still he is evil; maybe in some private way that relates only to you and me. And as unbalanced as you think I am these days, as unsure of myself, as unable to make you love me . . . aside from all this, I saw this one thing very, very clearly. He is evil.

— You're wrong, she said simply.

She looked over at Wu and they exchanged a soft but ambiguous glance. But when she looked back at me she seemed to waver, and I saw in her expression certain evidence of memory, about conversations we'd had, making love to each other, jokes, the things we liked to eat, my kissing her and exploring her mouth with my tongue, our rejoicing in the smell of trees or in open places to swim, or in things that reminded us of home.

In certain ways she was my partner so deep down that nothing could separate us. And I felt, as we looked at each other, like an uncertain tectonic movement of the earth, Kate's heart shuddering toward me as if in a series of jolts. It was there in her eyes. She did love me. She wanted me to see it, open and warm, and she let me in beyond her blue irises, and we gazed at each other with unembarrassed irony and admission of our love.

But at that moment I heard, as if on the other side of a dense wall, a sharp yell, high-pitched and to the point.

Half a second later I felt the onrushing sting of Wu's shoulder pounding into my gut at high speed. So that at one moment there was Kate, vaguely smiling, and the next I was flying backward over the ground with Wu's muscled arms clenched around me.

We crashed to the dirt, and at the same time I heard the *ping* of the sword, thrown out of my hand, hitting the ground in the distance.

There was a scattering of pebbles and dust, and together we made several acrobatic turns until we smacked sideways against the large white rock that had figured so prominently as a landmark. Wu, who had the advantage of surprise, managed to get on top and force my arms down. But I kicked a leg up and hit him in the back, so that his head smacked against the rock, and I gained enough time to throw him off me and jump to my feet.

He jumped up too, rubbing his head. Once again we faced each other. This time, however, we were both mad as hell.

Wu's face was a bright vermilion, just as it had been the night of the monkey-head party. And I noticed that his anger was so naked and clumsy on his face that I was almost compelled to feel ashamed for him. But I took only small consolation from this.

— You . . . you . . . Harry, he yelled, pointing at me with a jab. You . . . you . . . are definitely crazy! Nobody tells Kate what to feel for me!

He snapped into a defensive fighting stance and waved his flat palms in little slow circles.

— What is this, kung fu? Give me a break, Wu, I said, spraying saliva unintentionally when I sputtered "break," but still trying to remain composed.

— Harry, said Kate. Please. Can't we just drop this? Huh, Harry? I mean, is this what you followed us all the way up here for? A duel? Didn't you do enough back in Taipei? Do you know that your friend Mister Chen used that incident you concocted, that fight you started, to hold Wu for questioning for four days?

I glared at her, the whole time keeping my dukes up the way my brother had shown me years ago when we watched the Cassius Clay–Sonny Liston fight. I was very young, but he showed me. I wondered, very briefly, if Kate remembered that; whether her father ever talked about Cassius Clay. That's the way I stood. Listening to her, and her new indignation, and waiting for Wu to barrel into me again.

— Kate, you must have some doubts about this guy. There must be something in you that senses his snake of a soul. Look at him! Of all the people in our history, the history of *Amer-*

ica . . . of all people, this guy, your boyfriend, your Chinese lover admires most of all is . . . get this . . . William Tecumseh Sherman.

She gave me a blank look.

— That's right. The man who invented warfare against women and children as a way of furthering his cause. The man who burned every town in his path. . . . That's who this guy's hero is! Doesn't that make you wonder?

But as I was saying "wonder," and really rolling it on my tongue for all it was worth, there was a skitter and a flutter of movement, and when I looked, Wu P'ei-fu had somehow spanned the distance between us in a skip, and around about the height of my head I saw, like a beautiful, mechanical object tilted on its axis, his rigidly arched, perfectly vectored foot. And then, as I was observing, parenthetically, the movement of this ideal foot, this arched, silent, onward-rushing, elegant thing, it slammed directly into my jaw with great force.

I was thrown backward, past the white rock, and crashed to the dirt with a loud thump.

It was at that moment, when I tried to assess what had happened, that I saw beside me, when my eyes were level to the ground, the sword glinting dimly, curved in the dirt, looking like the last chance for victory, a remnant of the past, like a picture on a wall. Wu was approaching. And, although I felt woozy, I reached and grabbed it, jumping to my feet, wobbling, and thrusting it out to keep him back.

— Keep away, Wu! Keep aw . . . aw . . .

My jaw couldn't quite get out the words.

Very distinctly now, I envisioned Frederick with his sword, striding with big swoops of his arms. It fixated me for a second, the image of the gangly, mustachioed man dancing with his sword like an angelic giraffe. Was he here? No. I looked around. Yet if he had been there he would have intervened. He would be on my side. I knew it. Regardless of his contempt for me, he'd still help me. That's the way he was. But it was just me, with a bruised jaw, a shaky arm, an untied shoe, and dusty, ripped clothes, holding a tarnished, probably dull sword in my hand. There was a sweaty man, shorter than I, breathing heavily and rocking back and forth on his feet, eyeing me, waiting for me to move. And there was Kate. The woman I loved. She had her hands over her mouth.

Then again, I saw Frederick in my mind's eye, a memory of him, that is. He had a sword and was moving against the monkeys, as if in a collective trance with them, and they were all scattering, almost joyfully, in one big wave, as if it was their honor to participate in the display of his skill.

I jabbed the sword in the air in Wu's direction, and he flinched but stayed where he was.

— Okay, Wu, I said wearily. I'll stop. But on one condition.

— What? he said defiantly.

— What? said Kate, with a kind of howl in her voice. Please, Harry, she pleaded. What?

I paused and readjusted my grip on the sword. Then I coughed.

— That you admit you are what I say you are. That you say: I am the snake. What Harry saw was true. I am the reptile. The cold-blooded beast.

They both stared at me, flabbergasted. We all stood for a few moments with the wind blowing idly by and the clouds passing not far overhead, their fleeting shadows darkening and lightening our faces in bursts.

— Harry, said Kate. What is all this "evil" stuff?

— You know, Kate. Everything that seeks to do harm, or to cause pain for pain's sake. There's nothing evil in nature, Kate. It's just people.

— Harry, you don't seem to get it. Wu isn't at fault. *I* was the one who fell for *him*. He was the reluctant one. I lured him, I fell in love with him first. He didn't even want to come here. You don't understand. There's something I haven't told you.

— No, I said, chuckling. No . . . you were deceived, Kate . . .

— What is this? she yelled. Do you have some pathological fear of accusing me? *I'm* the one who started this whole thing, Harry. *Me.* I fell in love with Wu first. And on top of that, Harry, there's something else, something that you should know. There was only one way to get Wu out of Taiwan, and I did it, because I had to and because . . .

— Don't mock me, Kate . . .

— Harry. Wu P'ei-fu and I got married. We're married now. That was the only way I could get him out. He's an American citizen now. We're really in love, Harry. And we're married.

— What?

— It's true, Harry, said Wu, almost sympathetically.

— You married him?

— Why the hell didn't you challenge *me* to a duel? Kate screamed at me. I was the one who deceived you!

— You were deceived . . . you were deceived, Kate . . . I murmured, but it was getting confusing as to who had deceived whom.

So what is this? She's married. She's his wife. Wu and Kate. Mr. and Mrs. Wu. The man I fought, the man I hated, now has my beloved, my ex-beloved, as his wife.

All the muscles in my body began to unwind and uncoil like so many bound-up rags. She married him, she married the snake. I held the sword limply in my hand. She truly deceived me. I should have fought her, but long, long ago. She's right, I should have challenged her to a duel. I'd come all this way to find out I should have come all this way for another reason. But it was impossible to realign myself. The whole moment was drained of anger and filled with a large, windy sadness. And where I once stood I felt around me the body of a frustrated man resembling myself, but scattered into a moribund revenge. All genuine purpose felt old. I had lost my future wife. My sense of righteousness turned into a gray, generalized dust.

And then a balloon formed in my heart, and it began to fill with a variety of odd things about Wu, the things he cared about and the things he did well. And I thought, I could probably figure out why she loves this man. And each prospective reason stung into my flesh like a silver bullet. I could see, with sorrow, why such a man might be viewed as necessary, as vital, even as attractive. It wasn't that I despised myself. Even though I saw the reprehensible, reptilian man for what he was, on the other side I gradually began to see how his otherness was completely fresh.

But where did that put me? I was no longer a part of the circle. The circle had left me and gone elsewhere. Something else had taken my place. I was staring at them like a poor man gazing in on a banquet from a winter street. They were married. They were man and wife.

That's when it struck me: I was the dangerous one now. I was a threat to their union. I could see it in them, the will to protect something they'd created. The union always persisted, like an organism itself. And it sought to survive.

I felt my otherness increasing, and in her eyes I saw a fear of me, or possibly a revulsion. And Wu saw me the same way. They were together, firmly. I was like the border guard from some strange country accosting their new love with ugly mannerisms and foreign, intrusive ways. She watched me as if unsure of everything I was, she who once had known me so well.

But what a spectacle, I thought. Was my booby prize that I had now become another Wu? Ideas of disharmony began to leak into my blood. I'm free, I thought. I'm now free to want what others have. To see it all and feel it all, but this time from the outside.

The feeling was primitive and deeply mischievous. But it occurred to me that I was in a position to manipulate and transform their memories, to make them remember me always in an unfinished, uneasy way. That much I could do. That's one of the advantages of being on the outside, I thought. You get to dance around the included ones, circling them, bothering their consciences, putting into them the fear of chaos, the fear of unwinding hopes, the fear of losing what is precious. Maybe that's what being the snake is.

So I raised my sword. And with the most chilling yell I could summon from within, I rushed at Wu like a demon with his heart on fire.

He caught me, as I expected, quite deftly in the side of my head with a kick. As I went down, I had that profound peace of mind I suspect only the truly religious possess.